I0768592

A NOVEL

In the
MIST
of
TIME

W.G. STONE

This book is dedicated to my loving family and friends.

Your love is the light that shines upon my journey in this life.

To my dear father who awaits me in eternity.

Also, for those who search for meaning in the brevity of this life.

This world.

Your true meaning is found within… Love.

Prologue

THROUGH THE WINDOW of a country home in the south of Virginia, he lies on his bed looking up at the cedar wood ceiling. He is thinking about the love that he's scared to conquer. He takes a couple of deep breaths and gets up from his bed. On top of a desk near the closet, he takes hold of a piece of paper and pen. He begins to write a heartfelt poem.

When finished, he puts his pen down and walks back and forth anxiously. On top of his white t-shirt, he pulls on his black leather jacket that was resting in a wrinkled heap on the chair of his desk. He folds the poem and hides it in the inside of the jacket. Clothed in his blue faded jeans and cowboy boots, he heads down the stairs. As he passes the dining room table, he picks up a bouquet of roses wrapped with white paper around the bottom.

In a hurry, he leaves the house, heading straight to the motorcycle that he had parked in the driveway earlier. He picks up the helmet and fixes it to his head. He gets on the motorcycle and places the bouquet between his legs. Now with the motorcycle humming, he takes off to his destination. He makes a right turn on a narrow country road, surrounded on both sides by miles of wheat field standing about six feet tall. The moon is bright, behind it full of shining stars in the night sky without a single interruption of clouds. The wind blows in a soft manner, making the wheat field dance back and forth in a smooth rhythm.

As he rides down this road, he begins to feel anxious and impatient. He twists the handle toward himself to accelerate. Now at a fairly fast pace, he sees headlights down the road. He persists on his mission. The headlights are getting larger and larger, and after every electrical post he passes, his speedometer advances. As he gets closer to the moving headlights, he realizes that the road is too narrow for more than one vehicle. He signals the oncoming vehicle by flashing the motorcycle's high beam, but there is no response. No change.

Now he knows that there is a problem. Behind the bright light burning his eyes, he can see the fainted shape of the body of a truck.

The light of the truck blinds him as he tries frantically to slow down. The truck's horn begins to sound. The sound of both machines breaking to come to a halt is so loud as it shakes the night. The bright light gets brighter and brighter. Brake smoke clouds engulf the truck as it rises from the screeching tires. He swerves back and forth trying to avoid contact, trying to avoid the inevitable collision. He gives the light one final look as the truck inches toward him. There is a CRASH, a flash, then total silence.

Moments later, a police car arrives. The siren of the sheriff's car screams and the red and blue probe light covers the scene with an eerie glow. He gets out of his car and puts on his cowboy hat. He approaches the body next to the smoking motorcycle. He observes the perimeter looking for clues. He then spots a white piece of paper sticking out of the victim's black leather jacket. He reaches for it to see if it's the young man's identity.

As he unfolds the paper, he realizes it's a poem. He takes a moment to read it. When he finishes, he closes his eyes, recognizing the poetic irony of this tragedy. When he opens his eyes, he takes a step back and notices that he'd stepped on something. He raises his foot from the object. He frowns his eyebrows at the object on the floor, trying to decipher it. Astounded by what he is witnessing, he stoops down and grabs the bouquet of roses. The petals are dry and gray.

ONE

Liam

CURRENT DAY ... 11:11PM VIRGINIA, USA

I WAKE UP BREATHLESS, searching for air as my chest moves up and down and my forehead drips with sweat. It is as if I just woke up from a coma. Everything is so real, so tangible. I look around for about a minute or two trying to resituate myself in the world, a world apart from my dream. I jump out of my bed and go straight to my desk to find a pen and paper. I begin to turn my dream into a story. But something is different tonight.

While I'm writing, I keep losing my focus. Her image keeps flashing through my mind. Her mysterious eyes and baby-like smile captivate my heart. How I long to be near her, to hold her, and to kiss her soft pink lips.

For every second that drifts by, I yearn for her once more. Beatrice, a girl I fell in love with when I was younger.

We went to school together. We started as friends, and as time progressed, my feelings toward her kept getting stronger and stronger. So much so that now I call it true love.

My pen freezes. Then again, what is love?

I know she felt the same in school because we fell in love. We had a romance. We fought for love. Then, life changed. She changed. No! I've changed. Whatever it was it no longer matter. We are apart.

It's over!

Let it go!

Yet I just can't get her off my mind. Am I a fool to think that there's hope? Is love a game?

What are the rules? Move on.

After a couple of pages, I decide to put my pen down. Stretching, I get up from the chair of my desk, turn off the lamp, and head back to bed. As my head thumps against the pillow, I look at the night sky through my window. I ponder how my parents are dealing with the news of my departure. I advised them a week in advance and the whole week, they didn't show any sign of worry or emotion.

Maybe they think I might not go through with it? I think they just don't want to show me how saddened they are by my sudden journey. Come to think of it, it must be sad to realize that the child you've spent years raising, is all grown up and ready to head out on their own. I whisper a prayer and fall asleep.

The sun lights up my room as it has done every morning for the past nineteen years. I turn from one side to the other, trying to find a patch of shadow. Groaning, I eventually open my eyes and push myself up, rubbing the sleep out of them. I sit there for a while, reminiscing about the years I've spent in this room. How quickly it has gone by!

I get up and head downstairs to the kitchen to have some breakfast. Both my parents and my three sisters are there getting the table ready. I know I am going to miss these Saturday mornings, but I try not to let them notice my sadness. Before sitting at the table, I greet everyone with hugs and kisses. My two older sisters are murmuring about me leaving.

"So, Liam, tonight is the night," they say while putting coffee and milk on the table.

"I know. I can't believe it," I say as I pull a chair to the same spot I always sit.

"So, how do you feel heading out on your own? Are you excited?" Claire, the youngest, asks curiously.

"Yeah, I am. I mean, it's New York City!" I answer.

"Well, we hope you won't stay there for too long," Jennifer, my oldest sister, says.

"Jen, you know why I'm going. I'm going there to start my writer career, and also, I want to experience the life of a big city. I already know what goes on in a small town," I said, taking a bite out of my toast.

"You know that we are all here for you… right, Mom and Dad?" She looks around for corroboration.

My mother and father don't say a word, they just glance at each other with a reluctant expression, and then back down to their plates.

We all finish our breakfast, and I stay to help my sister and my mom clean up. I don't understand why but I feel guilty about leaving. I knew it brought pain to my mother's heart, but God put this dream in my heart and I know that I have to do it or I will regret it my whole life.

If my parents had their way, I would be attending one of the top universities in the state. However, I can't see myself doing that. *No!* My dream is much bigger than a degree. For now, all I need to do is explore and discover the world. If I fail, then and only then will I pursue a degree. But for now, I choose adventure.

I head up the stairs to get the rest of my things ready and packed. As I place one white t-shirt on top of another, the phone rings. I jump on my bed, trying to reach the phone perched on top of the dresser that's tucked behind a slew of boxes. I pick up the phone.

"Hello?!"

There is silence on the other end. Something inside me knows that it was Bia on the other end, but I have to find out.

TWO

Liam

7 YEARS PRIOR TO THE CURRENT DAY …

THE DAY STARTED out like every other first day of school. My mother wakes me up at the crack of dawn to help my father with some chores.

After slogging bucket loads of water to and fro, watering the plants, I head inside to find my mother and sisters busy in the kitchen.

"Go upstairs and wash up quickly. You are going to miss the bus," my mother orders, scowling sweetly as she sets down a jug of milk on the breakfast table.

I nod and rush to the bathroom. After washing up, I go to my room and find my freshly pressed clothes on my bed. My clothes were not brand new and slightly faded around the edges, but this didn't bother me much because they were always neat and clean. Looking presentable was something that my mother prided herself on.

After I pull on my red sweater and blue jeans, I slick my hair back and gather my school books. I shove the books into my brown backpack and look at myself in the little mirror on my wall.

"Liam, you are going to be late," my mother yells.

Slamming my door shut behind me, I raced downstairs. At the breakfast table, my father is reading the morning newspaper while sipping on his coffee, my mother is faffing around the kitchen preparing our school lunch. My bowl of porridge is steamy and delicious. I gobble down spoonfuls and when my bowl is empty, I get up and grab my bag ready to head out.

Before I am even two steps away, my mother says, "Where do you think you are going?"

I turn around and look at her confused. She points to her cheek and then I realize what she means.

"But mom," I begin to whine.

"Nah uh. I don't want to hear it. Come over here and give your mom a kiss." she says, not budging.

I sigh and accept defeat. After giving her a kiss on the cheek, I bolt out the door.

"Wait for me," my sister yells, but I spot the bright yellow school bus coming around the corner and ignore her because I want to beat the bus to the stop.

I gather all of my energy and run as fast as I can down the dusty path to the stop. My heart is racing and my adrenaline is pumping. Beads of sweat begin to form on my forehead as I come to a screeching halt at the bus stop with two seconds to spare.

This is pretty decent by my standards. My sister and I used to race to the bus stop all the time when we were younger, but now that she is a high school senior, she claims that it's too silly. I think that she just got tired of losing to me.

The bus stops in front of me and the doors fling open. I adjust my bag, wipe away the droplets of sweat on my forehead with the back of my sleeve, and walk onto the bus. My first day as a middle schooler has officially begun.

I see one of my oldest and best friends, Tommy. Rushing toward him, I take my seat. By this time, my sister finally catches up and gets on the bus. As she passes me, she hits the back of my head gently and I fake a yelp.

The bus doors close and off to school we go.

"Hey, Liam. How was your summer break?" Tommy asks me. I grimace slightly.

"Oh, you know. I just worked with my dad. How about you?" I say.

My parents chose to send us to the best school in town, despite the fact that we could barely afford it. This means that my vacations were never as exciting as my friends.

"Well, for my break we went to visit my grandparents in Florida," Tommy says as his eyes light up.

I could not help but be slightly envious of my friends when they told me about all of their exciting adventures all over the world. While I had never left this small town or even been to the next state.

We get to school and make our way to the classroom just as the school bell rings. I navigate my way through the desks in Miss Honey's classroom and try to find a seat. The rest of the class comes shuffling in and takes their seats. Tommy is sitting behind me and my other friend, Shane, is seated in front of me, but there is a vacant seat to my right.

Miss Honey breezes into the room and says, "Good morning class." In unison we all say, "Good morning, Miss Honey."

Then there is a soft knock on the door.

Miss Honey opens the classroom door and ushers in the most beautiful girl that I have ever seen. Instantly, my jaw drops as I watch her walk in clutching two books close to her chest.

"Class, please welcome our new student, Beatrice. Her family just moved here from Uruguay and I hope that you will all make her feel welcome," Miss Honey announces.

Beatrice smiles and looks a little awkward before Miss Honey tells her to find a seat. The beautiful girl scans the room. We make eye contact for all but a moment before she quickly looks away. Her cheeks turn rosy and she starts walking toward me. Her clothes are obviously brand new and designer.

She is well groomed, which means that she comes from money.

The girl takes her seat right beside me. She is close to me. Close enough that I can smell her rosy sweet perfume. I take a deep breath and only realize that I am staring at her when she looks up at me and smiles.

Tommy kicks my chair and whispers, "Dude, act cool."

I clear my throat, then sit up straight and turn my head to Miss Honey, who is standing at the front of the class and going over our reading list for the term. For the rest of the lesson, I try my best to concentrate and not look to my right. There was no way I could let her catch me staring again.

As soon as the recess bell sounds, I bolt out of class to the far end of the cafeteria where my friends and I chill. I didn't want to risk bumping into her.

Tommy and Shane catch up to me after a few minutes and take their usual seats. After a few moments of nervously sipping on my juice box I casually say, "So what do you guys think of the new girl?"

Shane shrugs and takes a bite of his sandwich while Tommy looks directly at me and asks, "Why? What do you think about her?"

His question catches me a little off guard so I casually say, "I guess she is okay. For a girl."

Tommy's eyes light up and Shane puts his sandwich down. They look at each other and then turn to me and start singing, "Liam has a crush, Liam has a crush."

At that exact moment, I spot her walking into the cafeteria. Panic fills my body as I see her walking in my direction.

"I do not. Girls are dumb," I blurt out loud defensively.

Beatrice stops right in her tracks. She looks at me and then I see something that makes my heart hurt. A look of sadness crosses over her beautiful features and I feel instant regret. All of me wants to go over and apologize, but I can't move.

She turns around and I watch as she walks away and goes to sit with a group of giggly girls at another table. With her exotic features, she sticks out of the group like a sore thumb. She was different from any other girl I had ever met before and I liked it.

I watch as she pushes away the sadness that I had caused only a few minutes earlier and makes friends with the girls at her table. They are all extremely intrigued by her.

Why wouldn't they be?

My mother would be so disappointed in me if she had seen what I just did. Sighing, I get up from the lunch table and tell my friends some lame excuse about me having some extra homework which is why I need to go to class early.

They buy it and leave, wanting to be alone for a bit. I go to the classroom and Miss Honey is there.

"Liam, is everything okay?" she asks in a concerned voice.

With my gaze downcast, I nod my head and reply, "Yes, Miss Honey.

Would it be okay if I did some reading in here until the break is over?"
"Of course you can. If you need to talk about what is bothering you,

I am here," she says and goes back to writing something down in her notebook.

The rest of my break is spent at my desk thinking about Bia. That look on her face is something that I will never forget. I silently promise myself that no matter what, I would never be the reason that she looks like that again.

THREE

Beatrice

FIRST DAY AT A NEW SCHOOL in a new town. The people here are so different from the ones I grew up around in Uruguay.

Honestly, I miss my home.

When my abuelo passed away a few months ago, I knew that my life would never be the same. My first memory of abuelo was the long walks he would take me on if I ate all my dinner. Our long walks in the cool afternoon were my favorite part of the day. Especially since our walks always included a quick stop at the corner shop to get the best soft serve in town.

My eyes fill with tears of joy as I reminisce about some of the happiest moments of my childhood. These were the most precious memories that I had. My abuelo would often take care of me because my mother and father would be out most nights attending galas and dinners with "important people." Before bed every night, abuelo would tell me stories about his childhood before tucking me in.

I can still remember that dreaded night. I thought that it was just another normal night. abuelo and I had dinner together at the dining room table.

After we were done, abuelo said that there was a storm coming, so we could not go for our usual walk after dinner.

After peaking outside, I noticed that the sky was clear.

"What are you talking about abuelo?" I whined and twisted my face into a knot.

He just laughed and gave me a gentle pat on the head before saying, "Go and get ready for bed, my nieta."

"That is so unfair," I spat back as I stomped all the way to my room to do as he said.

A few minutes later, as I was brushing my teeth, I heard the gentle pitter patter of rain. I shook my head, rinsed my mouth, and went to jump in bed and wait for abuelo to come and tuck me in. There was no doubt in my mind that I needed to apologize to him for not believing him and acting like a brat earlier.

I waited for about ten minutes and he didn't come. He was probably busy placing buckets all over the house to catch the water from the leaks in our ceiling.

So, I waited for a few more minutes and when I did not hear his footsteps approaching my room, I slowly crept out of bed to go and see what he was doing. Expecting a shouting if I was caught out of bed at this hour, I made my way downstairs as quiet as a mouse.

Holding my breath, I move from room to room until I see it.

My eyes move from the shattered glass vase to the gray rose petals on the floor until they finally land on my abuelo's limp, pale body lying on the floor.

A shriek escapes my lips as I rush over to him and realize that my worst nightmare has become a reality.

The next few weeks were a blur. It felt like my body was a machine and I had no actual control over it. Hours turned into days, days turned into weeks and before I knew it, my whole life was different.

After doing all of the funeral rituals, my father packed us up and took us all to the states. It had always been abuelo's dream to come to the states, but due to his old age and declining health, travel was not an option. That and the fact that it was not possible financially.

My father was the mayor of our small rural town and his salary was just enough to pay the bills and put food on the table while maintaining the rich façade that he and my mother had created. We always had to have the best clothes from some of the most well-known designers in town and latest cars while the roof in our house constantly had leaks.

Whenever abuelo would ask my father to get someone to patch the leaks up, his response was always that there was simply no money. Yet, a week later, father and mother would come home with brand new outfits for whatever dumb party they were attending that weekend.

It was all their fault that abuelo was gone. If only my father had fixed those dumb leaks, then abuelo would not have had to climb up that ladder and maybe he would still be here.

Instead of being home and tucking me in like they should have been, my parents were at some gala they were hosting for the town sheriff. Ironically enough, the night that abuelo passed away was the same night that my father got offered a job in America as a foreign ambassador.

Now, just two months after abuelo's death, here I am in a foreign country, at a new school with no friends. I felt like I was drowning and no one around me even noticed. This new town was so different from what I was used to. I didn't know anyone and they all seemed so stuffy and snobby. Our first week here, the only person that had actually spoken to me was our new house keeper and my new nanny, Dianne. She was a sweet, old lady with wrinkled skin, kind hazel eyes, and gray hair. Dianne took me on my first tour of the little town and showed me how beautiful it actually was. We spent most of the time hunched over books as she helped me to better my English. I knew the basic words, but she spent hours upon hours reading with me to help me build my vocabulary.

After one of our lessons, she took me out for a picnic in this huge field close to my house. From the field you could see a beautiful mountain range in the distance.

As I was looking at the mountain range in awe, Dianne said, "You know my dear, those mountains are called the Lovers Mountains."

I stared at her in confusion. While they were beautiful to look at due to their sheer size, I could not understand how such a daunting and hostile looking place could have a sweet name like Lovers Mountains.

"Di, why are they called that?" I asked curiously.

Dianne smiles at me sweetly before lying down on her back so that she could absorb the last rays of the sun. She sighs and says, "Well, my dear, legend has it, that long ago, there were two people, a man and a lady, that fell deeply in love with each other. After only two months, they knew that they wanted to spend the rest of their lives together.

However, the girl's parents didn't approve of their relationship as the girl came from a wealthy family and the boy didn't. So they decided to run away together and get married. In the dead of night, they crept out of their houses and met at the dock. The couple was never seen again and the next day, a fisherman found their little boat floating. The villagers say that not long after that, this mountain range appeared and they believed that it was the man and woman, finally together."

My small brain struggled to understand what she had just said to me. So instead, I decide to try and catch some of the beautiful yellow butterflies that were fluttering their wings nearby.

The next day, Dianne woke me up early for my first day at school. After washing up and getting ready, I head downstairs for breakfast only to find a lone bowl of steaming porridge on the dining room table.

"Your parents have gone to the office, dear. They had some important business to take care of seeing as it is your fathers first official day as the Uruguayan ambassador," Di says as she notices me looking around the kitchen for them.

I quickly try to hide the look of disappointment on my face and head over to the table.

Why would anything be different now?

It was my own fault for expecting them to be there, we hadn't had breakfast as a family for years. Di packs my backpack and walks me down the driveway of our fancy new house where a man dressed in a black suit who looks kind of like a penguin is waiting for me.

"This is Marc. He will be taking you to and from school every day," Di says with a smile as she buckles my seatbelt.

Marc seems to be around the same age as Di and closes the car door when she's done. He jumps into the car and drives off. I turn around to see Di standing and waving me off. I wave back before slumping into the seat. We pull up in front of my new school. It looks much bigger than the one I used to go to back home. The kids stare as Marc opens the car door for me and I jump out.

"Have a great day at school, little miss. I will be waiting right here for you when you are done," Marc says as I grimace slightly and walk away.

My new adventure is about to begin…

FOUR

Beatrice

I WALK DOWN the long hallways lined with lockers as I make my way to the principal's office. Clutching the strap of my little backpack close to my chest nervously as I get a few curious stares from bystanders.

"Miss Beatrice. Welcome to Starview Middle School. We are so glad to have you. I am Principal Stark," an elderly man in a button up white shirt with black pants and white gray hair says to me from behind his brown oak desk.

I smile nervously and return his greeting as I try not to stare at the pokey gray hairs sticking out of his nose. Clearing my throat, I try to stifle a giggle that threatens to escape through my lips.

The principal wiggles his nose and lowers his glasses before asking, "Will your parents be joining us for orientation?"

With a downcast gaze I shake my head, letting him know that they will not be coming. Principal Stark smiles and gets up. He walks past me and opens the door before saying, "That is perfectly alright. You can walk down the corridor to Miss Honey's classroom. It is the first door on the left. She will be expecting you."

"Thank you," I say meekly as I walk out. The secretary smiles at me sweetly as I walk down the corridor. Just like Principal Stark said, there was Miss Honey's classroom. I take a deep breath and muster all of my courage as I gently knock and push open the door.

As I walk in, I realize that everyone is now looking at me. My eyes fall on one boy in particular. He is seated right next to the window and his blue-eyed gaze is fixed on me.

"You must be Beatrice, the new ambassador's daughter. I am Miss Honey and I will be your teacher for this year," Miss Honey says sweetly.

She is pretty, very young, and has auburn locks that fall clumsily to her shoulders with bangs. Her oval tortoise shell glasses are much too big for her slim face and she's wearing a clumsy, oversized cream cardigan that has a big coffee stain on it. Overall, she looks so kind and harmless, I instantly feel welcomed.

I let out a breath and shift my gaze for a second only to realize that the cute boy with blond shaggy hair seated by the window is still staring at me. Shifting my weight from my right leg to my left nervously, I can't help but blush a little.

"You can call me Bia. It is lovely to meet you, Miss Honey," I say. "Oh my, what a well-mannered young lady you are," Miss Honey gushes. "Go ahead and pick whichever seat that is available and just before lunch, I will assign a student that will be your welcome buddy for the next week and they will show you around."

I nod and spot an empty seat next to the cute boy. We make eye contact again and it is almost as if he is in a trance-like state. I notice his friend kick his chair as I take the seat next to him and smile to myself.

Class goes by quickly as Miss Honey teaches us about citizenship and what it means to be a good citizen. Just before it is time for break, as promised, Miss Honey asks, "Okay class, who would like to be Bia's tour buddy for the week?"

A bunch of eager girls shoot their hands up instantly. From the corner of my eye, I see the cute boy almost put his hand up but then hesitates.

Maybe he's nervous.

"Okay. Settle down, class. I think that Mary should be Bia's tour buddy for the week," Miss Honey says.

I feel slightly disappointed that the cute boy isn't going to be my tour buddy, but I look over to see an excited girl with two braids on either side of her face smiling at me. I return her smile and the bell goes off for lunch.

Grabbing my stuff, I make my way to the door. As soon as I walk out of the classroom and into the hallway, Mary races over to me and starts speaking.

"Hi, my name is Mary, but you probably already know that," she rambles on energetically as she leads me to the lunchroom.

I grab a tray and join the line. All the while, Mary talks about her new obsession with some boy band. I hardly get a word in edgewise so I feel slightly relieved when I get out of the line first. Scanning the lunch room, I try to find a table quickly and get away from Mary. It isn't that I don't like her but everything was so overwhelming already. New school, new country, new everything. All I want to do right now is relax and sip on my chocolate milk for a second.

I see the cute boy from class looking at me and I decide that since he was too nervous to put his hand up, I would make the first move and try to be his friend by sitting with him. Clutching my lunch tray, I walk over determinedly.

As I approach, I overhear him say the most horrid thing. "Girls are dumb," the cute blond boy scoffs.

I cannot believe my ears. Here I was thinking that he was such a nice boy that I wanted to be friends with, only to hear him say something so silly. Turning swiftly on my heels, I walk away and see Mary waving at me to join her at the lunch table with a bunch of other girls.

Walking over, I try to ignore the disappointment that I am feeling.

Girls are dumb? No way. Only a dumb boy would say that.

I sit down at the table and all the girls start asking me questions about my life back in Uruguay. It feels like I am the new toy that all the kids are intrigued by. I try to answer all their questions briefly, not wanting to give away too much detail about my life back home. I'm not sure that they would understand and I don't want to feel like an outcast so I just stuck to the exciting stuff like the amazing food, beautiful beaches, and sunny days in the market.

The kids here were so different from the ones back home. Their interests were so peculiar. They wanted to know all the latest gossip about celebrities and knew all the details about some boy band called WestLife that I never really heard of and didn't care much for.

"You don't know who WestLife is?" Mary gasps, clutching her chest dramatically.

I shake my head and shrug.

"Well, get ready because I am about to give you the best crash course," Mary says excitedly.

The rest of the girls squeal in glee and sop up every word she says. I pretend to listen as I pick at the mac and cheese on my lunch tray. Eventually the bell rings, signaling lunch is over and I feel so relieved.

I wonder if there is anyone like me here? Someone that likes being outdoors and loves horses. These girls are so different.

Sighing, I empty my tray and head back to class. When we get back to class, Miss Honey gives us an activity that keeps us busy until the end of the school day.

As soon as the bell rings, I grab my bag and get ready to bolt out the door. Mary catches up with me in the school yard and says, "Hey Bia, I don't know if you heard about it but the town is hosting a carnival tonight. A bunch of us are going, would you like to join us?"

This day has been so tiring that all I want to do is go home and jump in bed, but I reply saying, "I will ask my parents and let you know."

"Okay great. Here is my number," Bia says as she hands me a piece of paper with her landline number scribbled on.

"Will do," I say with a smile and head in the direction where Marc is waiting for me. He is standing outside the car and reaches out to take my backpack as he opens the door.

"Wow, is that your driver, princess?" a boy from my class teases as I hesitantly hand Marc my bag.

I nod my head and blush as I jump into the car.

Why can't my parents just let me take the bus like a normal kid? Sinking into the back seat, Marc jumps in and starts the car. "How was your day, Miss Bia?" he asks kindly.

I sigh and lower my head. "That bad, huh?" he chuckles.

Marc is so kind, I can't help but smile.

Meekly, I ask, "Marc, do you mind calling me Bia instead of 'Miss Bia' and letting me open the door for myself?"

"But Miss Bia—" Marc begins and I scowl. "I mean, Bia, it is my job," Marc says.

"Please Marc?" I plead as the tears well up in my eyes, not wanting to be teased or called a 'princess' again.

"Okay," Marc says, defeated. "Thank you," I reply excitedly.

FIVE

Liam

I HUFF AND KICK the ground below me as I stomp out of the school yard.

How could I have said something so dumb?

There was no doubt in my mind that I had blown any shot of even being friends with the beautiful Bia by saying something that was so silly, something that I didn't even believe. I have two sisters, obviously I don't think that girls are dumb. I was devastated at the fact that I upset her, but more so disappointed in myself. This is not the way my parents raised me. If mother heard what I said, she would be so disappointed.

With my head hung low, I walk out.

"Hey, Liam," I hear someone screaming my name. I turn around to find Tommy sprinting toward me.

I slow down so that he can catch up.

"What's up?" I ask Tommy after he catches his breath. It is such a hot day here in Virginia. I watch as a bead of sweat falls off Tommy's face and evaporates as soon as it touches the ground.

"My brother is taking Shane and I to the carnival tonight. Do you want to come?" Tommy asks as we walk out of the school gate together.

Instantly I want to decline his offer. Right now I just wanted to go to my room and be by myself. The last thing I wanted was to be at a crowded carnival.

"I heard the new girl is going to be there," Tommy says and he gives me a nudge.

If she does actually come to the carnival, then maybe I will get the chance to apologize and make amends. Maybe we could even be friends.

Either way, I knew that I had to go to the carnival and hope for the best. "What time should I be ready?" I ask Tommy with a sigh.

Tommy chuckles and puts his hand on my shoulder before saying, "I knew you like her!"

"I do not," I protest half-heartedly.

"Sure man. We will pick you up at six," Tommy calls as he runs off to catch up with his older brother waiting to fetch him from school.

I say bye to Tommy and make my way to the bus.

Most of my friends got picked up from school by their parents, siblings, or a chauffeur, but I had to take the bus every day. It always smelled kind of weird and sometimes there was gum or some other weird substances on the seat.

Regardless, I was glad that at least I was fortunate enough to take the bus home instead of having to walk all the way to my house on the other side of town in this heat.

I sink into my seat and stare out the window. Right now, I don't want to talk to anyone. All I wanted to do was try and figure out how I was going to make things right with Bia.

Maybe I could beat her at one of the carnival games. Then she would see how good I am and want to be my friend.

No! That is such a dumb idea. Do better, Liam!

I scoff at how dumb of an idea that actually is. There was one thing that I was certain of and that was the fact that I had to think of something great to make up for my dumb comment.

The rest of my afternoon was spent role-playing different scenarios in front of my bedroom mirror as I tried to figure out what would be the best way to approach Bia and try to make things right.

My room begins to get a bit darker and I look out the window only to notice that the sun is setting. Panic starts to take over me as I rush to my closet and pull out my best shirt and pants. I have a quick wash and get ready, slicking my hair back as best as I could with my fine-tooth comb.

Tommy and Rio would be here soon and I still had no idea how I was going to make things right with Bia. I grab my most precious, little bottle of cologne and put on two squirts. My bedroom door creaks open behind me.

"Oh. Mommy, Liam's got a girlfriend. Liam's got a girlfriend," my oldest sister Jennifer yells teasingly from the hallway.

I feel my face heat up as she says this and I begin to chase her. Jennifer runs downstairs and to the kitchen where my mother is busy washing dishes.

"I DO NOT HAVE A GIRLFRIEND," I yell and stomp my feet in frustration as Jennifer hides behind my mother.

"Now now, Jennifer, leave your brother alone," my mother begins to say as she wipes her hands dry and turns to me.

She walks over and kneels down in front of me then reaches over and sorts out the collar on my shirt.

"Oh my, what a fine young gentleman you are," my mother says with a sweet smile as she pinches my cheek.

I pretend to yelp and rub my cheek in pain. My mother giggles and hugs me. I return her embrace.

"You will be on your best behavior at the carnival tonight. Won't you, my darling boy?" she asks.

I nod my head and watch as she reaches into her apron pocket. My mother pulls out a crinkled $5 bill and hands it to me. In the distance I hear the sound of a car pulling up and I know that it is Rio and Tommy. I pocket the note and give my mother a kiss on the cheek before racing outside to meet my friends.

"You be safe now," my mother calls out after me as I race down the path to where the car is parked. I wave at her and jump in.

The entire car ride to the carnival, I can hardly concentrate on a word that my friends are saying because I am so nervous.

I hope that she is there.

My tummy feels like it is twisted in a ball of knots at the moment. I see the glittery lights of the carnival appear and instantly my palms get sweaty.

The car stops and Tommy yells, "Come on, man."

I jump out of the car and we all race to the entrance. Once we are in, I look around, searching every face to try and find her. However, she is nowhere to be seen. I go along with my friends as they play Tin Can Alley, ring toss, and whatever other game they choose. It feels like hours have passed and I eventually give up hope.

"Guys, I am going to get a pretzel," I say to my friends before walking off. They are so engrossed in their game, they barely even acknowledge my departure.

I feel defeated. This entire afternoon, I had hyped myself up for this and she was not even here. My plan was to get a pretzel and then say goodbye to my friends before taking a slow walk home. I didn't want to be here anymore.

There is a huge line at the pretzel stand. I join without even paying attention to who was in front of me. I get caught up in my own thoughts and the time passes. As I near the front of the line, I look up and to my utter shock I see that the girl in front of me has beautiful black hair.

No. It can't be her.

I frown and get a glimpse of the side of her face as she turns to look at the menu.

It is! She has been standing in front of me this entire time and I had no idea.

Mustering up all of my courage, I gently tap her on the shoulder. As she turns around, I feel that knot start to form in my stomach again.

She realizes who is standing behind her and the beautiful smile that is on her face quickly turns into a frown. I clear my throat as I realize that I don't have much time before she has to order as she is the next in line.

"How much does a polar bear weigh?" I blurt out.

Bia's face scrunches up in confusion and the man at the counter yells, "Next please," before she can even answer my question.

She turns around, orders her pretzel and leaves. My heart sinks as I walk up to the counter and place my order. The man hands me my pretzel and I walk off.

To my surprise, Bia is seated at one of the tables near the pretzel stand. She looks up and waves me over. I walk toward her and she asks, "So, how much does a polar bear weigh?"

"Enough to break the ice?" I say sheepishly.

She chuckles and asks if I want to sit down. I nod enthusiastically and sit down with her as we both take a bite of our pretzels.

SIX

Liam

THE NEXT MORNING, I lay in bed and watch as the sunrise begins to brighten up my room. I barely got any sleep last night because I was so excited. Instead, I sat in the moonlight writing. Being with Bia inspired me to write. Writing has always been one of my passions, but I was inspired. So I sat on my bed in the moonlight writing about all the possibilities the future held. The words seemed to flow into the blank pages of the book in front of me and reminiscing on the special night that I just had with her.

After spending some time eating pretzels and talking to Bia, I asked her if she wanted to go on a bike tour of the town tomorrow. To my shock, she actually did.

We agreed to meet at the town square by noon. Ever since then, a goofy smile had been plastered on my face. I decide to get out of bed and go to wash up. When I am done, I go downstairs and find my mother at the stove.

"Liam, my darling, you are up early," she says with a smile. "Good morning, Mom," I say as I take a seat at the table.

"Good morning. I made your favorite for breakfast," she says as she places a stack of steaming flapjacks in front of me. It smells so good that my mouth starts watering instantly.

In between mouthfuls of delicious flapjacks and syrup I mumble, "'Thanks, Mom. These are so yummy."

She smiles and pats me on the head gently.

A few minutes later, my father comes down and sits at the table opposite me. My mother yells to try and wake my sisters up, but I have no time to sit around and wait for them today. I needed to finish my chores and get ready so that I could go and meet Bia.

Just thinking about it made me smile. I shovel in my last mouthful and stand up.

"What's the rush, son?" my father asks, raising one eyebrow. "Nothing, Dad. I just want to get to my chores," I say as I put my dishes in the sink.

"This early on a Saturday?" my father quizzes me further. "Yes, I am meeting my friend at noon," I say reluctantly.

"Liam's got a girlfriend," Jennifer says as she walks into the kitchen. "Mom," I whine.

"Jen, leave your brother alone," my mother says. Jennifer shrugs and sits down at the breakfast table.

I sigh and walk out. It is time to get those chores done. I fill the watering can and go to the vegetable garden behind my house. It is such a nice day. The sun is out and it is warm, the perfect day for a bike ride.

Bia is such a cool girl. Last night we spoke for so long and to my surprise, we actually have so much in common. She was so different than the girls at my school. She didn't crinkle her nose at my faded clothes or slightly worn shoes. In fact, she didn't care about those things at all. We spoke about horses, games, sports, and she told me about her home in Uruguay. Bia told me that she and her grandfather used to watch the NFL games together and she was an avid supporter.

I smile to myself as I water our cabbage patch. Last night with Bia was so much fun and I knew that the bike ride today was going to be even better. I race through the rest of my chores and once I am done, I go to the shed to fetch my bicycle.

It is a little rusty but otherwise seems to be in good condition. Then I see it and my heart sinks. One of my tires is flat. I kick the bicycle in frustration and slam the shed door shut. I sit in the backyard with my face between my knees.

How am I going to give Bia a bike tour with a flat tire?

Just then I hear my father's voice behind me asking, "Son, what is the matter?"

My voice croaks as I say, "The back tire on my bike is punctured." "Is that all?" my father chuckles and then says, "Bring it out. We will fix it in a jiffy."

I shoot up and grab the bike. My father takes off the wheel and patches it up. Within the hour, my bike is as good as new.

"Thank you, Dad," I say as I throw my arms around him.

He gives a hearty laugh and replies saying, "You are welcome, my boy. You best be on your way now. We wouldn't want to keep your friend waiting."

I nod and run inside to freshen up.

In my room, I pull on some clean clothes. Slick my hair back and race downstairs. As I rush past the kitchen, my mother stops me.

"Mom," I whine a little because I am already late.

"I packed you this for you and your friend," my mother says with a smile as she hands me a brown paper bag.

"Thank you, Mom." I say as I grab the lunch that she packed, give her a kiss on the cheek, and race back out to meet my father, where he's waiting by the gate for me with my bike and helmet. I put the lunch my mother packed in the little basket on my bike before securing my helmet on my head and jumping on.

"Be back home before the streetlights come on, my boy," my father says as I ride off. I pedal as quickly as my legs allow as I race to meet Bia. I get to the town square about five minutes late and look around to try and spot Bia. At first, I can't see her anywhere and I wonder if she changed her mind about meeting me. The town square is packed because every Saturday morning is market day. I greet a few people as I weave my way through the crowd trying to find Bia.

She isn't at the water fountain in the middle of the town where we agreed to meet. I sigh and kick the ground as I walk back to my bike. Then I hear her.

At first, I am not even sure if I actually heard her. I stop and try to listen.

"Hey, gorgeous boy," I hear Bia's sweet voice saying. Gorgeous boy? Who is she talking to?

I frown and follow the sound of her voice to Mr. Pruitt's fruit cart. "Liam, how do you do?" Mr. Pruitt asks me as I approach.

"Hi, Mr. Pruitt. I am good, thank you. How are you, sir?" I ask as I continue walking toward Bia's voice, which seems to be coming from behind him.

"All good. You be sure to pass on my regards to your parents," Mr. Pruitt says as he eyes me.

"Will do, sir," I say as I walk past him to the back of his cart to where he ties his horse, Jasper.

I see Bia standing in front of the large brown horse, petting his mane and calling him a handsome boy.

"Oh hey, Liam. I'm so sorry, I got so caught up playing with this gorgeous boy that I lost track of time," Bia says apologetically. Her long hair is braided in two pigtails with these ridiculous pink ribbons.

I try to stifle my chuckle but she notices.

"Di, my housekeeper, made me wear them," Bia says as she tries to yank the ribbons out of her hair. After her second attempt, she fails and sighs defeated.

I walk over and place my hand on hers saying, "Leave them. They look cute."

Bia looks at me and her cheeks turn rosy. "Liam, you still back there?" Mr. Pruitt yells.

"Yes, sir. Coming, sir," I yell back as I quickly take a step away from Bia. "Ready to go for that tour now?" I ask her with a smile. She nods and we walk toward our bikes. Mr. Pruitt hands us each a shiny red apple as we walk past and we say goodbye before racing off. There isn't much to see in our little town, but I am determined to give Bia the full tour.

After I show her the dinner, post office, and theater we head toward the little lake for a break. We find a tree and sit under it as we catch our breaths and enjoy the breeze.

"It is so beautiful here," Bia says in awe as she watches how the sunlight reflects off the water causing a faint rainbow to appear.

"It sure is. My mom packed us lunch," I say sheepishly as I pull out the brown paper bag and apples that Mr. Pruitt gave us from the basket on my bicycle.

I groan as soon as I realize what my mother packed us. The pungent smell is one that you simply cannot miss. I hand Bia her sandwich and watch as she excitedly picks up the top slice to see what filling was inside.

"What is this, Liam?" she asks sweetly with her head cocked to one side. "It is limburger cheese with sweet red onions. You don't have to eat it if you don't want to," I tell her.

The smell of limburger cheese is enough to put off any appetite. "Limburger. I have never heard of that cheese before," Bia says with a smile and takes a huge bite.

I watch as she crunches her way through the first bite. Not once did she twist her nose at the smell or make a funny face when chewing. If anything, her reaction was the complete opposite of what I was expecting.

"This is absolutely delicious!" Bia says after swallowing her first bite.

She takes another huge bite.

"Really? My mother baked the bread and my father made the cheese," I say with a smile.

"You really must ask your mom to teach me how to make such yummy bread. I used to bake bread with my abuelo all the time back in Uruguay. He would have loved this," Bia says with a sad smile.

She really is unlike any other girl I have ever met.

"So, you like Jasper?" I ask, trying to change the subject because I didn't want her to get sad.

"Jasper?" she asks, confused.

"Yeah, Jasper. The horse you were petting back at the town square," I say. A smile lights up her face and she gushes about how big, well-kept, and friendly the horse was. I sit next to her, feeling totally at peace as the sun begins to set over the water.

SEVEN

Beatrice

TODAY IS GOING SO much better than I expected. Finally, I found someone that I can actually get along with. Someone who has similar interests as me and someone that I enjoy spending time with. After the first day I met Liam, I would have never thought that we would be here, sitting beside a beautiful lake and having such a nice conversation.

Liam is kind, funny, and such great company. Maybe things were finally starting to look up for me. I had made a new friend; he was a cute boy and Di was so wonderful to me. I no longer felt like an outcast. The people at the town square this morning were so friendly to me and I even got to pet Jasper the horse.

"Who is your favorite superhero?" Liam asks.

This question kind of catches me off-guard. I am a bit taken aback so I take a few minutes to think before answering. I had not really given it much thought before.

"Well, I guess it would have to be Superman," I reply with a shrug. "What? How can you think that Superman is better than Batman?

Everyone knows that Batman is superior," Liam says passionately.

I notice the way his eyes light up when he talks about things that he is passionate about. It makes me feel warm on the inside and I stare at him for a moment before snapping out of it.

"No way. Superman can literally fly. He is hands down the best superhero," I say as a chill goes down my spine. The sun started to set and it was getting a bit chilly. Liam notices and he drapes his jacket around my shoulders. I smile and snuggle up, grateful for the warmth. The jacket smells just like him. A scent that is purely Liam, a little musky, earthy and strong. He really is such a gentleman.

"It is time to start heading back now," Liam says as he gets up and dusts a few blades of grass off him. My heart drops a little because I did not want this day to end. I had been having so much fun with Liam that the day seemed to just whizz by.

So I decided to make sure that this was not the end of the day. "Okay, but let's have a race to see who can get back to the town square first. The loser gets to go to the winner's house for dinner."

"Are you sure? Do you really think that you can take me and the bat-mobile on?" Liam asks as he raises one of his eyebrows and smiles.

I chuckle and nod my head. We throw away our trash in a nearby trashcan and jump on our bikes. Liam looks over at me and starts the countdown.

"On your marks… Get set… Go!"

We both speed off. Within a few seconds, Liam takes the lead. I did not care who the winner was, I just wanted to spend more time with him. The path ahead seems to be a bit dark. One of the street lights must have broken, I start to slow down and watch as Liam is engulfed by the darkness. He simply disappears. Then I hear a terrifying noise.

Crunch.

It sounds like a twig snapping or a bone being broken. This sound is followed by a shriek that stops me dead in my tracks. The sky above us is dark and the rain begins to gently fall. I stand there paralyzed as I have flashbacks of when I found my abuelo on the floor.

The sound of Liam groaning snaps me out of my paralyzed state. "Liam, where are you?" I call out as I slowly make my way down the path. I find him sitting on the ground with blood streaming down his knee. "Oh my goodness. What happened here?" I ask as I drop my bike and rush over to him.

Liam is holding his knee and is clearly in a lot of pain but he says, "Nothing. I am fine. I just need a minute."

His tough act is not fooling me. I go back to my bike and pull out the mini first aid kit that abuelo gave me. With the kit in my hand, I go back to Liam and do my best to bandage up his knee. He tries his best to keep his cool composure, but flinches a bit when I tighten the bandage. When I am done, he tries to get up by himself. It is clear that he is struggling.

"Hold on, Batman. Let me help you up," I say with a little laugh.

Liam tries to protest, but I wrap his arm around my neck and try my best to lift him off the ground. He groans as he tries to straighten up his leg so I urge him to take it slow. Once he is standing upright, he loosens his grip and then lets go of my neck altogether.

"Liam, wait," I yelp.

"I'm fine, Bia," he says solemnly as he begins to hobble over to his bike, which is lying on the ground a few feet away from where we are standing. He is so stubborn. It is infuriating. I follow him. Liam bends over to pick up the bike. His face scrunches up and it is obvious that he is in lots of pain.

I scowl as I quickly bend down and help him to lift his bike up. Then Liam tries to mount the bike and I am furious. "I have had enough heroics from you and your bat-mobile for one day," I say loudly.

For a second Liam stands still. He is shocked by my tone and then we both burst out laughing.

"Let's just push our bikes to the town square and I will use the payphone there to call Marc to come and fetch us," I say as I pick my bike up and walk over to where he is standing. To my surprise, Liam nods his head without protesting and we slowly begin to make our way back to the town square.

After a few moments of walking in silence, Liam asks, "So who do you think won the race?"

I burst out laughing at the ridiculous question and say that the answer is obvious.

"I am glad we agree then. You will be having dinner at my house," Liam says cockily.

I scoff, "There is absolutely no way that you won. You can't even get back on your bike."

"Well, I would have won if that silly twig didn't get stuck in my spoke and cause me to fall," Liam retorts.

"So that is what happened. All it took was a twig to bring down Batman and his bat mobile," I say with a giggle.

Liam and I both laugh as we slowly walk down the path to the town square—we are almost there now. I can tell that Liam is in pain and is going to need to take a break soon. Luckily, I spot a bench close to the entrance of the town square.

"You sit here while I go and call Marc," I instruct as I lean my bike on the bench and walk away before he even has a chance to argue.

The town square is quite beautiful at night. All of the people have gone home and it is so quiet that you can hear the way the water cascaded down the little water feature in the middle. I walk over to the payphone and call Marc hoping that he will pick up. He does.

"Bia, is that you? Where are you? Are you okay?" Marc asks. He sounds frantic.

"I am fine. My friend got hurt. Can you please come and pick us up from the bench in front of the entrance of the town square?" I ask. Marc agrees and says that we must sit tight and he will be there soon.

Walking back, I can already see the scowl on Liam's face.

"Marc will be here soon," I say. Liam nods and doesn't say anything. I sit down next to him and notice that his entire mood changed.

What happened while I was gone?

I look at him and he refuses to even look in my direction. "Is something wrong?" I finally ask.

Nothing.

He doesn't even respond. "Liam, what's wrong?" I plead.

He shakes his head and looks at me before saying, "It's nothing. I am just worried about how my mother is going to react when she sees this."

"We can call her from my house. Di will fix you up, then you can have something to eat and Marc will take you home," I say.

"You are very bossy," Liam says with a grin. I laugh and playfully whack him on the arm, grateful that his mood has lightened. Just like that, Liam and I became best friends. We spent every waking moment together after that.

EIGHT

5 YEARS PRIOR TO THE CURRENT DAY …

I CANNOT BELIEVE that today is my first day as a freshman in high school. My entire body is wracked with nerves. The only thing that is keeping me sane at this moment is the fact that I will get to see Liam today. Over the summer break, my family and I went back to Uruguay because my father had to attend an important summit and we had to prepare for my abuelo's tombstone ceremony. It has been over two months since I last saw Liam and I am so excited to tell him about my summer break and to hear about what he got up to over break.

The truth is that it is so much more than that. I missed him so much over summer break. Almost daily I would catch my mind drifting back to thoughts of him. What was he doing? Did he enjoy his summer break? And most importantly, was he missing me as much as I was missing him?

Thinking about this made me so nervous. Liam and I had been best friends for the past two years. It was always him and I. The two of us side by side against the world. However, being away from him during break made me realize that my feelings for him were so much more than just being best friends.

My train of thought is broken when I hear the familiar honk of a car horn. It is Marc. I grab my backpack, adjust a butterfly clip on my hair and get a final look at myself in the mirror before rushing downstairs.

"Bia, you are going to be late," Di yells from the bottom of the staircase. I shuffle down the stairs as fast as I can and hear her mumbling something in Spanish. She holds out a brown paper bag with my lunch and I give her a quick hug before sprinting out the door with a pop tart in my mouth.

Marc is waiting for me with a huge smile on his face. "Hello, Bia. It is so nice to have you back," he says genuinely as he opens the back door for me.

"I missed you," I say between mouthfuls of my strawberry pop tart. I jump in the backseat and smooth over my skirt as Marc starts the car and drives me to school. Once I am done eating my pop tart, I rummage through my bag and I try to find the gift that I got for Liam, but I cannot seem to find it. My heart sinks as I realize that I had left it on my dresser.

"Are you excited for your first day of high school?" Marc asks warmly. "I am," I tell him as I nod my head enthusiastically, shaking off the disappointment from having forgotten Liam's gift.

"Well good, because we are here," Marc replies as he stops the car.

I peer out the window and look at my new school. It is so much bigger than my previous one. The kids here look more intense and definitely way more daunting. My excitement begins to wane and fear starts to creep in. I shrink into the backseat.

"Hey, don't be scared, little miss. You got this," Marc says encouragingly. I take a deep breath and get out of the car. I hear Marc call out to wish me good luck as I close the door and walk toward the school. There were kids everywhere and they were all taller and bigger than me. It felt like I was drowning in a crowd of people. I accidentally bumped into a guy wearing a black t-shirt with a skull on it. After quickly apologizing, the scary guy just grunted and walked away. I search the crowd, trying to find a familiar face.

As I walk in through the school door, I enter a long hallway with lockers on either side of the wall. I know that my locker number is 324 so I decide to try and find it before the school bell rings. Making my way down the hallway, I look at all of the numbers until my eyes finally find mine. I go over and unlock it before jamming in my lunch and a few textbooks from my bag. As I am doing this, I feel someone tap my shoulder.

I whirl around to see Liam standing there. At least I think it is him. He's gotten so much taller, probably grown a whole foot since I last saw him. I don't know what comes over me, but in that moment, I am so excited and grateful to see a familiar face that I drop my backpack to the ground and throw my arms around his neck. He welcomes my embrace and I take a deep breath as I inhale the scent that is so unique to him.

"It is nice to see you too," Liam says with a chuckle.

I snap out of it and quickly take a step back before clearing my throat and saying, "Sorry. I don't know what came over me."

"It's okay. I missed you too, my Bia," Liam says tenderly.

His voice had cracked over break and he no longer sounded like a little boy. Actually, he sounded like a man. His voice was so deep and just hearing him calling me "his Bia" sent shivers down my spine. I look at him and our eyes lock. In that instant, it feels like there is electricity buzzing between us. Even now, in this busy corridor, all I see is him and I know he is feeling the same way—I can tell by the look of tenderness on his face.

The school bell rings and a woman's voice announces over the PA system that all freshmen are to report to the gym immediately.

Liam clears his throat and says, "We better get going." I nod, grab my bag and follow him to the gym.

We take our seat on the bleachers and the principal gives us a speech to welcome us before we are separated into groups for the school tour and dismissed. Liam and I end up in separate groups, but before we part ways, he comes over to me and says, "I will meet you in the cafeteria for lunch." I silently hoped and prayed that we would have at least one class together.

There was one familiar face in my group though and that was Mary. She came over to me as soon as Liam left and began asking me about my summer break. Turns out that Mary and her family had gone to Texas for break to visit family. She told me all about the Texas heat and the delicious barbecue. The conversation was actually decent now that she had gotten over that boy band. Things were already starting to look up and it was time to start another chapter in my life.

We set off out the gym door and down the halls for our school tour. Our guide was a cheerleader and a senior. She showed us where all of the different classrooms were and took us to the football field. Just as our tour was about to end, she came up to me and handed me a flier. It was for cheerleader tryouts.

"Tryouts are tomorrow afternoon in the gym. You should come," the girl said with a smile before leaving. The bell sounds and without giving it much thought I shove the flier in my bag and head to my first class. By third period, I was already exhausted both mentally and physically because I had gotten lost four times and had to ask the not so friendly kids in my school for directions.

When the lunch bell sounds, I breathe a sigh of relief. Finally, I get to catch up with Liam. I grab my bag and stop by my locker to fetch my lunch before speeding to the cafeteria. When I get there, I see Liam sitting at a table to the far left. I make my way over to him but as I am walking, the cheerleader that gave me the tour this morning stops me.

"Hey. I didn't get a chance to really speak to you earlier. My name is Chelsea, I am the cheer captain and you must be Beatrice, the ambassador's daughter, right?" the senior asks with a smile that does not reach her eyes. "Hi, uh, yes. I am," I reply as I try to get past her. She sidesteps and blocks my path to Liam, who I can see is staring at us.

"You should come and sit with us," Chelsea says as she points to a table where the other cheerleaders are seated.

I smile and say, "Maybe next time."

Chelsea looks surprised at first and then nods and walks away. Finally! I sigh and walk over to Liam who is staring at me curiously. "What was all of that about?" Liam asks.

"She wants me to try out for the cheer squad and she asked me to have lunch with them," I say with a huff.

Liam laughs. Like actually laughs until there are tears streaming down his cheeks.

I frown. "Why are you laughing?"

Then Liam sobers up. "Wait, you are not actually considering joining them. Are you?"

I stutter and say, "Well… I don't know."

"Bia, you're joking right? Just look at those girls. They're so… I don't know and you are you," Liam says.

I feel hot tears begin to sting my eyes now. "What's that supposed to mean?" I ask as I choke back a sob.

"Bia, just look at them. They're so girly and fake. What would you even talk about?" he asks.

One tear escapes and trickles down my face. "So you don't think I'm girly? I think I forgot something in my locker. Maybe I'll see you later," I say as I quickly get up and make my way out of the cafeteria before the tears start pouring down my face.

I hear Liam call out after me, but I just walk faster. At this point, I'm practically running as I make my way to the girl's bathroom. I lock myself in a stall and burst into tears.

NINE

Liam

THIS IS DEFINITELY not how I expected this day to go. Clearly, I upset Bia. All I meant was that those girls seem so pretentious and unlike her. Bia is the most genuine and beautiful person that I have ever met on the inside and outside. Over the break, there wasn't a single day when I did not think about her. Sometimes, on the days when I missed her a lot, I would ride past her house or go to the lake and sit under our tree. The tree where Bia and I spent our first day as friends together.

I was so excited to see her today and I had planned on telling her how I felt, but there was no way that I could do that now. Not after I had upset her so much. I have to figure out a way to make things right. I reach into my backpack and pull out my notepad. The only way for me to make things right and express myself properly is for me to write her a note. I end up scraping the first two attempts, but then the words start flowing. The rest of lunch is spent working on this note. I write:

My Dearest Bia,

You are the kindest and most genuine person that I have ever had the privilege of meeting. I am really sorry for what I said earlier. It did not come across the way I meant it to. Please let me make it up to you. Will you meet me at 6 PM tonight? I will be waiting for you by the Ferris wheel at the carnival.

Liam

The bell sounds to let us know that lunch is over and I slip the letter into my bag before heading to my next class, which is French. Bia told me that she also picked French so I cross my fingers and hope that she is in the same class. I walk into the classroom and my eyes instantly fall on my beautiful Bia. She is seated in the second row and there is an empty seat next to her.

As I walk closer, I notice that her eyes are red and puffy, something that only happens when she cries. My heart sinks as I take my seat next to her. She refuses to even look at me.

Before I can say anything, a slim, tall lady with a high bun that looks like it is so tight that it is pulling the skin on her face back walks into the classroom and introduces herself as Mrs. Du Fleur, our French teacher. She tells us that no one is allowed to speak in her class unless they are spoken to and lays down a few other ground rules. Honestly, she is kind of scary.

I know that there is no way for me to talk to Bia and try to make things right now. It feels hopeless sitting next to her not being able to do or say anything. The only thing I can do is slip her the letter that I wrote her and hope that she decides to read it. Bia eyes the letter suspiciously and quickly pockets it when she notices the strict French teacher walking toward us.

Sitting this close to her without being able to say a word to her, knowing that she is hurting and I am the reason why, is nothing short of torture. I just want to put my arms around her and hold her close while I tell her how much she means to me. For now, I can't do any of these things. The only thing that I can do is hope that she reads my letter and agrees to meet me tonight.

Throughout the rest of the lesson, I steal a few glances at Bia when Mrs. Du Fleur has her back turned to us. I notice that Bia hasn't even looked at the letter yet. When the French class is over, Bia grabs her stuff and bolts out of the room before I even have a chance to say anything to her. With my spirits low, I get through the rest of the day before the final bell sounds and it is time to go home. Not exactly how I expected my first day as a freshman to go. I had only seen Bia in the hallway one time and she completely ignored my existence. The only thing that I can do now is hope that she will actually show up later.

I get home and as soon as I walk through the front door, my mother asks, "So how was your first day of freshman year?"

Trying not to grimace, I put on my best smile and say, "It was okay. I upset Bia, but I am hoping to make it right tonight at the carnival."

My mother smiles sympathetically and puts her arm around my shoulder, "Bia is a very special girl. I know she means a lot to you so be sure to not let small things come in between what you two have."

Taking a deep breath, I nod and get started on my chores. After watering the plants, I go to the shed and check if my dad needs any help. He asks me to complete a few small tasks. Before I know it, time has flown by. It is almost 5:30 PM and I need to freshen up and start making my way to the carnival.

The walk there is nerve-wracking. My palms are sweaty as I walk down the long windy road toward the bright, blinking lights of the carnival. I stand beside the Ferris wheel and wait patiently. I look at the watch on my wrist. Every time the hand moves and a minute passes, I look up and scan the crowd. With each second that passes my pulse quickens. The heat of the day is still lingering and I feel beads of sweat start to form on my forehead as my sleek, straight hair gets damp and sticks to the back of my neck.

Looking at my watch again, I notice that only a few minutes have passed but it feels like I have been standing here forever. The carnival is getting busier and I begin to scan the crowd more frantically. There are so many faces, a few of them are even familiar but none of them are my Bia. Then a chilling thought runs through my mind.

What if she doesn't show up?

My blood runs cold. Each breath I take feels like it is scorching my lungs and making it even more difficult to breathe. Just when it feels like I am about to pass out, I see her angelic face. Someone turns on a spotlight behind Bia as she walks toward me giving her a halo. She is wearing a flowy white dress with daisies on it and her long hair is flowing on either side of her face. Her eyes land on me and her rosy lips curl into a small smile.

Bia wafts her way to me and says, "Hey."

She is looking at the ground the entire time and twiddling her fingers. "I uh… I thought you weren't going to come," I say.

Bia rocks back on her heels and says, "Yeah, sorry for being late. I had to wait for Marc to finish up a few things."

A strand of her hair falls over her eyes and instinctively, I reach out and tuck it behind her ear. I let my hand linger on her cheek. Her skin is so soft and Bia leans into my touch. We are drawn to each other like magnets. Before we know it, Bia and I are standing right in front of each other. There is hardly any space in between us. Slowly, I move my mouth toward her. Just as our lips are about to touch, I hear someone say, "Bia!"

We spring away from each other at lightning speed. Bia and I look and see her friend Mary and a few of the other girls from school heading toward us. Behind them, I spot Tommy and Shane walking toward us.

"I hope that I am not interrupting anything," Mary says mischievously as she eyes Bia and I. My cheeks are hot and my palms start getting sweaty all over again.

Bia clears her throat and says, "Oh no. Not at all. I didn't know that you guys were coming to the carnival tonight."

Tommy and Shane join our group and we are all standing in a circle now.

"Liam, my boy. Let's go on the Ferris wheel," Tommy says, saving me from the awkwardness of this conversation. We all head to the Ferris wheel behind us and I make sure that Bia and I are seated together. Tommy and Mary end up getting seated together and I can see that Tommy is less than pleased as they enter their pod below us. Slowly Bia and I go higher and higher. The people below us look smaller as we go up and the sky above dazzles with the light of the stars. It is a perfect night.

TEN

Beatrice

MY BREATH IS STILL a bit shaky. I cannot believe that Liam actually tried to kiss me only a few moments ago. What is even more unfathomable to me is that fact that I actually wanted him to and as soon as Mary showed up, I felt the bitter taste of disappointment in my mouth. Now, as we are seated in silence beside each other on this Ferris wheel I cannot bring myself to even look at him. I am grateful for the darkness of the night that encases us as we go higher up the Ferris wheel because the darkness helps to hide my embarrassment and flushed cheeks from Liam.

I try to sit back and enjoy the beauty of this moment, but my heart is pounding in my chest. Being this high off the ground makes me feel slightly anxious. I don't particularly have a fear of heights. Well, that is when my feet are planted on the ground or I am horseback riding, but sitting here with my feet dangling in the air makes me painfully aware of the distance between me and the cold, dusty ground below.

Clutching the safety bar, I feel my palms getting sweaty against the iron rod with a few rusty spots on it. My fingernails dig into the soft flesh of my palm as I try to tighten my grip and try to calm myself down.

Just then it is as if my worst nightmare becomes a reality. The Ferris wheel begins to make a weird screeching noise. Our capsule begins to rock and comes to a halt right at the very top of the Ferris wheel. I freak out and clutch on to Liam when I hear Mary's shrill scream as a cloud of smoke rises from beneath us.

"Don't worry! We will have everything sorted out in a few moments!" the ride operator yells from below.

Liam clears his throat and I realize that in the heat of the moment, I had flung my arms around his neck and clasped my fingers tightly. The heat rises in my cheeks and we make eye contact. I still haven't removed my hands from their spot around his neck. A part of me is afraid that if I do, I might fall to the ground below. I try to convince myself that my fear is completely irrational, but being this close to Liam is making my brain a bit fuzzy.

He looks at me and without even saying a word, swoops his head down and covers my mouth with his. At first, I am slightly taken aback, but I warm up as my body yields to his gentle assault on my mouth. My lips part and welcome his tongue as we both explore each other. The kiss starts off so gentle and then keeps growing in passion. Liam weaves his hand in my hair and pulls my head closer to his, I moan as he kisses me even more deeply and passionately than anything I could have ever imagined. We are both so caught up in our passionate make out session that we completely forget that we are in a public space with our friends just below us in the other capsules.

"Oh get a room you two," Tommy yells from below us.

I pull away from Liam and I am certain that I am about to spontaneously combust on the spot. My cheeks are burning with embarrassment and I am a bit breathless for our intense make out session.

"Get lost, Tommy," Liam yells and then turns back to me as I am frantically trying to pull myself together and set my tousled hair. Liam flashes me one of his dazzling smiles and I feel chills run up my skin. Goosebumps prickle my skin.

Liam leans closer and asks, "Are you cold?"

I shake my head as I try to mask the surge of excitement that goes through my body as a reaction to having him so close. He places his warm hand on mine. I feel the rough calluses on my smooth skin and I'm reminded of what a hard worker he is. Smiling internally with pride, I look at him curiously wondering what he is about to say.

"So, I told you that I wanted to speak to you," Liam says meekly. "You did," I reply. For some reason, I am so nervous.

What could he possibly have to say to me? Will he say that the kiss was just a mistake or he doesn't want to be my friend anymore? Oh goodness, I hope he doesn't. I am certain that I will burst into a thousand little pieces if he does.

Shuffling in my seat, I try to search his face, illuminated by the moonlight, for answers. However, Liam has a straight face and is hiding his emotions so well. I am a bit frustrated that I am drawing blanks here, but I do know that whatever he has to say to me, it is important. I can tell by the way he is looking at me with so much intensity, it is like he is looking directly at my soul. In this moment, I feel so exposed and vulnerable. No one has ever looked at me like this.

Liam squeezes my hand gently and says, "You know how over break we were away from each other for such a long time?"

Of course I knew we were away from each other for the longest time over break. I missed him every single day that we were apart. Was that a goodbye kiss?

I can feel tears begin to pickle my eyes as these painful thoughts cross my mind. Stop it! I begin to scold myself. At this point, I know that I am just hyping myself up, so I try to ignore my thoughts and focus all of my attention on Liam instead. Nodding my head in agreement, I urge him to continue.

He clears his throat and when he speaks his voice is slightly hoarse as he says, "Well, in that time I could not get you off my mind. Will you be my girlfriend, Bia?"

Joy courses through my body and I feel the hair on the back of my neck stand up. "Yes. Yes, I will be your girlfriend," I say as the tears stream down my face. Liam just made me the happiest girl in the world. I wrap my hands around his neck and kiss him. The capsule wobbles, but we are too caught up in the moment to pay any heed to it. Liam suckles on my lips gently and ignites a fire in my belly.

Just then, we hear the wails of a siren.

"Yo, is there a fire or something?" Tommy yells as the flashing red lights of the firetruck become visible. A man's voice booms over a megaphone letting us know to sit tight and not panic. He grunts and says, "That is easy for you to say. You aren't stuck looking at a smooch fest."

My cheeks turn hot and Liam and I both giggle. I tuck my head into his neck and he cuddles me. We stay there until we are rescued by the town firefighters. This night sure had taken an unexpected twist. A few unexpected twists actually. I walked in here thinking that the friendship between Liam and I was over and here I am walking out of the carnival as his girlfriend.

Once we are on the ground Mary rushes to me and says to Liam, "I just need to borrow Bia for a second."

She drags me to the corner of the Ferris wheel and asks, "So what was all of that about?"

I try to brush it off and act like I don't know what she is talking about but she is having none of it.

"Come on, Bia. I totally saw you and Liam up there. You were all over each other," she says as she rolls her eyes and places her hands on her hips dramatically. She arches one of her fuzzy brows and looks at me.

Her words send shivers down my spine as I recall the precious moments that Liam and I just shared together.

"Okay, Liam asked me to be his girlfriend," I say.

Mary squeals and grabs my shoulders, "You said yes, right?"

I nod my head shyly and she throws her arms around me saying, "Congratulations! I am so happy for you two."

Gasping for breath as I try to recover from Mary's death grip, I take a step back and say thank you to her. Glancing over, I notice that Liam is looking at us curiously. Smiling at him, I look back at Mary. I can tell that she did not pull me over here to ask me about Liam.

"Thanks, Mary. What about you and Tommy?" I ask.

Instantly, her cheeks turn red and she can't seem to look me in the eye. "Come on, spill the beans," I say with a chuckle.

Mary looks over at Tommy goofing off with one of the guys and I see her facial expression soften. "I think I have a crush on him," she says meekly.

I giggle and link my hand in hers. "Come on girl. I am going to be the best wing woman ever." We walk back to our group of friends and I say, "Hey guys, who wants to go and get some ice-cream at my place?"

Most of them do not seem interested but Mary and Liam agree. I chime in saying, "Hey Tommy, you live a few houses away from me. You should come too. It is on your way home."

Tommy shrugs nonchalantly and agrees to join us. We all walk out of the carnival together and Marc drives us all to my house for a little snack. Mary is trying her best to hide her excitement but is doing a dismal job as the entire car ride to my house she yaps all our ears off. I smile sweetly and try to engage with her. She is such a sweet person and the first friend that I made here, besides Liam, of course.

We spent the rest of the night playing card games and eating ice-cream together. Liam even manages to sneak in a few cheeky kisses every now and then. For the first time in a while, I feel so content as I look around the table at my friends and now, my boyfriend.

ELEVEN

Liam

3 YEARS PRIOR TO THE CURRENT DAY …

BIA AND I WALK into school holding hands. As we enter the building, the halls are buzzing as students excitedly empty out their lockers.

"Just imagine, next year that is going to be us," Bia squeals with glee.

It is so hard for me to believe that in just one short year Bia and I will be graduating high school. The future seems so bright, but also so daunting. A part of me was absolutely terrified. Just 12 months until I start the rest of my life. The prospect of the future is both exhilarating and incredibly intriguing.

Looking to my right, my eyes fall on the beautiful girl walking beside me. She looks around at the seniors who are emptying out their lockers with such anticipation. My nerves settle and in this moment I realize that regardless of what the future holds for us both, as long as we are together, we could conquer anything.

The school bell sounds and it is time for us to get to class. Bia turns around to face me and says, "I will catch you at lunch." She gives me a peck on the cheek and then skips away to her first class. I watch as her long, dark hair catches the rays of the sun, making them glisten and creating a celestial-like aura around her.

How did I get so lucky?

Bia disappears around the corner and I smile to myself as I think about the past year that we spent together as boyfriend and girlfriend. Our relationship was not perfect. We bickered and argued, but we could never stay mad at each other for long. I know that I will never love anyone as much as I love Bia. She is the one and only girl for me and I plan on telling her that later.

The periods fly by as I eagerly anticipate the evening that I have planned with Bia. Even my math class feels somewhat bearable because of how excited I am for what is to come. When the bell sounds for lunch, I scurry out of the classroom and head down the crowded halls to the cafeteria. After scanning the room, I spot Bia sitting with our friends and head over to them.

"Hey, beautiful," I say and I plant a kiss on the top of her head. Bia smiles and scoots aside to make space for me beside her.

Across the table from us, Mary sighs and says, "You guys are the cutest. I wish someone would take some notes," as she shoots daggers at Tommy who is too busy shooting spitballs at some guys to even notice her snarky comment. Mary rolls her head and stuffs a brownie in her mouth.

Bia and I giggle. She leans closer to me and whispers, "I am so excited for our little adventure tonight. You are coming to my house at 4 PM, right?"

I nod and take a sip of my water.

Just then, one of the most annoying and pompous seniors named John walks up to our table. I feel my skin tingle with anger like a feral cat when I notice the way he is looking at Bia.

"Hey gorgeous," he says in a slimy voice.

Bia grimaces and says, "Hi John."

I cannot stand the guy and it isn't just because I know that he has eyes for Bia.

"So are you coming to the lunch that they are hosting at the country club after school?" John asks.

Bia tenses up beside me.

This is the first time that I am hearing about this. How come she never told me and why is she tensing up? What about our adventure?

"Yeah, I will be there. My parents are forcing me to go," Bia replies dryly. John smirks and turns his gaze to me before smirking and saying, "Guess I won't be seeing you there." Without even waiting for me to reply, he turns around and walks away.

Geez. That guy gets under my skin.

I take a deep breath to calm myself down and then turn to Bia, who is nervously nibbling on a grape and ask, "What lunch is he talking about?" "Well, they are hosting an end of year lunch at the country club and my parents are making me go. I know you hate these pretentious social gatherings so I didn't even bother inviting you," Bia gushes without even stopping to take a breath between her sentences.

She is right. I do hate these events. The last dinner I went to at the country club was an absolute disaster. I ended up accidentally spilling cocktail sauce all over one of the ladies who frowned at me with so much disdain.

Just thinking about that experience leaves a bitter taste in my mouth and do not even get me started on all of the fake and pretentious conversations I was forced to engage in. These events were such a drag, but a part of me can't help but feel like Bia didn't tell me about this lunch because she is embarrassed of me.

Bia probably notices the look of discomfort and anxiousness on my face because she goes on to say, "You are more than welcome to come with me if you want though."

Shaking my head, I reply and say, "No, thank you. But will you be done in time for our little adventure?" I ask knowing how long these sorts of things tend to go on for.

"Yes. Definitely, I will be ready on time even if I need to sneak out early. If I do happen to be a little bit late for whatever reason, Di will let you in," Bia says with a smile.

All of my doubts evaporate as soon as I see her beautiful smile and the way that her eyes light up when she talks about the adventure that we have planned. To be fair, it is nowhere near as fancy as the lunch that she is going to be attending at the country club, but I can see the excitement on her face when she talks about our adventure.

The bell signaling the end of lunch sounds and I give Bia a quick peck on the cheek before saying, "Okay. I will see you later. Enjoy your lunch." Grabbing my bag, I hurry out of the lunch room and to the gym for my next period.

By the end of the school day, I am exhausted, but also very excited that it is over.

"Can you believe that our junior year is finally over?" Tommy says as he throws his arm around me. His arm lands like a weight on my shoulders due to his large build.

"Yeah, man. We are going to be seniors next year," I reply as I try to shrug his arm off.

Tommy moves his arm to high five one of our friends and then turns his attention back to me.

"What are you and the missus doing to celebrate?" Tommy asks.

I smile and reply, "We are going for a hike up the mountain in her backyard and we plan to camp at this nice spot we saw on our last hike up there. What about you?"

"Ugh. Bro, that sounds chill. Mary is dragging me to some snooze fest at the theater," Tommy replies.

In my opinion, Tommy and Mary made the oddest couple. They basically have nothing in common except for the fact that they both love sucking each other's face off. But who am I to judge?

"Haha, enjoy. I will catch you over break," I say before we part ways. The bus smells extra funky today for whatever reason. I make my way to the back and plonk myself down on one of the empty seats. The entire ride home, I stare out the window and daydream about the incredible afternoon that I am about to have with my beautiful girlfriend. I picture us, standing in each other's arms under the starry night sky. It is so perfect that I get so lost in my thoughts and almost miss my stop. The bus driver yells my name and I get up hastily and make my way to the front. Before I jump out, I apologize to the driver and then start walking up the long and windy path to my house.

As I walk, I find my thoughts wandering to Bia.

I wonder what she is doing right now? She is probably already at the country club by now. I bet that sleazy John is there. Is she talking to him? Nah, she wouldn't. I know that she cannot stand the guy just as much as I can't, but of course she is too polite to say anything. Regardless, I hope that she is having a good time.

From a distance, I see my mother busy taking the laundry off the line with my little sister on her heels and my father's shed door is open, which means that he probably has a new order. As a carpenter, he works odd hours and the income is not exactly steady, but somehow my parents still manage to make ends meet. I cannot wait to finish school and start working so that I can help them out.

When I get closer my mother spots me. "How was your last day as a junior?"

My little sister runs over to me and wraps her hands around my leg. I chuckle and pick her up, swinging her around until she giggles uncontrollably.

"Hi, ma. It was good," I say and give her a kiss on the cheek.

She begins to tear up and says, "You all are growing up so fast. Just look at your older sister already working and you are almost done with high school."

"Don't cry," I say softly.

My mother brushes me off and says, "Don't mind me. Are you still going camping with Bia tonight? Mrs. Blooming mentioned that there is some event happening at the country club today."

"Yes, I am. Bia is going to leave early," I say as I walk past her into the house.

"Okay. I made you a plate. Warm it up and I will pack a little picnic basket for you and Bia for later," my mother calls after me.

I know better than to argue with her or tell her that Di is already packing food for us, so I thank her and walk in. After scarfing down the food my mother left for me, I go outside and get started on my chores before heading upstairs and getting ready for the exciting night ahead.

TWELVE

Beatrice

I SHUFFLE IN MY SEAT as the itchy, pink polyester material sticks to my skin. Sighing, I wish that I was anywhere but here. My mother, who is seated beside me, notices me shuffling and flashes her emerald eyes at me before harshly whispering, "Stop shuffling and sit up straight."

Then she turns around and plasters her pearly white smile on. It was the type of smile that did not quite reach her eyes and never seemed genuine. I roll my eyes and do as she says, longing for the moment that I can rush home and get out of this ridiculous, frilly dress.

The country club is decorated according to a floral theme. There are loads of flowers everywhere and each place setting is a little graduation hat. This lunch is in honor of all the seniors that are graduating this year. They spared no expense from fancy cutlery to an elaborate setup at the front of the country club ballroom. There are even tiny graduation hats shaped cookies on the table.

"Hey, Beatrice. So lovely to see you here," Chelsea the cheerleader from school says as she walks past our table.

Ever since I turned down the opportunity to be a cheerleader, Chelsea and her groupies have been anything but kind to me. In fact, on more than one occasion she has 'accidentally' tripped me while I was walking through the cafeteria or down the hallway at school. To make matters worse, Chelsea seemed to have a crush on John that was not reciprocated. I smile at her meekly and take a long sip of my sweet tea.

"Hello, Mrs. Varela. How are you?" Chelsea says sweetly as she flutters her lashes at my mother.

My mother and Chelsea engage in some polite, pretentious conversation for a few moments before Chelsea excuses herself and walks away in her brick red, sweetheart neckline, silk gown.

"Such a lovely girl. You really should be more like her," my mother gushes as Chelsea walks away. I pinch at the dainty cream puff on my plate and hope that this little façade is over soon. The only time I got to spend any time with my parents is whenever we attend these social events, forced to grin and play happy family. I do understand that my parents are busy trying to create a better life for me, but I just wish they would spend time with me.

When I was little, my abuelo would insist on having a family dinner at least once a week. That was the only quality time I spent with my parents and since his death, we haven't had a family dinner. So I take what I get and grit my teeth to attend these pretentious events just so that I can spend some time with them.

I wish my family was like Liam's. They have dinner as a family every day and his house is so warm and homely because of how much love they all have for each other. He has such a precious bond with his mother and father. I can't help but feel slightly envious whenever I go over.

One of the high society mothers goes up to the platform and calls the graduates to the front of the room. I look around and spot John as he straightens his coat and makes his way to the front. He is pleasant to look at with his short blonde hair, chiseled jaw, blue eyes, and broad shoulders.

What he had in looks, he lacked in personality though and whenever he was around, I instantly felt uneasy. Just then, I make eye contact with Chelsea. She shoots me a venomous look which I ignore and instead take a bite of my cream puff. The delicious flaky pastry melts as soon as it touches my tongue and the fresh cream coats my tongue luxuriously. It is pure decadence in a bite.

The lady at the front of the room announces the name of each graduate and congratulates them by handing each one a little Louis Vuitton bag. I finish the treats on my plate and as soon as she announces the name of the last person, I get up, ready to dash off. Just then, my mother grabs my hand.

"Where are you going? I thought that we could go and get some ice-cream to spend some time together and celebrate the end of your junior year," my mother says.

Looking through the window, I can see that the sun is already starting to set and I know that Liam will most likely be on his way to my house already. Panic sets in and I know that I need to get home as soon as possible.

I hesitate and say, "Sorry, but I already have plans."

My mother raises her brow and looks over to John who is chatting to a few ladies only a short distance away from our table. I can already tell what my mother is thinking without her saying a word.

"I have plans with Liam," I correct her before her mind wanders anymore.

My mother scrunches up her face disapprovingly and sighs. I take this as my cue to leave and rush out of the country club to the parking lot where Marc is already waiting for me.

"Please hurry, Marc. I promised Liam that I would be home on time," I say breathlessly from running to the car.

"I will get you there as soon as I can," Marc says reassuringly and drives off.

In the backseat, I kick off my high heels that my mother insisted I wear and breathe out a sigh of relief as my aching feet feel some comfort again. After tugging out the ridiculous flowers that my mother pinned to my hair,

I look at the clock in the car and realizing that I was supposed to be home 20 minutes ago, I say a silent prayer and hope that Liam won't be mad at me. He was already upset about the fact that I didn't invite him to this event. Now that I am late for our plans, I can only hope that this doesn't add to the fire.

A few moments later, Marc pulls up our driveway and I fling the door open before rushing inside. Bursting through the kitchen doors, I see Liam, snuggling a mug, seated at the table, and smiling happily while talking to Di.

He looks up and a mischievous grin appears on his face. "You look like cotton candy," he teases.

I playfully whack his shoulder and feel a sense of relief. The fact that he is making jokes means that he isn't mad at me.

"Your bags are packed. All you need to do is go upstairs and get out of the ridiculous dress," Di says to me.

I chuckle and say, "Thank you, Di," before going upstairs and changing into my sweatpants. When I am done, I head back downstairs to find Liam standing at the back door with both our backpacks and the picnic basket. "Do you have everything we need for our little camping trip?" I ask as

I suspiciously eye the bags or lack thereof.

Liam laughs and assures me that we have everything we need. We both say goodbye to Di and start our trek toward Lovers Mountains. The last rays of the sun are shining and we try to hurry as much as we can while enjoying our hike.

When we are at the base of the mountain Liam asks, "Hey, Bia, why were you late?"

I clutch the straps of my backpack nervously and say, "Oh, sorry about that, but the lunch went on a bit longer than expected and my mother wanted to go and get ice-cream after, but I told her that we already had plans."

Liam stops in his tracks and turns around to face me. His brows are knit together and he has a look of tenderness in his eyes. Walking toward me, he takes my hand and says, "Bia, why didn't you go?"

"Well, we had plans and I knew that you would be waiting for me," I say.

Liam cups my cheek with his palm gently and says, "My Bia, I know how much it means to you to spend time with your parents. You should have gone."

I shake my head as the tears well up in my eyes. Liam is such a gentle, understanding and compassionate person. *How did I get so lucky?*

"Today is special. I would rather spend it with you," I say as I choke down the sobs of joy that threaten to escape.

Liam smiles and swoops his head down. His lips touch mine with such gentleness, I melt against him. He loops his arms around my waist and deepens the kiss. The fresh breeze blows against us and I hear the birds happily chirping in the trees above us. Everything about this feels so magical. I nestle my head against his chest as I experience the bliss of being here in his arms and I am certain that there is nowhere else that I would rather be.

THIRTEEN

Liam

BIA AND I MAKE it up Lovers Mountains with just enough time to set up our camp before the sun sets. I stood behind her with my arms wrapped around her waist. She was pressed up to me and when the wind blew, it carried the scent of her strawberry shampoo along with it. The sky in front of us looked like it had been set alight as its amber hues glowed magnificently.

We stood there in silence as we appreciate the splendor of the sight in front of us. While Bia appreciated the beauty of the sunset, I appreciate her beauty. The way her emerald eyes twinkled, the way her long, dark hair blew in the wind, the way her flawless skin glowed as it caught the last rays of the sun.

There is one thing that I am certain of, this is a moment that I will forever treasure. It is the exact moment I realize that I cannot even begin to imagine my life without my Bia. She is and will be the only girl for me.

In this moment, I know that she is my forever person. The sun sets and the air becomes chilly. A gust of wind blows and sends shivers coursing through Bia's body. Taking off my jacket, I wrap it around her shoulders and lead her toward our campsite a few feet away from the edge of the cliff of the mountain.

The campfire I started when we got here makes a sizzling pop sound as we get closer. Even though I am not standing directly beside it, I can feel the heat that it is emitting. Going over to the picnic basket that my mother packed for us, I pull out a flask and grab two cups before making my way back to Bia, who is now snuggled up beside the fire. I sit down next to her and open the flask before pouring out the piping hot contents.

The luxurious smell of chocolate combined with the musky smoke of the fire is intoxicating. I hand a cup over to Bia and hold mine in between my palms as I watch the steam gently wisp its way out of the cup.

"Hmm, this is delicious," Bia says, licking her lip after taking a sip.

I blow on the hot chocolate before taking a sip of my childhood in a cup and smile.

"This is exactly how my mom used to make it for me when I was little," I reply.

Bia snuggles closer to me and we sit there again for a few moments in silence. Both of us just stare at the fire in front of us, enjoying the warmth that it brings. The silence is broken by the sound of Bia's tummy grumbling. She looks up at me and we both burst out laughing.

"Shall we have dinner?" I ask with a chuckle.

Bia nods and says, "Yes, please. I am so hungry I could eat a horse."

I laugh and reply, "Well, you are just going to have to settle for Di's corned beef sandwiches." After we are done eating, we lay on the ground near the fire. The dark night sky above us is aglow with loads and loads of tiny little twinkling stars and seems to stretch to infinity as it disappears beyond the horizon.

Propping myself up on one hand, I look down at my beautiful Bia lying beside me.

"I wish it could be like this forever," she sighs and continues, "just you and I. On our own little farm. That is my dream, you know? One day, I want to own a farm, and on that farm I want to have a white horse. Not just any horse though. It has to be a Cremello horse with a spotless white coat. In the evenings, after we put the kids to bed, I want to sit on a rocking chair on the porch and look up at the stars, just like this, with you beside me. What is your dream, my sweet guy?" Bia asks as her eyes widen and she looks at me curiously.

Without even hesitating I tell her, "My dream is to become a world-famous writer one day so that I can buy you the farm of your dreams and raise a family with you. I can picture us with our two boys and one girl, all going to the farmer's market on a Saturday morning after having a delicious breakfast of chocolate chip pancakes."

She smiles and her eyes soften and her beautiful features are illuminated by the amber glow of the sizzling fire beside us.

"You really want to start a family with me one day?" she asks in a hushed tone.

I nod and Bia puts her hand around my neck and pulls my face to hers. She covers my mouth with her soft, luscious lips and kisses me tenderly. I yield to her touch and our bodies melt into each other. She traces the outline of my lips teasingly with her tongue and my body goes limp. Desire and passion course through me. I gasp and open my eyes to look at her longingly for a moment. She really is the most gorgeous girl that I have ever seen.

Lowering my head, I move slowly and return my lips back to her warm and welcoming lips which part as soon as our lips meet. In this moment, only Bia and I exist. We are solely focused on each other, on our special, intimate moment. No one else in the world matters right now. It is just us.

When the fire starts to die down, Bia and I make our way to the tent that I set up earlier. She snuggles close to me in the darkness as the wind howls outside. A few moments later, I feel her breathing settle and she falls peacefully asleep in my arms.

Lying here with her in my arms, I imagine our future together. When she asked me what my dream was earlier, I never thought about owning a farm, but now that I think about it, I cannot imagine a better place for Bia and I to raise a family. This is just the beginning of our perfect fairytale. With this thought, I fall asleep with a smile on my face and my beautiful Bia in my arms.

The next morning, I wake up at the crack of dawn. Bia is still asleep beside me. I give her a gentle kiss on her forehead and try to shimmy my arm from under her head without disturbing her. She shuffles a little before settling and falling asleep again.

I unzip the tent as silently as possible and creep out, making sure to zip it back up before walking away. Looking around, I don't see any kindling, so I decide to take a short walk to gather some to start the fire with and make us breakfast.

The sun's rays have barely started peeking through and lighting up the dark sky. Dry leaves and small twigs snap and crunch as I make my way around the cliff. The icy mountain air is crisp and fresh. Taking deep breaths, I fill my nostrils with the refreshing piney scent. Enjoying the serenity of the scenery, I gather some kindling and head back to camp. After starting the fire, I brew some coffee. Just as I finish preparing the oats that my mother packed, I hear the tent unzip behind me.

"Good morning, my beautiful," I say as I pour her a steamy cup of coffee.

Bia takes the drink and groans as she rubs her eyes. "Good morning," she mumbles and stands beside me. We both look at the splendor right in front of us. The air has warmed now and the sun is lighting up the horizon. Birds chirp happily as the morning starts.

I snuggle up next to Bia and we both enjoy our breakfast as we watch the sunrise.

"Did you have a good sleep?" Bia asks me sweetly between mouthfuls of oatmeal.

Smiling, I nod my head. Last night, I probably had the best sleep I have had in a while.

"We should get going in a bit. I don't want to be hiking down the mountain during the heat of the day," I say as I eat my last bite of oatmeal.

Bia pouts and says, "I wish we could stay up here forever."

I chuckle and kiss her on the forehead before replying, "We will come back soon."

With that, we finish what is left of our breakfast and begin to pack up our campsite. I wish we could stay up here longer, but I need to get back and help my father. This morning, I woke up with a clear goal and in order to make this goal a reality, I knew that I would have to do loads of hard work.

Bia and I begin our hike down Lovers Mountains. All in all, our camping trip was a huge success and I had a wonderful time. If I am being honest, I always have a wonderful time when my Bia is around. Just being in her presence makes me feel so much joy.

FOURTEEN

Liam

IT IS THE SUMMER of my senior year and almost two years since Bia and I officially became boyfriend and girlfriend. For the past year, I have been working with my father during my vacations and saving up all my earnings. After our first overnight camping trip on Lovers Mountains, I set a goal for myself and I have been working toward achieving that goal every day I possibly could for the past year.

Wiping the sweat off my brow, I screw on the last leg of the wooden table in place and step back. This is my final project. Once I sand and varnish this piece, I will receive the last paycheck I need to reach my goal and make my beautiful Bia's dream a reality by buying her a Cremello horse with a pristine white coat. Mr. Pruitt has been so kind as to get me in contact with a horse breeder that lives two towns over and he assured me that as soon as I have the money, he will deliver the horse.

All of this hard work and saving will be worth it once I get to see the smile on my Bia's face when she sees the horse of her dreams. Just thinking about it makes me feel warm on the inside and smile.

"Son, are you almost done with that table? Mr. Robin will be over to pick it up tomorrow," my father says as he walks into the shed. Stepping back, I look at the almost completed table in front of me. "It will be done by morning."

Behind my father, I see that the sun is starting to set and I know that I am probably going to have to work throughout the night to get this done. The image of pure joy on Bia's face is the only thing that is driving me right now.

My father nods and walks out of the shed. I get back to work as I try my best to fight off the exhaustion that is slowly creeping in. Grabbing the sandpaper, I get to work trying to smooth out the edges and surface to make sure that it is ready and smooth for the varnish. I get so caught up in the task at hand that I don't even hear my mother walking into the shed until she speaks.

"My darling, I brought you a plate because you didn't come in for dinner," she says as she sets down a plate of food on the workbench in the corner of the room.

Dusting off my hands, I look outside and realize that it is pitch dark outside now. I stretch and walk over to the small basin so that I can wash my hands and eat. If my mother hadn't brought me a plate, I would not have even realized how hungry I was. Walking over to the work bench, I get the aroma of her meatloaf and my mouth instantly begins to salivate. "That smells delicious. Thanks for saving me a plate," I say to my mother as I pick up the plate and begin to scarf the food down. My mother inspects the table silently while I finish my food.

"Don't stay up too late," my mother says as she cups my cheek gently before walking out of the shed and back to the house. Sighing, I look at the wooden table in front of me and I already know that it is going to be a sleepless night for me.

I step outside the shed for a quick breath of fresh air. A cool, refreshing gust of wind blows and it feels invigorating against my clammy skin. I do a little stretch to relieve my aching muscles and look up at the sky littered with stars. It is a beautiful night which makes me reminisce of my first overnight camping trip with Bia. I can still remember every little detail from the way her flawless skin was illuminated by the glowing fire, to the way her eyes twinkled like the stars when she was watching the sunset in my arms, I can even remember the piney smell of the trees as we laid in each other's arms and shared our dreams and aspirations.

With that, I marched back to the shed feeling more determined and energized than ever.

I will finish this table tonight and get the horse for Bia tomorrow so that I can surprise her with it for our two-year anniversary.

Picking up the brush, I begin to apply my first layer of varnish. While waiting for each coat of varnish to dry, I manage to catch a few short naps and by the time the sun has risen, the table is completed.

"Looking good," my father says as he walks into the shed.

Nodding my head, I take a step back and stand beside him and admire my handy work.

"It does look pretty good," I say in agreement with his observation.

My father places his hand on my shoulder and squeezes it affectionately before asking, "So are you ready to get that horse?"

The corners of my mouth stretch into a huge smile as I take the paycheck that he is handing me.

"Why don't you go and freshen up and then I will take you to Mr. Pruitt so that you can sort things out," my father says.

"Thank you," I say and head out the shed and to the house overwhelmed with excitement. I walk into the house and see my sisters seated at the table eating breakfast.

The eldest one scrunches her face as soon as she sees me and says, "What happened to you?"

Rolling my eyes, I walk past them and get washed up before returning to have my breakfast. I can barely sit still as my mother places a bowl of steaming porridge in front of me.

"Slow down or you are going to burn your tongue off," my mother scolds when she sees me shoveling the hot porridge into my mouth. My father is seated at the head of the table reading the daily newspaper and sipping on his coffee.

My mother comes over and scoops in an extra spoon of porridge into my bowl. "Today is a big day, you are going to need a little extra energy," she says.

"Liam and Bia sitting in a tree. K-I-S-S-I-N-G," my elder sister sings teasingly.

Frowning, I tell her to be quiet, but she ignores me and continues to sing her dumb song.

"Leave your brother alone," my mother says. My sister stops singing and rolls her eyes before sticking her tongue out at me.

My father puts down his newspaper and asks, "Are you ready to go?"

I basically inhale the contents of my bowl, wipe my mouth with the back of my hand, and nod.

"Good. We need to leave now if we are going to catch Mr. Pruitt before he leaves," my father says as he puts on his signature black and gray pinstriped beret that is just two shades darker than his already graying hair and gives my mother a peck on the cheek before walking out the door.

Grabbing my brown sheepskin wallet—which was a gift from Bia for my birthday last year—I follow him outside. About 15 minutes later, we get to the town square to find Mr. Pruitt packing up his cart and getting ready to leave.

I race to him and catch his attention in the nick of time.

"Liam, how are you, my boy?" Mr. Pruitt says with a wide smile. His graying mustache is so long that it covers half of his front teeth when he smiles.

Returning his smile, I say, "Hello Mr. Pruitt. I am ready to buy the horse now," I say.

"Oh, that is wonderful. Would you like to come with me? I planned to stop by farmer Brown's anyway so you will be able to see the horse," Mr. Pruitt asks.

I nod excitedly and Mr. Pruitt scooches over, making space for me beside him.

"See you later," I call out to my father as Mr. Pruitt and I leave.

About 20 minutes later, Mr. Pruitt takes a right onto a long, dusty road and I assume that this is the way to the farm. As we make our way down through the dust clouds, I see the horse. My jaw drops.

"He is a beauty, isn't she?" Mr. Pruitt asks. I am too awestruck to even respond. All I can do is shake my head in agreement.

Bia is going to love him. I already know it.

Mr. Pruitt stops the cart and hands me a carrot from the back. "Well, go on, boy," he urges.

Clutching the carrot, I nervously walk over to the wooden fence that the horse is behind. Up close she is even more majestic and he is everything that Bia wanted. There isn't even a spot on his shiny white coat. As I walk over, he trots toward me slowly. I extend my hand with the carrot and after a quick sniffle, he opens his mouth and munches on it. When the horse is done eating the carrot, he playfully licks my hand. I am amused and slightly grossed out at the same time.

I cannot wait for Bia to meet him.

FIFTEEN

Beatrice

TODAY IS THE LAST first day of school that I am ever going to experience. More importantly today marks two whole years since Liam and I officially became boyfriend and girlfriend. On my way to school, I sit nervously clutching my hands together over the gift that I got him.

It is a gray Hollister hoodie that I had seen him eyeing in the storefront when we went to get ice-cream a few days ago. I also got him the cutest brown leather journal because I remember him telling me that he wanted to become a writer.

I wonder what he got me, it honestly doesn't even matter. The most important thing is the fact that I get to spend the day with him.

"Enjoy your day, kiddo," Marc says as he pulls up to my school and lifts his hand for a high five. Nervously I give him a high five and jump out of the car clutching that gift wrapped present in my hand. My palms are clammy and my heart begins to pound louder and louder in my ears with each step I take toward the school yard. I know that Liam will probably be waiting for me at the bench in the courtyard like he usually does every morning. However, when I get to the bench, he isn't there.

My heart drops a little in my chest. Maybe he is just running late today. So I decide to take a seat and wait for him. Seconds turn into minutes and then finally the bell sounds for the beginning of first period.

Where is he? On today of all days, what could possibly be more important? I hope that he has a really good explanation.

I walk over to my locker and grab a few books before shoving the gift into my locker and sighing.

Guess I will just have to give it to him at lunch.

First period passes by and I barely pay any attention. My mind is too caught up in trying to figure out what happened to Liam this morning. Luckily, my second period is French and I know that I will definitely see Liam there.

As soon as the bell sounds for second period, I race out and head to Mrs. Du Fleur's class, scanning the hallways for any sign of Liam as I go along. There is none.

I sit at our usual table and keep my eyes fixed on the classroom entrance. The class starts to fill up and there is still no sign of him. A senior that I barely know sits down next to me and every cell in my body wants to yell at him and tell him to move but Mrs. Du Fleur is standing at the front of the class now and I wouldn't dare. My heart begins to pound as the most terrifying thought crosses my mind.

Is he okay? What if something bad happened to him? Oh my gosh.

Tears begin to well up in my eyes and my heart begins to pound. The room around me starts to get a bit hazy and just as I am certain that I am about to pass out. I spot him.

He shuffles into class and mumbles an apology to Mrs. Du Fleur before taking a seat at the front of the class without so much as giving me a glance.

The nerve that this boy has. Not only does he show up late to class, but he doesn't even acknowledge me. What is going on with him today? The last time I saw him was two days ago when we went to the town square to get ice-cream and he said that he couldn't stay long because he had an important project to finish. I didn't think much of it then, but his odd behavior coupled with the way he is acting today is just very suspicious.

I am determined to ask him what is going on when this period is over, but as soon as the bell sounds, Liam bolts out of class before I even have a chance to get out of my seat.

Sighing, I shove everything into my backpack and head to my next class. As I am walking down the hallway to the biology lab, Mary spots me.

"Hey, girl. How are you?" she says chirpily. "Hi," I mutter and start walking faster.

She speeds up to keep up with me, "Are you okay?"

I inhale sharply and say, "No, Mary. I am not," before walking into the biology lab and slamming my book on the table.

Massaging my temples and squeezing my eyes shut, I try to calm myself down. After a few seconds, I take a deep breath and open my eyes to see a stunned-looking Mary standing in front of me.

"I am sorry about that," I say genuinely.

Mary brushes it off and takes a seat next to me. She squeezes my hand and whispers, "I am here if you need to talk."

Our biology teacher stands in the front of the class and begins the lesson about Eukaryotes and Prokaryotes. I try my best to pay attention and take notes as he progresses with the lesson, but my mind keeps going back to the Liam situation. When it comes time for lunch, I am determined to get some answers.

I grab the lunch that Di packed me and shove the gift that I got for Liam in my bag before heading to the cafeteria. Sitting at our usual table, I scan the busy room for him. Just when I think he isn't going to show, he walks in and takes a seat next to me.

"Hey," he says casually and kisses me on the cheek.

Hey? Is that all he has to say?

At this point I am seething with anger, but I try to pull myself together and say, "Hey yourself."

Liam seems indifferent to the snarky remark and continues to eat his lunch and talk to Tommy like nothing is wrong for the rest of lunch. When the bell sounds to indicate that lunch is over, I yank the gift out of my bag and shove it at him.

"Happy two-year anniversary, you jerk," I say before storming off to my next class. I spend the rest of the day actively avoiding him and by the time school is over, I rush out of the school yard and jump into the car, slamming the door behind me.

Marc stares at me curiously and drives off without saying a word. When we get to my house he says, "Hey, kiddo. Whatever is bothering you, I am sure it will get better."

"I hope so. Thanks, Marc," I say and I go inside.

Walking in, I smell Di's famous chili cooking, but I have no appetite. After saying hello to her, I head straight up to my room and jump onto my bed where I plan to spend the rest of my afternoon sobbing my eyes out.

I can't believe that Liam treated me like that today. What is his problem anyway? Did he actually forget that it was our two-year anniversary today? The tears soak into my frilly pink pillow as I think about today's events.

Honestly, if Liam had just confessed and told me that he forgot, I would have been a little upset but not to this extent.

I just cannot figure out why he acted the way he did.

Tears keep flowing and flowing until the one side of my pillow is drenched. I hear a gentle knock on my bedroom door. It is Di.

"Bia, are you okay?" she asks sweetly.

Clearing my throat, I try to pull myself together and manage to croak out, "Yes."

"I made some of my famous chili. I know you love it, why don't you come down and we can go have a little picnic in the backyard. The weather is so nice today," Di says.

At first, I try to refuse, but Di doesn't back down and I know better than to fight a losing battle with her. Eventually, I agree and let her know that I will meet her downstairs.

Dragging myself off the bed, I stand in front of my mirror and can't help but be slightly scared by what I see. My mascara has left black streaks all down my cheeks. My eyes are red and puffy and my hair is a tangled mess and I have snot running down my nose. I do my best to make myself look presentable and quickly change into a knee length, cream, floral dress before heading downstairs.

Di is waiting at the back door with the picnic basket in hand. She smiles sweetly and says, "You look gorgeous."

We walk to our usual grassy spot under the big oak tree in the backyard.

I help Di to set up the picnic.

"Oh goodness. I seem to have forgotten the lemonade in the fridge," Di says and she gets up.

I stop her and say, "Wait. I will go and get it." But she insists that I relax after my day at school. Instead of arguing, I sit back down on the picnic basket and watch as she walks back to the house. I decide to lay down and close my eyes as I soak up the sun. Birds are happily chirping in the trees, the insects are buzzing merrily, and the warm breeze is blowing.

Di was right. It is a lovely day out. I am glad she dragged me out of my room because being out here is actually making me feel so much better. Then I hear something odd. It sounds like leaves crunching on the ground. I bolt upright and open my eyes to see what is coming toward me.

My heart is racing.

I squint as the glare of the sun blinds me momentarily.

Then I see it. Liam is walking toward me with a stunning white Cremello horse. I am dumbstruck. He walks over to me and hands me the reins saying, "Happy two-year anniversary, baby."

SIXTEEN

Liam

2 YEARS PRIOR TO THE CURRENT DAY …

I WAKE UP at the crack of dawn to the sound of the rooster crowing in the backyard. Wiping the sleep away from my eyes, I stretch and yawn in bed. Lying in bed, looking at the ceiling, I take a moment to reflect on the year.

Today is my final day of senior year and after this summer, I know that my real life begins. I have a goal, but I haven't quite ironed out all the details of my plan just yet. Looking at the little square box on my bedside table, I smile to myself in the darkness.

This past year with Bia has been nothing short of magical. We spent every single day together in school and on weekends, I would work with my father. Sometimes Bia would come and watch me work or she would just meet me when I had finished for the day. I still remember our two-year anniversary. It was a day unlike any other.

Every moment leading up to it, I felt so overwhelmed and nervous. At school, I tried to avoid Bia because I wasn't sure that I would be able to keep this secret from her any longer. It felt like I was about to burst at the seams, but I was not going to let that ruin the surprise. So I walked to school ensuring that I would be slightly late. I accidentally forgot my French textbook in my locker so I had to run back and get it which meant that I was late for the class and didn't get to sit with Bia.

Lunchtime was by far the worst. I tried my best to avoid having a conversation with her at all costs. Even if it meant me talking to Tommy about cars, about which I knew nothing about, just to avoid talking to her. As much as I tried not to be too suspicious, Bia is a smart girl and she figured that something was going on.

I remember walking into her backyard with Snowball and seeing the look of confusion on her face turn into pure bliss when she realized what I had done. Since then, I have been working and saving up to buy her a ring.

When I told my mother about it, she refused to let me buy one. Instead, she raced to the room. I sat at the kitchen table and waited as she fumbled around in her room.

When my mother came back into the kitchen, she blew some dust off a little red box and wiped it in her light blue apron before handing it to me.

"What is this?" I asked her with my one eyebrow raised.

My mother's eyes begin to tear and she says, "This is your grandmother's ring. I kept it safe so that one day when you found someone special enough to give it to, I could hand it over to you. If you think that this is meant for Bia, then I trust you."

Holding the little velvety red box in my hand, I flip it open to see one of the most beautiful rings ever. It has a simple sterling silver band with a round diamond in the middle.

"Thank you, Mom," I say and clutch the ring box to my chest. We embraced each other as the tears fell down our faces.

Now, lying here in my bed, on the final day of my senior year, I know that it is the perfect day to propose to Bia. After school, we planned to take Snowball up Lovers Mountains and camp. I have it all planned out in my head.

It is going to be perfect.

Excitedly, I get out of bed and start to get ready for the exciting day ahead. When I go down for breakfast, my father is sitting in his usual spot, sipping on his coffee and reading the newspaper as he normally does every day.

When everyone is seated at the table, I pluck up the courage and clear my throat before saying, "Guys, I have an announcement to make."

My middle sister stops munching on her toast and slowly wipes the sides of her mouth, looking at me curiously. The oldest one sighs and says, "Spit it out already. I have to leave for work soon."

My father lowers one corner of his newspaper and looks at me while my mother has a huge, beaming smile on her face because she already knows what I am about to say before I even say it.

"Well, I am going to propose to Bia today," I say all at once. The words just tumble out of my mouth and I watch as my family registers what I just said. All of their reactions are different.

My father nods and goes back to reading his newspaper. My oldest sister says, "Well, it is about time," before grabbing her last slice of toast from the plate in front of her and rushing out the door. The middle sister whispers, "Congratulations, Liam." My mother squeals with delight as she feeds my youngest sister Claire, who is indifferent to the news, her porridge. Knowing that my family approves of my decision just makes this moment all the more special. I finish my breakfast and grab my stuff before heading out.

"I hope you have a wonderful day, my darling," my mother calls after me as she stands on the bank outside our house with Claire holding the hem of her dress.

Waving goodbye, I make my way down the path to where Tommy's brother's car is parked.

The car door fling open and Tommy yells, "Last day of senior year, let's GOOOO!"

I jump into the car with a huge smile on my face and head to school with my friends. A part of me isn't ready to tell them that I plan to propose to Bia yet. Knowing these guys, one of them would accidentally let it slip and ruin the entire thing.

Nope. I can't let that happen.

For now, I keep the secret close to my chest. My own little secret mission if you will. The school is buzzing with excitement as seniors empty out their lockers and run around trying to get all of the students to sign their yearbooks.

As we walk in, one of the student council representative's hands me a yearbook. I flip through the pages nonchalantly until I see page six. At the very top is a picture of Bia and I.

No way.

We were voted "most likely to be together forever." My lips curl in a smile when I see this and it feels like somewhat of a confirmation to me. It reinforces the huge, life changing event that I have planned for later. I head to the bench where Bia and I normally meet before class and see her surrounded by a group of Mary's cackling friends as they all fawn over the yearbook.

I awkwardly smile and wave at Bia as I walk away. She looks at me helplessly and smiles back. Bia knows that I cannot stand Mary and her friends for more than a few seconds when they are this hyped up and given the fact that three of them were voted "most likely to meet someone famous," I think it would be in my best interest to avoid them for the rest of the day.

The only time I see Bia for the rest of the day is in French class. She sits next to me and whispers, "So we are the most likely couple to stay together forever."

I smile and hold her hand under the desk. Even though I do miss her, I am kind of relieved that the girls keep her busy for the remainder of the day. My nerves are pretty shot at this point and I am grateful for the time apart. This way I know that the secret will not be ruined and Bia won't notice if I am acting strange. At this point, she knows all my quirks so there is no doubt in my mind that she would figure out that something is going on if we spent more time together.

When the final bell sounds, all the seniors yell with glee and fling the papers on their desks into the air. I join them as I holler, celebrating the end of my schooling career.

"We made it, bro," Brett yells as he throws his arms around my shoulders. "You're coming to my party tonight, right?"

I shake my head and tell him some lame excuse. He is bummed out for a second but gets over it quickly as Tommy, Brett Donnelly, and the rest of our friends begin to pelt us with eggs. We run out of the school as we try to dodge the projectiles that are being aimed at us.

We get to the bus stop, breathless, gasping in surrender and we all burst out laughing. Just as I am about to get on the bus, Tommy stops me. "No way, you are coming with us," he says and it is clear that he is not about to take no for an answer so I go along reluctantly.

I see Bia in the distance and she blows me a kiss before jumping into the car with Mary and a few other girls.

"Where are we going?" I ask Brett, one of our friends seated beside me in the backseat. I hear the clinking of bottles in the trunk as Tommy's brother drives onto a bumpy road in the opposite direction of our houses.

Brett smiles and says, "To celebrate."

A few moments later, we pull up to this secluded dock by the lake with a "NO ENTRY" sign on a chain at the entrance. Tommy's brother ignores the sign and jumps over the chain. Not wanting to be a buzzkill, I follow them.

He leads us to a shabby building. It is clearly abandoned and it looks like there are no signs of life anywhere.

"Welcome to The Retreat," Tommy's brother says proudly as he pulls open a huge wooden door to reveal a decently set up room with disco lights, beach chairs, a jukebox, and what seems to be a makeshift bar and poker table.

Not wanting to be rude, I sit with them and sip on my Coca-Cola as I play a few rounds of poker. Before I know it, the sun is already starting to set and my friends are getting more and more drunk.

Pushing back my chair I get up from the table and say, "Guys, I need to leave now."

Tommy wobbles as he stands up beside me and belches loudly before slurring, "Come on, bro. One more round."

I hesitate and then sit down for just one more round. One round turns into three and it is almost dark out now. I have to get going. As I am saying goodbye, Brett spills half of his glass of beer on me. Sighing, I race home to fetch what I need before heading to Bia's. I am already so late and there is no time for me to change my clothes.

SEVENTEEN

Liam

AS I RUN up Bia's driveway, I stop at the front door, panting and trying to catch my breath before knocking. The sky is now a pale gray and it is going to be dark soon. How I managed to run this fast all the way from my house to Bia's with our camping gear remains a mystery to me.

There is a slight chill in the air already, so it is probably going to be a rather cold night. The front door creaks open and instead of Di or Bia, I see Mrs. Varela.

Why is Bia's mother home? Her parents are never around. I can count the number of times I have seen them in the past four years of knowing Bia on one hand.

Her face drops when she sees me and she tries to hide her disappointment before I notice, but it is too late.

"Oh, Liam. It's you. When Bia said she had plans tonight, I thought it was something a little more, you know…" she trails off and waves her hand in the air without continuing her sentence.

I swallow hard and look at her blankly.

A little more what? I honestly had no idea how she was going to finish that sentence, but I do know that it wasn't anything good. I dare not ask.

She scrunches her nose and looks at me.

Oh damn! She probably smells the beer. I knew I should have changed before leaving.

I brace myself as I wait for her to question me but she doesn't. Instead, she smirks and says, "Bia will be down in a minute." Then she walks away, leaving me standing at the door.

What do I do now? Should I just stand here or go in? Technically, she hadn't invited me in.

So I stand there twisting the strap of my backpack around my index finger nervously and wondering if she actually did smell the beer on me.

"Hey you," Bia says as she walks down the spiral staircase with a huge smile on her face.

I clear my throat and say, "Sorry I am a bit late."

Bia shrugs off the apology and says, "Are you ready to leave?" I nod excitedly.

Today was not going the way I had thought it would, but now that I am with my Bia, that is all that matters. As soon as she wraps her arms around me, all the anxiousness and nerves I had been harboring all day evaporate.

"I was thinking that instead of hiking today, we could take Snowie for a ride," Bia says as she stands on her tippy toes with her arms draped around my neck.

Smiling, I agree. This way we will get up faster and before dark.

Bia scrunches up her nose and steps away from me, "Have you been drinking?"

I chuckle and shake my head before saying, "No, but Brett Donnelly did spill half of his beer on me when I was saying goodbye to him."

This answer puts her at ease and we head to the backyard where her parents built a little stable for Snowball.

I load all of our gear onto Snowball and we are ready to set off. We mount the horse and begin to make our way up the mountain.

"Hey, where is Di by the way? I didn't see her anywhere," I say to Bia as she clutches onto me. Her arms are wrapped tightly around my waist and her body is pressed up against my back.

Bia sighs. "Di took a few personal days. One of her grandkids is not doing so well," Bia says solemnly.

We ride up the rest of the way in silence. The ring box is in the chest pocket of my jacket, right against my heart. I try and figure out what would be the perfect way to propose to Bia.

I hope we make it up in time for the sunset, but I highly doubt that we will. Although, a proposal under the night sky with a blanket of twinkling stars hanging above us does sound pretty close to perfect.

Sighing, I decide to just wait for the perfect moment. I am sure that when the moment does present itself, I will know. Trusting my gut instinct is the best option right now.

When we get to our spot at the top of the mountain, I jump off and help Bia down. As I go to offload our stuff, Bia follows me.

"Is everything okay?" she asks.

Her question catches me off guard and I have to take a moment to gather myself before answering in the least suspicious way I can possibly think of.

"Yeah. Why wouldn't it be?" I say, making sure I do not look her in the eyes and continue to offload our things from Snowball.

Bia eyes me curiously. I can feel her gaze prickling against my skin even with my back turned toward her.

"No reason. You just seemed preoccupied on the ride up," Bia says as she walks over to stand in front of me.

She is watching my face, scanning it for any hint of emotion. I clear my throat and say, "I was just thinking about poor Di."

This isn't really a complete lie. I was thinking about Di and her family on the ride up. Well, for a small part of the ride up anyway.

"Hmm, okay," Bia says. I know she isn't fully satisfied with the answer, but she backs off, for now anyways and helps me to unpack and set up our camp.

I just get the fire started and the darkness creeps in. The wind howls and Bia jumps onto my lap. We both burst out laughing.

"Are you scared of some wind, baby?" I tease.

She playfully whacks me on the arm and laughs. I hold her close and I can feel the way her body vibrate against mine as she laughs heartily. These moments are priceless.

It is time.

I kiss her on the nape of her neck and feel the shivers run down her body as soon as my lips make contact with her soft, smooth skin. She turns to face me, her eyes filled with desire and longing.

Now! I have to do it now.

Clearing my throat, I gently push her off my lap and onto her feet. She frowns as she tries to figure out what I am doing. I fish out the box from my pocket and get down on one knee. Bia gasps and covers her mouth with her palms as the realization of what I am doing sets in.

"My beautiful Bia, ever since I met you, you have filled my life with love, laughter, and loads of joy. The prospect of living life without you in it seems grim. Will you make me the happiest man in the world and be my wife?" I ask shakily as I open the little velvet box to reveal the elegant diamond ring inside.

Bia is frozen and for a moment there is silence. I hold my breath as I wait for her answer. Even the wind has stopped howling. The fire cracks, breaking the silence.

Tears stream down Bia's face and she says, "Yes! Yes, a thousand times yes!"

I let out a sigh of relief and slide the ring on her finger. It fits perfectly.

My eyes fill up with tears as I look at the beautiful ring on her finger. Bia crouches in front of me and flings her arms around me. The force knocks me to the ground and she comes tumbling on top of me. Normally, we would both be in stitches, laughing at what just happened, but not today.

I pull her face toward mine and kiss her passionately. We are tangled in each other's arms as our innocent, gentle kiss erupts into somewhat of a wildfire as we are both set alight with the desire and passion that we have held back for the past few years. Tossing around as the leaves crunch beneath us, our hands begin to wander and explore each other's bodies.

The sticks on the ground beneath me prick my back, but that is the least of my concerns right now. All of my focus and attention is on Bia. She pulls her lips away from mine and sits upright, straddling me. Fluttering her lashes at me, she slowly begins to pull her shirt over her head.

I gasp as I feel my loins grow taut and passion surges through my body. She tosses her shirt to the side and smiles at me mischievously.

"Are you sure you want to do this?" I ask. My own voice sounds so raspy, I barely even recognize it as the words leave my mouth. Bia doesn't answer me, instead she leans over and covers my mouth with hers.

"Does that answer your question?" she whispers seductively. Her breath is hot against my icy skin. She gently nibbles on my earlobe and I groan as I am overcome with desire.

I kiss every inch of her body, trying to restrain myself as much as I can. This is a special moment for the both of us and I want to make it last as long as I can. Bia playfully grinds her hips on me and it takes every bit of self-control that I have to stop me from grabbing her and making her mine right this instant.

Groaning, I scowl and warn Bia.

"Stop or this is going to be over before it even starts," I say.

Bia's tongue snakes out and she licks her lip before biting down on her bottom lip seductively. This sends me toppling over the edge and no amount of restraint can stop me now. I rip off the layers of clothes that are between us and make her mine.

We ride our waves of pleasure and crash together beside the fire. Bia collapses on me breathlessly as we both try to recover from the after effects of our lovemaking. The flames of the fire reflect off the diamond and the glare catches my eye. Smiling in the darkness, I wrap my arms around her and hold my Bia close. Now, she is mine in every sense of the word.

EIGHTEEN

Beatrice

SITTING AT MY DRESSING TABLE, I stare out the window. It is a lovely day out. The sun is shining and the sky is blue and bright. I hear the birds chirping happily in the trees and there is a slight breeze that is refreshing as it blows through the open window. From my spot, I can see my Snowball happily munching on his hay in the little barn that my parents built for him.

My eye catches the diamond ring on my finger and I sigh contently, smiling to myself. Everything feels so surreal. Liam and I had the most amazing time at our secret spot. Yesterday, Liam rode down Lovers Mountains as not just my fiancé, but also as my lover. My first and only love.

Mrs. Beatrice D'Fiori. That actually has a nice ring to it.

"There is no time to day dream. Your parents will be home any second now," Di says as she bursts through my room doors.

I spring up from my seat and rush to her. Flinging my arms around her, I hold her close.

"Goodness. I have missed you so much, my Di. Are you back? How is your grandson?" I ask her all at once.

Di guides me back to the chair at my dressing table and makes me sit down while she brushes my hair.

"We will talk about that later, for now, I believe that congratulations are in order," Di says as she starts to braid my hair.

I frown as I try to figure out what she is referring to and then it dawns on me.

"Oh yes! Thank you," I say as the heat rises in my cheeks. I see them turning a rosy red in my reflection. Di pins my hair and then steps back to admire her handy work. There are two thin braids on either side of my head which are pinned together at the back. The rest of my hair cascades down in wavy curls.

Di smiles and says, "All done. Are you ready?"

I nod and get up from my chair. Smoothing down my dress, I go over to my bed to pull on my cream espadrille wedges. Looking at myself in the full-length mirror, I take a deep breath and brace myself for what is about to happen. My strappy, knee length, floral dress looks stunning and the sleek, elegant diamond ring on my finger is the perfect accessory.

This is really happening right now.

The urge to pinch myself to wake up from this sweet dream is overwhelming. I just truly cannot believe that this is my life right now. The sound of the doorbell pierces through my thoughts and I gasp.

"That must be Liam. I will go down and let him in, you come down when you're ready," Di says as she squeezes my shoulders gently before walking out of the room.

Exhaling sharply, I try to calm myself down.

You got this, Bia.

Mentally, I give myself a pep talk as I look at my reflection in the mirror, smoothing down one of my stray strands of hair. I wipe my sweaty palms on my dress and give myself a quick shake to try and get rid of some of my nerves.

In the past, my parents never really cared for Liam. They kind of just tolerated him and my mother always seemed to be pushing me onto one of her friend's sons from the country club. So I had every right to be this nervous about telling them that Liam and I are now engaged.

Walking down the stairs, I see Liam standing in the foyer and talking to Di. He stops mid-sentence when he sees me. The look on his face is so tender and my heart swells with joy. I walk down and stand beside him. Liam holds my hand and as soon as he does, he looks at me curiously.

"Are you that nervous?" he asks with a chuckle. I nod.

He smiles sweetly and pulls out something from his jacket pocket. "I got this for you," he says as he hands me a rectangular white box. It has the name of the fancy jewelry store in town engraved on the front in small, gold letters.

"What is it?" I say excitedly as I clutch the box in my hand.

Liam shrugs and replies, "Just a little something to commemorate our first official day being engaged."

Slowly, I open the box to reveal the daintiest and most beautiful necklace. It is a thin silver necklace with two little lovebirds kissing while perched on a branch.

"Turn it around," Liam says.

I do as he says to reveal an inscription on the back.

To being together forever and a day. My love for you will never run dry.

Tears trickle down my face as I read the words. I throw myself at him, wrapping my arms around his shoulders as I sob into his shoulder.

Why was I even so nervous? When my parents see how amazing Liam is, there is no way that they can disapprove of us being together.

"Thank you, my love," I say between sobs.

Liam tightens his grip around my waist and hushes me soothingly.

I get my emotions in check and step back, wiping away the snot and tears from my face with the back of my hand.

"Sorry. I am such a mess today," I say.

"It is going to be okay," Liam says reassuringly, "Do you want me to put it on for you?" he asks as he points to the necklace in my hand. I nod and smile.

My parents show up half an hour after the expected time that they were supposed to be home. My mother rushes into the room in a huff. "Sorry, darling. You know how these events tend to drag on."

I bite my tongue and put on my most pleasant smile. Nothing is going to ruin this day. Nothing.

We sit around the table in the dining room. All of us pick at food on our plates in awkward silence for a while.

Liam clears his throat and says, "So, how was the council meeting in Washington DC, Mr. Varela?"

My father and Liam have a brief conversation before the room reverts back to awkward silence.

"You look lovely today, Mrs. Varela," Liam says. I can see that he is trying his best to ease the tension in the room.

Under the table, I squeeze his hand appreciatively.

My mother's smile is more of a grimace as she replies, "Thanks, Liam." Back to the silence.

Why are they being so cold and standoffish to him? They also haven't noticed the engagement ring on my finger.

At this point, I am burning up with rage. My parents can charm and strike up a conversation with anyone. I have seen them do it with total strangers at their social events. Why are they acting like this toward Liam?

I sit there as the anger builds up in me, seething from every pore. My pulse gets quicker and quicker until I feel like I am about to explode.

"Liam asked me to marry him and I said yes," I yell.

Everyone is in shock, including Liam. I hear my mother gasp and the sound of her cutlery clinking as she drops her fork on the floor. My father takes a sip of his water and then says, "Liam, can you please wait in the foyer? We would like to speak to Beatrice privately."

"No. Anything you have to say to me, you can say in front of my fiancé," I protest.

Liam gets up from his seat, gives me a kiss on the top of my head and says, "It is okay, Bia," before walking out of the room.

As soon as he walks out my mother says in a low, venomous voice, "How could you disgrace us like this?"

I am taken aback by her banal accusation.

Disgrace her? How could I have possibly disgraced them? They have known that Liam and I have been dating for years now.

"Now, calm down," my father says to her. Okay. It seems like he is on my side.

I smirk at my mother smugly.

"You know that it is beneath us to marry someone from… a lower class. You need to call off the engagement as soon as possible. It is a good thing you told us about this so soon this way no one has to know about it and we can make it go away quietly," my father says.

My head is swimming. I cannot believe this.

"I love him and he loves me. Why can't you see that? Why can't you both just give him a chance?" I plead with them as the tears flood down my face.

My father sits upright and my mother scrunches her face before saying, "I am sure that he is a lovely boy, but this just won't do. What will everyone think? No! It is final, you will call off this engagement now."

I stand up and throw my napkin on the table in frustration, "No. I will not. Whether you two approve or not, I will marry Liam and we will be together forever," I say as I march out of the dining room and to the foyer where Liam is. I hear my mother call after me, but I ignore her and slam the door behind me.

Rushing to Liam, I wrap my arms around his waist, I search for comfort. Instead, I am met with none. Liam's skin is pale and drained of all color. Stepping back, I look at his expressionless face and realize without a doubt in my mind that he had just overheard the entire conversation. I look at Di who is standing in the corner of the room. She shakes her head and shrugs at me sympathetically.

Liam takes a deep breath and then says, "I think I'm going to leave now."

His voice is shaky and it sounds like he is trying to repress the sobs that threaten to erupt from his throat. Without even waiting for my response, he grabs his jacket and walks out the door. I am frozen. My mind is screaming and telling me to run after him, but my body just won't cooperate. Instead, I stand there staring at the shut door with tears streaming down my face.

NINETEEN

Beatrice

TWIRLING THE RING around my finger, I sigh as I cradle a steaming cup of tea on my bed. The weather outside is an accurate representation of the way that I am feeling on the inside at the moment. The sky is gray and looms with big, dangerous looking dark clouds whose threat can be felt in the icy wind.

It has been two weeks since that dreaded day. The last time I saw Liam was when he was walking out my front door. Ever since then, I had not heard from or been in contact with him. My heart is shattered. There is an all too familiar ache in my chest. The ache of loss, it is the same way I felt when I lost my abuelo.

Things between Liam and I had never been like this.

We have fought previously, but never about anything this serious. Even though I try to convince myself that we can work through this, deep down I know that things are looking bleak. When I hugged Liam that night, despite the fact that he was in my arms, we felt miles apart. My eyes have been constantly red and puffy, my skin is dull and lifeless, my hair is a tangled mess and I am too afraid to even look in the mirror.

I have barely gotten any sleep since that dreaded night. Most of the time, I cry through the night. When my eyes close from sheer exhaustion, I am awoken by horrid dreams. It is the same one every time.

In my dream, Liam and I are standing on opposite sides of a long corridor. He has his back turned toward me. I call out to him, but he is too far away to hear my pleas begging him to stop, to wait for me. Instead he keeps walking away, into the light. Despite my best efforts to run after him the dream always ends the same way.

Liam goes further and further away from me. His figure turns into a distant outline which eventually disappears altogether into the light. Then, the floor beneath opens up and swallows me whole. I wake up, screaming. My pillow is usually drenched by my tears and the sweat droplets that are pouring down my forehead. Night after night, I always experience the same nightmare. Two weeks of pure torture.

During the daytime, I spend my time in bed wondering what Liam is doing.

Does he miss me the way I miss him? Is he feeling our separation as deeply as I am? What is he thinking about?

Today, for the first time in a while, my eyes are dry. It is as if I have cried myself dry and am unable to shed a single tear. The pain is still there, gnawing at me from the inside during every waking moment, but the tears refuse to fall. It is as if my body is rejecting this sorry state that I am in.

Di knocks on my door and carries in a tray with food on it. She has been doing so every single day and she sits with me until I have eaten everything. If it wasn't for her, I don't know what I would have done. After Liam left that night, Di practically carried me to my room and tucked me in bed. She stayed with me all night until she fell asleep on the couch beside my bed.

"Di, I am not hungry," I groan as she makes her way over to my bedside.

She ignores me and proceeds to place a bowl full of her homemade quesadillas in front of me. The gooey cheese is melted perfectly and the smell of the spices tantalizes my taste buds.

"How are you feeling today?" Di asks as she fusses over my dresser, tidying whatever is out of place.

I shrug and say, "The same."

Di walks to the couch and sits down before saying, "I know it may not seem like it now, but this is not the end of the world. It will get better."

My eyes burn but no tears fall. I reply meekly, "When, Di? It feels like my heart has been shattered into a million little pieces and I am hopelessly trying to put the pieces back together."

Di places her palm on mine. "A broken heart can be healed and my homemade quesadillas just so happen to help the healing process. Now, eat up before your food gets cold," she says sternly.

"Where are they?" I ask Di. Without me having to say more, Di knows that I am referring to my parents.

She sighs and says, "They are out of town for some important conference."

Of course they are. Like a whirlwind, they came around and turned my whole life upside down before leaving just as quickly. They have no worry or remorse for the devastation that they have caused. At this point I don't even know why I am surprised. Maybe I should have just kept the engagement to myself and not even told them in the first place. However, never in a million years would I have expected them to act the way they did. I also believed that Liam and I would be strong enough to face any obstacle thrown at us.

I sink into my pillows and take a bite of my quesadilla. Then there is a knock on the door.

"Are you expecting anyone?" I ask Di.

She shakes her head, signaling that she isn't expecting anyone and gets up to check who is at the door. I go back to eating my quesadilla and trying to forget my painful existence until Di walks back in. The expression on her face makes it seem as if she has seen a ghost or something.

"What's going on? Who is it?" I ask her suspiciously.

Di shuts the door behind her and sits at the foot of my bed and takes a deep breath before saying in a hushed tone, "Bia, Liam is here to see you."

All of the warmth drains from my body and a nervous chill sets in. "Now, I can send him away if you really want me to, but I think you should talk to him. There is a lot that needs to be said between you two and you really cannot keep moping around like this," Di continues.

I take a moment to think. A part of me wants to jump out of bed and race down the stairs to him, but there is something holding me back. The image of him walking away from me pops in my head, triggering some pain in my chest.

What should I do? Of course I want to talk to him, there is so much that I have to say, but what if he ends things officially. Can I handle that? What if he wants to make things work between us? How am I going to get that past my parents?

It feels like the weight of the world is on my shoulders at the moment, but I know that Di is right. She always is. I nod my head slowly and say, "Please tell him to wait for me in the study. I will be down in ten minutes." Di nods and leaves the room. I jump out of bed and hurry to my dressing table. Struggling, I try to make myself look presentable. Some things even makeup can't hide. After pulling, patting, and prodding, I am finally ready. I don't look my best, but after the past two weeks it is the best that I can do.

My light blue bell-bottom jeans and juicy couture hoodie were the first things I saw when I opened my closet. After pulling on my white sneakers, I head downstairs.

As I walk around the corner to the study, I see him. There he is, seated on the salmon couch staring into space blankly. His eyes have dark circles around them and he looks just as bad as I do. A small part of me can't help but feel some sort of relief after seeing that this whole thing took just as much of a toll on him as it did on me.

When he sees me, he springs up from the couch and starts walking toward me, but stops after only taking two steps. He frowns and says, "Hi, Bia."

"Hello," I say in almost a whisper.

I walk toward him and take a seat on the couch opposite him. "How are you?" he asks awkwardly.

"Fine and you?" I reply bleakly.

His eyes light up as he notices the engagement ring is still on my finger and the chain that he bought me is still around my neck. Even though he sees it, he doesn't say anything and instead replies to my question dryly.

After engaging in polite conversation for what seems like an eternity, he finally says, "I thought we could take Snowie out for a ride to our favorite spot."

I hesitate at first, but then agree reluctantly. We go to the barn and saddle up before heading to our secret spot on Lovers Mountains.

TWENTY

Liam

MY BIA AND I ride Snowball up Lovers Mountains. Her hands are wrapped around me and she is so close that I can feel the warmth of her body radiating against my skin, her strawberry-scented body lotion overwhelms my senses as the wind carries the smell to my nose. I feel the dampness of her sweaty palms against my chest and I can tell that she is nervous.

If I am being honest with myself, I am nervous as well. I have no idea how she is going to take this news and I hope that she can try and see things from my perspective. All I want is to build a future with her, that is my only goal… or at least that is what I keep telling myself.

We ride up in silence. The clouds above us are looking even more threatening with every moment that passes, but we trek on up the mountain regardless. This spot is where it all started and it only feels appropriate for me to tell Bia the big news here. Eventually, we reach our spot. We jump off Snowie and I tie him to a nearby tree.

Bia walks over to the edge of the cliff and is looking over. As I walk toward her, she asks, "Why did you bring me here?"

She doesn't turn to face me, but keeps staring into space.

I clear my throat and say, "Well, we need to talk and I thought that this would be the best place for us to do that. Here, we can always be ourselves. Truly ourselves. There is no one watching, no one around to overhear our conversation or judge us. Up here, you can scream at me if you want to or say any ridiculous thing that is on your mind freely, without the fear of someone overhearing."

Bia nods and keeps looking over the cliff. She stares into the vast, open space in front of us as the wind howls, blowing through her long hair. The combination of her standing at the edge of the cliff with the dark gray sky looming above creates such a menacing scene. She sighs and turns to me, her eyes red and puffy. A telltale sign that she has been crying. My heart aches when I see the look of sorrow and brokenness on her face. All I want to do is take her in my arms and tell her that everything is going to be okay. "Well, you wanted to talk right? So, let's talk," Bia says as she walks over to one of the fallen down logs nearby and takes a seat.

I gulp and take a seat beside her.

Am I ready for this? I don't know if I can do this.

Clenching my hands together, I try to relieve some of the nerves and tension that is building up in my body.

"Okay, you know how your parents said those things to you that night," I start shakily.

Bia's emerald green eyes widen, but she doesn't say a word. She just sits there and waits for me to continue.

"Well, I overheard them and I think that what they said was right. I cannot give you the life that you deserve, the life I want to give you. It is just not possible if I stay here and help my father," I say. My momentum is starting to build and, with it, my confidence.

Bia tries to interrupt, but I cut her off because if I don't say what I need to right now, I fear that I may never have the courage to.

"Let me finish. These past two weeks, I have spent thinking, brainstorming trying to figure out what I can do to give you everything that you desire and so much more. Bia, you are my princess and I want you to have the life of one. I don't want you to ever experience wanting something that you cannot have because I can't afford to give it to you. The dreams that we shared with each other, about our future together, I want us to have that," I say passionately as I move closer to her and grab her hands.

"Bia, I want to give you the farmhouse and so much more. You deserve the very best that this world has to offer. So, I have decided to move to New York," I say.

As soon as the words leave my mouth, it feels like a weight has been lifted off my shoulders. I breathe out a sigh of relief, which is short lived as I turn to face Bia. The expression on her face knocks the air right out of my lungs. Her face is just as stormy as the clouds above us. Behind her emerald green eyes, I see a storm brewing. I brace myself for whatever is about to spill out of her mouth.

The frown on her forehead deepens and she exhales sharply. It is as if she is trying to contain her emotions and calm herself down before she explodes.

"Liam," she says in a low tone, "the only thing that I want is you. I don't want any of those things if it means that I have to be away from you."

The calamity in her voice catches me off guard, but I know that below the cool demeanor that she is trying to maintain, lies something dangerous.

I have to tread carefully.

Merely thinking of a life without my Bia in it makes me feel sick to my stomach.

"But Bia, I need to do this. It is not just for you. After hearing what your parents said to me, I feel like I need to make a name for myself. There is this need to prove myself. A little voice in my head telling me that I am not good enough for you and no matter how hard I try to silence or ignore it, it always gets to me. This is something that I need to do for myself as much as it is for you. For us, for our future," I explain.

She shakes her head and tears begin to stream down her face.

"No," Bia spits out venomously, "Don't you dare pretend like this is something that you are doing for me, for us. No! I thought that you were different, Liam, but you just proved to me that you are just like them. Always trying to put on a façade and worrying about what others think about you regardless of the pain that it caused to those around you. Do not, for one second, stand in front of me and pretend like you are doing this for me. You are doing this because you feel like you have something to prove, but you don't. Why can't you see this? Why isn't my love for you enough?" she screams as the tears continue to pour out of her eyes.

Her words cut me like a two-edged sword. I know that she would be upset, but this... I never foresaw this. I try to step toward her and take her in my arms. Every fiber of my being wants to hug her and take all of the hurt and pain that is now so clearly etched on her face away. But as soon as I step toward her, she steps back.

"Don't," she threatens. "Stay away from me. You promised me that we would be together forever. You said that you would never leave me, you said that life without me seems grim and now you tell me that you are leaving?"

It feels like someone shoved their hand through my chest and squeezed my heart.

"My Bia, I never meant to hurt you," I whisper as I try to close the gap between us.

She shakes her head and walks toward the edge of the cliff. I follow her, fearful of what she might do next.

"Bia, think about what you are going to do," I say as calmly as I can.

She whips around to face me and says with a devious laugh, "Oh, I have thought about it. You broke your promise to me Liam and maybe it is a good thing that you are going because I never want to see you again."

Within the blink of an eye, everything happens so fast that I don't even have time to register what is going on before it is too late. Bia yanks the ring off her finger and throws it over the cliff into the forest below. She races past me and jumps onto Snowball. Bia gives me one last look before turning around and taking off, leaving me standing at the top of Lovers Mountains by myself.

I sit down in the ground and bury my head between my knees as I try to comprehend what just happened. My mind goes blank. Thunder cracks above me and my body goes into autopilot. I need to get off this mountain.

Up here I have no protection from the storm that is brewing. As I start walking down, big drops of rain fall as the sky above me begins to cry. I walk the rest of the way home as the rain comes pouring down. Despite being soaked to the bone, I feel numb.

TWENTY-ONE

1 YEAR PRIOR TO THE CURRENT DAY …

I SIT ON THE TREE swing in my backyard swinging back and forth. The rhythm is hypnotic and puts me in a trance-like state. Brown and yellow leaves litter the ground in front of me and they serve as the only indication that time is passing by. I hear Snowball neighing in the barn behind me and the sound makes me think of him…

It has been just over a year since I have seen Liam. The last time was that dreaded day on Lovers Mountains when he shattered my whole world. Every single day since then there hasn't been a moment that I haven't thought about him. Even now, I know that if he had to come to me and tell me that he is sorry and he wants me back, I know that without a doubt in my mind I would go rushing back into his arms.

Everything is different now that he isn't around. Wherever I go, I am haunted by the memories of him, of 'us' and what we could have been. All of the rooms in my house contain special moments that we spent together, every corridor, hallway, my backyard, and especially the mountain. I have not been able to ride Snowball up there since. To be honest, I have barely been able to ride Snowie at all. Everything I do, say, and even eat reminds me of him. I go to the farmer's market with Di sometimes on Saturdays, hoping to catch a glimpse of him, but I never do.

Just then, Di walks out the back door and yells, "Bia, you have a visitor." "Coming," I yell back.

I already know who it is. There is only one person that comes to visit me now. I hop off the swing and head inside. I would recognize those frizzy red locks anywhere.

"Hey, my girl," Mary says as she flashes me a big, toothy smile. I smile back and say, "Hello. Would you like some tea?"

Mary nods and we head to the parlor where I know Di has already laid out a tea spread for us. Mary visits me every Wednesday afternoon without fail. Come rain or sunshine, I can always count on her to be there for me. She started doing this after I saw her at the farmer's market one Saturday. When she asked me how things were going with Liam and I, well, I burst into tears. Right there, in the middle of the market. It was quite the spectacle.

Well, ever since then, Mary and I have tea every Wednesday afternoon.

She is the only person I keep in contact with from school. "So, how was your week?" she asks in a chipper tone. I sigh and pour her some tea.

"Uhm, it was the same as it always is. How was yours?" I reply nonchalantly.

Mary is my only line of connection to the outside world and Liam. She keeps me updated on everything that is going on around town.

"Well, I got into a huge fight with Tommy for being such a tool and going out drinking with the boys the entire night," she says as she rambles on about some dumb fight that she had with Tommy.

I nod and try my best to pay attention to what she is saying.

"The next day, we found out the most tragic news," she says. Her entire demeanor changes and her tone becomes serious. "What happened?" I ask as I stir a sugar cube into my tea.

Mary slowly picks up her cup of tea and takes a sip. The suspense builds with every second that passes.

"Do you remember Brett?" Mary asks.

The name sounds vaguely familiar. I rack my brain as I try to put a face to the name. As I comb through my memories, I notice that Mary is watching me intently.

That is kind of odd.

Then a lightbulb goes off in my head.

"Oh yes! Brett Donnelly, he is one of Liam's friends. Such a lovely guy, how is he doing?" I ask.

"Well, he passed away yesterday. The rumor that is going around town is that he got involved in street racing because he was trying to make money to support his family and he got in an accident. It is really tragic. Mrs. Donnelly is distraught," she tells me before taking another sip of her tea.

She helps herself to a slice of Di's pineapple upside down cake.

My poor Liam. I wonder how he is coping with this heartbreaking news. I know that he was pretty close with Brett and the rest of his friends. A part of me wishes that I could go over to his house and see how he is doing, but I still can't face him. Not after everything that has happened.

"You should come to the wake with Tommy and I. Our entire senior class is going to be there and you will probably even get to see you know who," Mary says.

I couldn't. Could I?

Just then the front door opens and my mother breezes in.

"Oh, Mary darling, how lovely to see you," my mother says as she air-kisses Mary.

My friend looks a bit awkward with the whole interaction but goes with it and says, "Hello, Mrs. Varela."

Then my mother turns her attention to me saying, "Beatrice. Your father and I will be attending the wake of a young boy tomorrow. I believe that he was in your class, so it is only fitting that you join us. Marc will pick you up at noon. Anyway, I got to run. My Pilates class isn't going to do itself. Enjoy your afternoon, my dear."

Just like that, she is gone before I can even say anything or protest. My relationship with my parents is still kind of rocky, but it is a work in progress and things are kind of getting better. After I broke the engagement with Liam, we had a family meeting and aired all of our grievances. My father, being the politician that he is, decided that it would be best if we started having dinner as a family at least once a week.

They try their best and we do have dinner together most weeks. At first it was rather awkward, but it slowly started getting better.

"Well, I guess I will see you at the wake then," Mary says between mouthfuls of her pineapple upside down cake.

I sigh. "I guess so."

That night I toss and turn in bed, unable to fall asleep. My thoughts are all over the place.

What if I see him? Do I go up to him? If I do go up to him, what would I even say? Does he want to speak to me? The last time I saw him, I told him that I never want to see him again. I wonder if he remembers that.

I shove my face into my pillow and let out a muffled scream.

The next morning, Di wakes me up. My eyes feel like there are a thousand grains of sand on them. This is most likely due to the dismal two hours of sleep that I got.

"It is time for breakfast," Di says as she pulls apart my curtains and lets in the rays of the sun. I groan and pull the covers over my head.

I hear Di's footsteps getting louder and louder as she walks toward me on the hardwood floors. She stops beside my bed and yanks the covers off my head, "Come now. You can't be late for the wake of the poor Donelly boy."

Di walks out of the room and I huff as I drag myself out of bed. After showering and eating, I head back upstairs to try and find something to wear.

After scouring through my closet, I finally decide on a simple, straight cut cotton black dress. I pull on my strappy black sandals and pin my hair back.

Marc presses the horn to let me know that he is outside and I spritz myself with some perfume before rushing out.

I walk in and search the crowded room for my parents. Then my eyes land on him. Well, it is just his back, but I would know those broad shoulders anywhere. I am frozen.

"Come on. Let's go take a seat," Mary whispers as she appears behind me. She ushers me to a seat two rows behind Liam and I sit there just staring at his back. He is wearing a light brown shirt and chocolate brown pants. Not much seems to have changed with him except that his hair is slightly shorter and he seems to be more muscular.

Mary holds my hand and I try to steady my breathing. I can't do this.

Without even giving it a second thought, I get up and sprint outside knocking over one of the floral arrangements as I do. Everyone turns around to see what happened. I look at the vase that is shattered on the floor and as I look up, I see Liam staring right at me. We make eye contact and I bolt out.

TWENTY-TWO

Liam

CURRENT DAY …

IT IS NOW four o'clock. My family and I get into the car and head to the bus station. The bus is set to depart at five, but I want to get there early so my family and I can have time to say a proper goodbye. Deep inside, I am nervous and somewhat afraid. I have never lived without my family's comforting presence. I know I'm going to have to be strong.

When we arrived at the bus station, there was about forty minutes to spare. We sit on some wooden benches and start a light conversation, mainly rehashing some past memories. We are all laughing, remembering the time when I got stuck in a tree and my parents had to call the fire department to get me down, when the announcement comes on the overhead speakers. "Bus R destination New York City, now boarding all passengers. Departing in ten minutes."

We stand up and head toward the entrance of the bus. Before leaving, I decide to call Bia. The last time I saw her was about a year ago at Brett Donnelly's wake and then she was hastily running in the opposite direction of me. Aware that I can only have a few minutes, I search for a phone and find a payphone by the information department. I put the money in and dial. As it rings, my stomach starts to twist, my legs start to shake, and my heart pounds faster and faster. On the fourth ring, someone picks up.

"Hello?" I stand there frozen for a couple of second. "Hello?" she says again.

"Bia," I answer, clearing my throat. "Liam… hi… how are you?" she says softly.

"I'm okay… I just called to say goodbye." It's a little dramatic, but I have no other way to say these words.

"Liam, before you go, I want to tell you something," she whispers, as if she is going to make a confession.

Finally, this is the moment that I've been waiting for! She's going to tell me how much I mean to her and that she can't let me go.

"Really… what is it?" I say, waiting for a reason to change my mind about my departure.

"I just want to say that I… I… I lov…" This is it. She's going to say she loves me, she's going to voice what I've been feeling inside about her all these years, and now she's going to tell me that she feels the same way and that she wants me to stay!

With a low tone of voice she finishes, "… I hope that you find what you are looking for."

My heart shatters. For a moment, I didn't think she was going to let me go.

"Thank you… I also hope you find what you are looking for," I say. But really, I want to say *that what I'm looking for is you, your smile, your presence, your hugs, and your love.* Deep inside, I know I have to do this. I have to live something new. I have to give the world a chance.

There is a silence on the phone and my folk start to wave at me, signaling that the bus is only minutes away from leaving. I try to hold on to the moment as much as I can.

"Bia, I have to go. The bus is about to depart."

"Be careful out there, okay. Remember to call me," her voice trembles, trying to hold back tears.

I swallow hard, trying to keep my composure. "I'll keep in touch."

Silence. "Bye Bia…" I linger. All I can hear is the sound of our breathing. "Bye, Liam…"

I hang up the phone and wipe a tear from the corner of my eye. I take a deep breath and go to say my farewell to my family. I can feel their sadness about me leaving. I know it's painful, but it's something that I have to try or I'll never know what can happen.

My mother and sisters start to cry as they hug and kiss me. As my father gives me a hug and tells me to stay strong, I see his eyes getting watery, but not a single tear drops. My father never really shows his emotion. Growing up, he would buy us gifts or take us somewhere we wanted to go. I guess that was his way of expressing his love.

I pick up my bag from the floor and head for the bus as they announce the last boarding call. I look back as I step up onto the bus because as much as I know I should go, deep down inside, I want to stay. I sigh, and keep walking, looking to find my assigned seat. I stow my suitcases overhead and sit down by the window.

The bus sounds its horn, and as we pull away from the station, I look for my family on the platform. When I can no longer see them, I look down at my watch. It's a nine-hour bus ride to New York. I get comfortable and start to think about my arrival in New York City.

The further I inch away from home, the more excited I feel. I haven't felt this way for a long time. One of my childhood friends, Shane, has planned to pick me up at the bus station. We used to be very close until he dropped out of high school and took a faithful leap to New York City. We have kept in touch and he told me how good he was doing and that school wasn't necessary to achieve the American dream.

When we talked, I told him about my situation over the phone and he offered to let me stay with him while I'm in the city until I get myself settled. So that is the plan. I'm going to stay with Shane for a while. I haven't seen Shane in three years and I'm a little curious to see if his appearance has changed.

Suddenly exhausted, I close my eyes to catch some zzz. By the time I open them, we are approaching the station. I get my suitcases from overhead and walk to the nearest exit. When the bus comes to a halt, I get off with my book-bag balanced on one shoulder and my suitcases in both hands. I have to find the main lobby where I'm supposed to meet Shane. I go up and down some stairs, following the signs to the lobby. It takes a while to find the lobby because every turn I make seems like the wrong one.

Finally, I find my way around this maze and arrive at the lobby, but Shane is nowhere to be found. So I put my suitcases down and stand there, waiting. As I'm standing there, I noticed that I am probably the only guy wearing a cowboy hat, a white shirt, blue faded jeans, and brown cowboy boots. But as I observe my surroundings further, I realize that everyone is wearing something more ridiculous than the last. Then again, I'm in New York City! Nothing is too shocking for this town!

I look at my watch and it is more than a half hour past the time that we had set to meet. I sigh, and keep looking around. The bus station is an interesting place. It's funny to think that about a million different people must pass by here every day. Everyone with a destination, a story, or any other reason that might drive these people to get up each morning. I tap my temple.

Right there and then, I begin to have ideas for a book. I look to my left and see a man sitting in a café drinking coffee while reading a newspaper. The longer I watch him though, the more I realize that this man does something unusual every two minutes or so: he uncovers his face from the newspaper so that just his eyes can scan his surroundings. Perhaps searching for something suspicious? Maybe he could be a detective and I could write a whole story about how this man is spying on a mafia boss sitting two tables from him with two other very well-known mobsters.

At about this time I feel a poke against my side, and the next thing I know, I'm caught in a choke hold.

"Give me your money, cowboy… throw it on the floor now…" the man who is choking me demands with an intimidating tone.

"Hey, man, I'll give you my money, just don't get crazy okay… but you're gonna have to let me go because my money is in my bag."

"Don't play with me, cowboy, or you're going to spit bullets, now come on!" he says in a raspy voice. My mind goes wild; I can't believe that in my first twenty minutes in New York City and I am already getting mugged. I have never been in a situation such as this before. My body begins to shake, my stomach drops, giving me the sensation that I am falling into an abyss. For a moment, I think my heart is going to jump out of my chest.

"Please, please don't hurt me," I implore. "I just arrived from a small town and it's my first time in the city, so please, please I just want to live," I say frantically, quickly losing control of my emotions and my legs.

After that speech, there is a sudden silence. His arm around my neck starts to loosen. Maybe my plea worked. I don't want to turn around, but when I start to hear laughter, I take a glimpse over my shoulder and see two men hysterically laughing. As my fear subsides, I take a closer look. Shane looks back at me. How can I forget that Shane, by the age of fifteen, had his master degree in pranking.

"Oh man, I can't believe you fell for that!" Shane says with his hand on his stomach to ease the cramp of laughter.

"Shane… Shane, man what is wrong with you? What, are you mental?" I say, kind of upset and still tense.

"Ha… I'm sorry, I'm sorry, but that was the perfect opportunity! I couldn't let it go…" he says, calming his laugh. After gaining control of himself, he gives me a welcome hug. "So how was the trip man?"

"Well, I slept the whole ride here so I couldn't tell ya," I respond. Shane takes a step back and puts his right hand on my shoulder. His eyes examine me from head to toe.

"Wow, man. You've changed since the last time I saw you, you seem taller, and heavier. Are you working out?"

"No, I don't work out, but I've been working with my father. You know, carpentry, so maybe that's it."

Shane is a regular guy; he's kind of tall and light skin. Not too fit but not too skinny. My mother used to think that he looked like James Dean. He certainly has the coolness of James Dean. He's very mellow, mellow to the point that when he smiles, it's not a full one from ear to ear, it's just a dog-eat-dog sly smile.

"Shane, what happened to you? You look different!" I ask, noticing the suit.

"Oh I know, the suit, right! Well, I'm working on Wall Street. I'm a businessman now," he says sarcastically.

"Really? Just a year ago when I called you said you were waiting tables?" I ask, confused.

"Yeah, I was, but you know, you meet people here and there so… hey, let me get that for you," he reaches for my suitcase, clearly trying to avoid an explanation.

"Oh by the way, that's Kyle. He's my business associate," Shane introduces the man beside him and Kyle and I shake hands, greeting each other discreetly. Kyle is modestly built, with a body also clad in a suit, his blond hair slicked back. While we are walking out, I look at their hands swinging in front of me, and notice that both of them are equipped in Rolexes.

TWENTY-THREE

Beatrice

JUST WHEN I THINK that things are starting to get better, when my life feels like every day is not a struggle and become more tolerable without him, finally when I feel like I can go at least two hours without breaking down, some stupid phrase or some dumb flower reminds me of him.

I cannot believe that he is actually gone. It took everything in me not to burst out in tears and beg him to stay, to beg him not to leave me. As the emotions welled up inside me, I put on my best façade, gritting my teeth and wishing him the best on his new adventure.

It has been two days since he called me from the bus station to tell me that he was leaving and since that last call, I have not fully recovered. For the past two nights, I have cried my heart out and I even asked Di to cancel my Wednesday afternoon tea with Mary because I just don't have the energy. Snuggling under my covers, I try to muffle my sobs and pretend like I am asleep as soon as I hear footsteps approaching my door.

The handle clicks open and my mother walks in. I can hear the tick tock sound of her heels against the hardwood floor.

She pulls open my curtains and says, "Goodness, Beatrice. It is almost noon and you are still in bed. Enough moping around, it is time for you to get back on your feet. Please meet me in the foyer in exactly twenty minutes. I have an exciting day filled with pampering planned for us."

With that she turns on her heels and walks out, leaving my bedroom door opened behind her.

An entire day with my mother is the last thing that I want right now.

I throw my pillow on the ground and groan in frustration.

"Don't make me come up there and drag you out of bed, darling," my mother calls in a sugarcoated threatening tone.

What if I stay in bed and refuse to listen to her? Then what? It isn't like she can come up here and actually drag me out of bed, forcing me to go with her… can she?

Di walks into my room and smiles.

"Come now, Bia. A full day of pampering sounds like it is right up your alley," she says sweetly as she tries to coax me out of bed.

I do love being pampered and going to the spa but with my mother? Plus, I really don't feel like being around people right now.

Scrunching my face up I look at Di and don't move a single muscle.

Di sighs and says, "Well I guess those yummy chocolate brownies I made are just going to have to eat themselves."

I spring up in bed. "You made brownies?"

Di's brownies are the best brownies that I have ever tasted in my entire life. They are gooey on the inside and crispy on the outside, not to mention, they are super-duper chocolatey and filled with yumminess.

The smell of freshly baked brownies wafts in through my opened bedroom door. My mouth instantly begins to salivate as my taste buds get tantalized. If anything is worth getting out of bed for it is definitely Di's freshly baked chocolate brownies.

I freshen up and rush downstairs making a b-line for the kitchen. As soon as I walk in, I see that Di has placed a delicious corner piece of the brownie in a bowl and is walking away from the refrigerator with a tub of vanilla ice-cream.

"Sit down and eat up. Your mother will be ready to leave any time now," Di says as she scoops some of the vanilla ice-cream onto the brownie and pushes the bowl toward me.

I do as she says without any complaints. The brownie is warm and gooey. Its chocolatey goodness coats my tongue in the most luxurious way. This is pure decadence. I sigh with pleasure as I devour the brownie in front of me.

"That smells delicious, Di," my mother says as she walks into the kitchen and pinches a piece of the brownie from the tray.

Di smiles and asks, "Would you like me to cut you a piece?"

"Oh no, I really shouldn't. I have got to watch my calories," my mother replies as she filches another piece of the brownie and pops it into her mouth. I roll my eyes and eat my last spoonful of the brownie and ice-cream.

My mother grabs yet another piece of the brownie before she dramatically pushes the tray away with one of her perfectly manicured fingers.

"Beatrice, are you ready? We have to get going," she says dramatically. I nod and make my way to the sink to wash up and pop in my dirty dishes in the washer before following my mother outside. Marc drops us off outside the fanciest hotel in town.

"Wow, you got us an appointment here?" I gasp as I walk in through to the reception and gawk at how exquisite this place is. My mother sees one of her friends and excuses herself so that she can go and say hello.

Standing there, I feel so out of place in my shorts and flip flops. I wander around the giant waiting area and spot a beautiful painting on one of the walls. The huge painting is off a beautiful landscape with a mountain range that looks eerily similar to Lovers Mountains. As I walk closer to inspect the painting, I realize that I was right. The painting portrays the cliff at the very top of the big mountain. I gasp. That is our secret spot.

He really is everywhere I go. In this town there is no escaping the memory of him. I am so caught up in my thoughts that I do not hear the footsteps that hastily approach me until someone clears their throat behind me. Turning around, I see an older man looming over me. His thick mustache is so long that every time he speaks the strands of the graying hair tickle his nose causing him to scrunch up his face. This makes it appear as if the man is constantly in a state of constipation.

"How can I help you?" the man asks impatiently, without even waiting for me to answer he goes on to say, "Only hotel guests are allowed in the lobby."

The man looks at me from head to toe and doesn't even try to hide the look of disgust and annoyance on his face. His tone and attitude catches me totally off guard. I spot a name badge on his perfectly pressed, pinstripe black suit. It says "Peter Hughes—Manager."

"I, uhm… I'm just waiting for my mother," I stammer my way through the sentence.

The man scoffs and says, "Well, the workers entrance is down the alleyway to the left. Please wait there and let your mother know that having visitors during working hours is strongly frowned upon."

I watch as the man finishes his sentence and my mother stands behind him with a look of disgust on her face.

She clears her throat when he is down and he swiftly turns on his heels to face her.

"Oh, Mrs. Varela. Sorry about that, you know how it is when you have 'those types' of people hanging around in the hotel lobby. Once you allow one in, they all think they're welcomed," the manager says in an obnoxiously self-righteous and apologetic way. His entire stance and tone have changed in an instant.

My mother tries to keep her facial expression neutral and says, "Oh, who are those people exactly?"

The manager seems visibly uncomfortable by her question.

"You know, those who aren't exactly welcomed at an establishment such as this splendid one," the manager replies.

My mother nods her head and walks around him to stand beside me. "In that case, let us take our business to an establishment where we are more welcomed darling," my mother says as she puts her arm around my shoulder and ushers me out of the hotel lobby with her head held high.

As we walk out, I turn around to see the look of embarrassment and confusion on the manager's face as he tries to make sense of what just happened.

"The world is full of guys like Peter. Don't let it get to you and keep your head up, mija," she says as she walks out the hotel doors with her arm around my shoulder. In that moment, all the built-up resentment that I had been harboring toward her evaporates and it is replaced with adoration. She handled that situation with such grace, kept her cool, and managed to get her point across without causing a scene.

If I was in her position, I wasn't sure that I would have been able to keep it together the way she did back there.

My mother sighs and says, "Well, there goes our spa day, I guess. Should we go and get coffee instead?"

I nod my head and we head to the little café down the road.

TWENTY-FOUR

Beatrice

MY MOTHER AND I sit on the curbside of this little café under an umbrella. Luckily for us, it is a nice, cool day in Virginia. The sky above us is gray and there is a cool breeze.

"You know, I heard that the chocolate chip pancakes at this place are phenomenal ever since they got a new chef," she gushes casually as she browses the laminated menu in front of her.

Chocolate chip pancakes are Liam's favorite.

I sigh.

"Hey, don't let what happened back there get to you, Beatrice." she says, mistaking the reason behind my sigh.

Shaking my head, I say, "I won't. It is just so unfair to think that people actually get treated like that." My mouth fills with bitterness as I speak.

Recalling the unpleasant memory, I feel anger begin to bubble and brew in the pit of my stomach.

"Life isn't fair. If you want to see a change, then you have to make an effort, create waves and bring about that change on your own. You cannot just sit back and expect things to happen. I know that you may think that all your father and I do is go to fancy dinner and galas, but what we do is so much deeper than that. Yes, we do dress up and go for outings at the country club, but that is only to earn the respect of the people at these places. You see, once we have their respect and they view us as equals, we are able to get what we want, which is for them to contribute to our projects. Did you know that we run a soup kitchen for the needy just a few blocks away, or that since we have got here we have been working on a campaign that makes immigrating to America easier for people from other minorities?"

I shake my head.

For the longest time, I have always thought that my parents were such phony people. This was my initial judgment, clouded by the bitterness of losing my abuelo and them not being around. I never questioned my judgment because I had no reason to, until now…

"We have worked hard to give you a good life. A life that is far better than what your father and I had growing up. My mother died during childbirth so it was always just my dad and I. When I was little, my father used to be a gardener and groundskeeper at the house of a really rich man. He kept the grounds in immaculate shape and would keep busy, working at all odd hours to ensure that they stayed that way. He tried his best to give me everything that I needed by even working extra hours and doing whatever the rich man told him to so that he could afford to send me to the fancy private school so that I could have a better future.

One night while he was trimming the rose bushes, my father saw something that he shouldn't have. The next morning, my father's remains were found on the grounds. After 'investigating' the police determined that it was a suicide, but I knew my dad. There was no way that he would do that. So, I decided to do my own investigating and uncovered some ugly truths. Even then, no one believed me. I had to learn lessons the hard way. One of the most valuable lessons that I learned is that having money gives you power. When you have power, you have influence and influence is what you use to make changes," my mother says.

The entire time she had been talking, not once did she look up at me. She stared blankly into the cup of steaming coffee in front of her, but when she was done, she looked up at me and I could see the unshed tears in her eyes. The scars of pain and anguish were so clearly etched on her face. I couldn't help but reach over the table and give her a hug.

As I wrap my arms around her, I feel her body tremble with sobs. I grip on tighter and we stay like that for a moment before she gets a grip on herself.

She chuckles and pulls away from me as she says, "Ah, I am being so silly."

Just like that my mother regains her composure. She wipes away the tears and sits up straight. Clearing her throat, she takes a sip of her coffee before saying, "So, you see Beatrice, the point of my story is that your father and I have fought so hard to give you a voice. We didn't agree to your marriage to Liam because that would basically be throwing away the voice and influence that we worked so hard for you to have. You are so special and we only want what is best for you."

Before I could argue or even respond the café doors open and out walks Liam's mother holding a plate of steaming hot chocolate chip pancakes. When she sees me, she stops dead in her tracks. The expression on her face looks like she has just seen a ghost. Quickly, she shakes her head and hides the shock.

"Here are your pancakes," she says sweetly as she places the plate down on the table. "Will that be all?"

I just stare at her for a moment as all of the memories of Liam come flooding back. Tears sting my eyes and I just stare. She looks so much like him. Their bright blue eyes, complexion, and even their jawline are so similar.

"Beatrice," my mother scolds.

Snapping out of it, I say, "No thanks, Mrs. D'Fiori."

My mother's eyes widen across the table from me when she realizes who the woman is. Mrs. D'Fiori nods and walks away.

I want to call her back and beg her to tell me every little detail about Liam but something is stopping me. Of course, I want to know everything, but is it okay to even ask? Surely she knows why he is leaving. He left because of me. I am sure that I am the last person she wants to speak to now anyway.

"We can leave if you want," my mother suggests.

I shake my head and pour syrup all over my pancakes. Every now and then, I would catch glimpses of Mrs. D'Fiori in the café window. A few times, I even thought it was Liam. Seeing her was comforting in an odd way.

This is probably the reason why I would find myself coming to this café every Wednesday for the next few months.

There was just something about seeing her and being around her that made me feel at ease. It was almost as if he was still there, like there was still a connection between him and I.

I also decided that it was time to get off my butt and do something with my life. After my interaction with Peter and my heartfelt conversation with my mother, I was determined to give those less fortunate than me a voice. So, I decided to apply to study law at Virginia State University.

When I get home, I download the application and start filling it out. As I write the words on this piece of paper, my emotions begin to grow stronger and stronger.

I had no idea that I could be this passionate about something. Every nerve of mine was tingling by the time I completed the application. Saying a little prayer, I lick the envelope and seal it shut.

Walking out of my room, I clutch the envelope and head downstairs to tell my parents. I hear them speaking in the study. Standing at the door, I take a deep breath and pipe my sweaty palms on my jeans before knocking on the door.

"Come in," my father says.

I walk into the study and see that my father is seated behind the desk with my mother standing beside him, hunching over and inspecting a document on the desk.

"Is this a bad time?" I ask nervously.

"Not at all," my mother says as she stands up straight. "What is it?" I place the envelope on the desk and take a step back.

"What is this?" my mother asks as she eyes the brown envelope suspiciously.

I gulp and reply, "It is my completed application to Virginia State University. I have decided that I want to pursue a career in law."

They both stare at the envelope in front of them for a moment as they compute what I just said. A few moments later my mother rushes over to me and throws her arms around me saying, "That is wonderful news."

My father remains behind his desk and says, "Congratulations. We are very proud of you."

For a moment, I am almost certain that I see a tear trickle down his face, but he quickly picks up a document file in front of him and 'inspects' its contents hiding his face from my view.

TWENTY-FIVE

Liam

NEW YORK CITY, NY USA

WE HEAD OUT of the bus station and signal for a cab. It's around nine o'clock when we finally get in the cab and head to West 4th. On the way there, I stare out the window, trying to capture every image I can because New York is a stimulating city, and it seems to me that no matter how long you live here, you won't ever get to see everything. It's Saturday night and New York is packed with people at this time. In Virginia, everyone would be at their home enjoying some quiet time with the family. But not in this town, when the moon hits the sky, the party goers come out to play.

Upon driving down FDR Drive, I get a quick glimpse of the Manhattan bridge and the iconic Brooklyn bridge. It is spectacular. I cannot believe that I am finally here. It all feels so surreal. I'm left wondering how this is even my life right now.

Shane doesn't say a word; he just lets me enjoy my first fifteen minutes in The City That Never Sleeps. There are so many buildings that I can't even get a glimpse of the moon. This place looks like a jungle, a concrete jungle. We approached West 4th Street, and Shane signals the driver toward his apartment complex. We pay the cab and go inside his apartment. The lobby of the building is very fancy with a bellboy and expensive furniture decorating it. The elevator light blinks red. We get inside and head to the seventh floor.

The elevator door opens and I see a short corridor leading to Shane's apartment. The apartment door is a big sliding metal door that shines like silver. He opens it and I am surprised to see how grand his apartment is. I can't believe that at the age of 21, he is able to afford such a luxurious pad.

I walk into the main room and see that the living room and the kitchen are only separated by a marble balcony in the shape of an L. On the left side of the room is Shane's room and across the wide living room is where I'm going to stay. I look around for a bit.

His apartment is decorated with some bougie looking furniture, the type that you see on the pages of those fancy "House and Home" magazines. He has an ultra-wide screen plasma TV, a state-of-the-art sound system, a fine leather couch, and the floor of the kitchen and the living room are made of marble with artistic designs on them. The living room has a three-piece couch and in the middle is a white bear fur rug with a glass table on top of it.

I take my suitcase and head to my room. I open the door, turn on the light, and take a look around. It's a nice room with a king bed, different color walls, and aluminum designer lights all around the ceiling. I put my suitcases down by the drawers and without even taking the clothes off my body, I throw myself on the bed to get some rest. It feels so good to just lay here after a long trip. I shut my eyes for a couple of minutes with no intent to sleep.

No more than two minutes later into my rest session, Shane opens the door.

"Hey, Liam… get up! I've ordered some Chinese food. Come have some." I get up and walk to the kitchen. Shane and Kyle are sitting around the counter on some barstools, making up their plates. I approach them and start preparing my own.

"Liam, so what brings you here to the city?" Kyle asked. "Hmm…

actually, I just needed a change, you know." I answered. "Any ambitions?" Kyle asks, attempting to get to know me.

"Well… I write. I'm thinking of writing while I'm here. Take advantage of the city of opportunity."

"Wow, I didn't know you were a writer," he says with a look of enthusiasm.

"Yeah, becoming a known writer has always been a dream of mine," I declare.

"Yeah, hum… that's great, but what do you plan on doing before you 'make it'?" Shane cuts in.

I shrug. "To be honest with you, I don't know yet… I'll do whatever I can to get my writing career started."

"Well, in the city, there are lots of things you could do like being a waiter at a restaurant or working in a bar, there are plenty of those jobs here. All I'm saying is that if you want it, there is always work available. You just got to be willing to work," he suggests. I just kind of nod to him in agreement.

"What do you guys usually do on a Saturday night?" I ask, since it is eleven o'clock and they're still just sitting here taking their time eating.

"We always go to this nightclub called 'Raven.' It's one of the hottest places in the city right now," Shane says.

"So lose the cowboy hat and get ready, cause we're heading out!" he declares.

We head out to Raven where many of Shane's friends join us. As a group, we proceed to the door where there are two tall and muscular bouncers. Shane walks up to them, gives them a choreographed handshake, and they politely step aside from the red carpet and open the door for us. Shane lavishly makes his way to the bar, greeting all his friends along the way. I, on the other hand, walk inconspicuously toward the bar where Shane and his friends are gathered. The music is blasting with the sound of techno and house. Back where I'm from, I don't recall ever listening to this type of music. In Virginia we are more into country and contemporary music.

I stand there leaning on the bar. Shane whistles and shouts.

"Hey Donny… what's up, man?" Donny appears to be the bartender and from the looks of it, it seemed like they were best friends. Donny has a Latino look to him; he is tall, well-built, with dark features. Donny comes over to us after he takes care of a customer and gives Shane a homeboy handshake.

"Donny, what up, my man? Hey, I'd like you to meet my friend who just got here from Virginia," Shane introduces.

Donny approaches me with his palm toward me, and introduces himself, but as he starts doing his choreographed hand shake, I get lost in it and so I end up giving him a businessman hand shake.

"Dude, how's it going?" he says, releasing his hand from mine.

The music is so loud that I have to lean toward him to respond. "I'm all right… Wow this place is really something, huh!" I look all around the room.

"Yeah, man. The best place in town. So what are you doing in the city?" Donny asks while wiping a white towel across the bar counter top.

"Well, I came here to be a writer… Do you know someone that's on that field?"

"Wow, maybe one day when they make a movie out of your book then you can hire me as an actor!" he laughs. I can't tell if he is being sarcastic.

"Why, are you an actor?" I asked.

"Dude, everyone in New York City that is a waiter, bartender, or bus boy is a struggling artist," Donny says as he nods his head. After he makes this statement, I think about it. What he said sort of got to me because I don't want to just be another struggling artist in a huge city.

Donny rearranges a couple of bottles and throws the cleaning rag on his shoulder. He turns to me and asks, "Hey, so what are you doing now?" "Hum… I just got here today really. I didn't even have time to unpack my bag," I chuckle. "But tomorrow I plan on getting up early and going door to door looking for a job."

"What kind of job are you looking for?" Donny asks.

"Anything really… Just something to get my foot in the door, ya know," I answer.

"Well, if you want, we might need some help in the bar!" he yells. "What kind of help?"

He strokes his chin as a gesture of someone gathering their thoughts. "Well, we need a bar-back. I could ask Craig, the manager, to see if he'll let me bus you."

This catches me by surprise. "Yeah, that's a great idea. I would love it!"

Donny yells at one of the bartenders and asks them to cover him for a minute before turning to face me again.

"Give me a second, I'll be back." Donny says.

He leaves the bar to talk to his manager to see if they are hiring. I can't believe my luck! In only one day in the city, I got a job proposition without even trying. That goes to show that things do happen for a reason, or perhaps I was at the right place at the right time. I look around to see if I can find Donny. In the corner of my eye, I can see him talking to someone who looks like the manager.

The man looks slightly older than Donny with his silver-gray hair and is wearing a black suit. He looks like those men that you see in gangster movies. He has a cigar in his mouth and talks with his hands. For a second, I assume he is angry at something, but then I think that he could also be expressive. I notice that Donny shakes his hand. A few minutes later Donny approaches me.

"Do you want a job?"

"Yeah… I would love a…" I hesitate a little bit.

"You start tomorrow at 2 PM. Be here on time so that I can show you the way around this joint, all right!"

"Yeah… yeah, no problem." I say excitedly.

"Do you have any bar experience?" he now asks.

"No, I was a carpenter back home," I respond, thinking that now I've blown my opportunity. Donny examines me for a second.

"Well, that is going to be a little problem, but you look the part and that's all you need to get by in this city."

I thank Donny and go looking for Shane to tell him of what had occurred. When I tell him I have a job, he is surprised. We stay in the bar for about another hour. During that time, I take a walk around to see the people. I have never seen such a variety of races in one place. In the club there are three floors, each with different type of music and different themes.

As I make my way down the stairs, I notice Shane in one of the VIP booths. Making my way over, I see that he is surrounded by beautiful women and what seem like expensive bottles of champagne. He lights a cigar and winks at me as a cloud of smoke covers his face. Shane does a dance move and we both chuckle. He throws his hand in the air and screams, "Paaarrttyy!!!," just as the DJ drops the beat and everyone begins to jump and dance to the beat.

The following day, I woke up around noon. I set my room in order and decided to call my family. My mother picks up the phone. She is so happy that I called. I tell her what is going on, that I found a job on my first day here. She can't believe it. We talk for about a half hour. When I hang up the phone, I know that I am missing something. Something deep inside my heart tells me that I'm incomplete. I'm already missing Bia.

She's always on my mind, but I'm too afraid to pick up the phone. I always hesitate to pick up the phone because I left her. I left her after I promised to marry her. Instead, I chose my ambitions over love. I left for the conquest of my dreams. I've broken a promise. Like a con-artist I lead her along. Even after all this she forgave me. Still accepted my friendship. A privilege for me. However, I deeply hurt her. How can our lives ever be the same again?

Well, there's always tomorrow! As time flies by, I get myself ready to try out my new job. A new job could be very exciting, but it also makes me nervous. I'm not a city boy and from what I've seen so far, the city life moves way too fast for me. I just hope I can catch up.

TWENTY-SIX

Liam

SINCE THE PLACE wasn't that far, I decided to walk. I arrived at Raven a half an hour early. Donny is already at the bar cleaning and checking inventory. I walk in and give him a smile as I approach the bar. "Donny, how's it going?" I say, approaching the counter.

"Hey, man. Same old, different day. Come on dude let me get you started," he replies.

Donny spends some time showing me how to work my way around the bar. He teaches me the duties of a bar-back. My basic duties are to fill the bottles when they are running out. Bring beer up from the basement, so that the beer can be iced. Also, to make sure Donny has enough straws, napkins, and garnish available to him.

I know that tonight will be a hard night because it's Sunday night. Sunday night in New York City is very much alive, from what I'm told.

It must be way different than Sundays in Virginia. In NYC, everyone is out to party. In Virginia, people didn't go out very often, and if they did, it was probably to watch a movie or just to hang out at the local bar. The difference is that in NYC, there's this trend called "club hopping" in which a group of friends go from club to club, bar to bar, all night long.

As the clock ticks, it gets closer and closer to 8 PM, the opening hour of the bar. As the night goes on, and the bar starts to get packed, I realize that I have never seen so many beautiful people in my life. I run around like a headless chicken: going back and forth with the garbage and bringing out cases and more cases of beer.

Donny, the whole night, keeps yelling my name: "Liam, get me this. Liam, get me that." It gets to the point that I can't stand my own name any more. I look at the clock and it's only 1 AM, which means four more hours to go. My feet are killing me and at this point they are wet and tired from all the running around.

As the end of the night approaches, I am tired and can't wait to go home. When it hits 5 AM, the manager closes the club doors. Everyone that worked tonight helps put the club back in place. I walk over to the bar to give Donny a hand. While I am cleaning the bar, Donny is counting the money he made that night. I am putting the drinks away when Donny walks toward me and says, "Here's for your hard work." He hands me a bundle of cash and I think that there must be at least a thousand dollars here, but unfortunately, to my dismay, they are all one-dollar bills. Donny taps me on the shoulder. "Hey, you did well today, being your first day and all!"

I take the money and count as Donny walks away. I count a total of $235. I can't believe that in one night I made all this money just being a bar-back. I put the money in my pocket, finish cleaning everything up, and head on home. On my way home, I feel so tired that I can't wait to hit my bed. I get home and Shane is sleeping.

I sit on my bed and take off my soaking wet socks, lean back, and instantly fall asleep. At this point it is probably six in the morning. Back home, I know that the rooster crow is making everyone get up, and that the sun is coming up from the horizon, starting to peek itself through the windows, it's rays breaking through the wheat on the field making a beautiful orange yellowish glow.

I wake up at 2:30 PM in the afternoon. I wake up to find that there is no one home. I go to the kitchen and make myself some spaghetti. I sit down at the table as I eat and start to think about my current situation. If I work Friday and Saturday nights, I could probably make about $500 a week. That would be enough to make ends meet and still leave me some time to pursue my writing career.

I spend the rest of the day in my room writing. In the midst of all my brainstorming, I notice my heart leaning toward thoughts of Bia. I stare at my notebook and begin dreaming of her shy smile, her green eyes, her long brown hair, and when she speaks it is as if she is whispering in a sweet soft tone. I remember when we would talk, I would just listen to her speak softly to me about her life.

For me, anything she said was interesting and joyful to my heart. I could listen to her for hours and not get tired. I could look at her a lifetime and still be mesmerized by her beauty. Every time we spoke, we would look into each other's eyes the whole time, and I kept trying to imagine what her heart tried to tell me.

She's not like other girls. She has that something that my heart searches for. Bia has that Latin charm to her. Her Uruguayan roots are undeniably deep, for she still (in her shy and reserved ways) can charm the eyes of any man. She came to America with her parents when she was still young.

I try and try, but no matter where I go nor what I do, I can't deny what I feel in my heart for this person. I can't say that I moved to another city just to chase a career. I'd be lying to myself. But I can truly say that one of the driving forces that made me choose to "run away" was my fear of not being able to provide the life that she dreams of. I just feared that maybe if I was not successful enough, she would walk away. Instead of taking a chance and finding out, I took the safe way out.

Plus, her parents never did approve of me. They are ambitious and astute folk. I, on the other hand, am the son of a waitress and a carpenter.

Four Months has passed since My arrival. everything's been going great. I keep writing two to three times a week, and have been sending my book proposal to publishing companies, but no answers yet. During this time, I've got in touch with Bia about every two weeks. It seems like we've gotten closer since we've been distant from one another.

I don't really know, but I've begun to notice, over the phone, that Bia and I are able to express ourselves more intimately. Maybe because now we realize that life and its circumstances can drift people apart. It seems that she doesn't want to lose the intimate moments that we have together. Could it be that her feelings are strong toward me again?

As I'm getting ready for work, all these thoughts are racing through my mind. I'm going to call her and let her know how I feel. I reach for the phone and dial. On the third ring she picks up.

"Hello," Bia answers. "Hi," I say.

"Liam… Hey, sweetheart, how are you?" she asks cheerfully.

It feels so good that she already knows my voice, and answers me so warmly.

"I'm doing fine just getting ready to go to work," I reply.

"I'm so glad you called me. I was looking at our middle school yearbook, and I thought about 7th grade. That was when we became friends. Remember?" she asks.

"Yeah, I remember. It was at the carnival, right?"

"I was standing there, waiting in line to get a pretzel and you asked me the most ridiculous question."

"Time flies, doesn't it? It seems like it was yesterday!" I respond.

"I had fun that year. You know, you and I were always around each other," she says. As she says it, I know it is the right moment to say something sentimental. I take a leap of faith, and say, "I miss you."

There it is. I said it now. I feel like my stomach just dropped because I made my sentiment toward her show. There is a moment of silence. Now my emotions are telling me that I just blew my friendship into the wind.

"Liam… I miss you too," she says, with a lower tone in her voice. There is another awkward silence for a moment. Without wanting to reveal too much of myself to her, I decide to end the conversation.

"Bia, I'm sorry, but I have to get ready for work. I'll keep in touch, okay?" I murmur.

"Oh… Okay, I guess we'll talk some other time, right?" she says, noticing that I am doing what I had done for years. I was running away from emotional intimacy.

"Yeah, we will. I'll talk to you soon… Bye," I say. "Bye."

I hang up the phone and finish getting ready for work. I try not to dwell much in fear and insecurity. Instead, I channel these emotions through my writings. That's the only place where situations can turn out the way I want them to. I go down the elevator, and head out to Raven.

It's a Saturday night, and I know I'm going to have to run around like a maniac again. I get to the club, greet everyone, and get myself ready. The night goes on, and the crowd keeps coming, demanding their drinks be served faster and faster. So Donny keeps me going back and forth, with beer case after beer case.

By now it's one o'clock and I see Donny gesture with his hand for me to hurry up. I'm carrying five cases of beer, how can I be fast? I decide to go through the dance floor, because it is more convenient. As I make my way across the dance floor, I fail to notice that someone has dropped their water bottle. Leaving a nice little puddle.

As I'm politely walking across, I feel my feet slip and my whole body lose its balance. I can see the boxes in the air as my back hits the floor.

Everything happens in slow motion, and I still have time to pray. "Oh please, God, don't let these boxes fall on me!" The probe lights keep flashing, making the scene appear to have a two-second delay.

When the boxes come down, to my surprise, they hit a middle-aged man, and he falls on the floor with me. I get up as quickly as I can to try to help the man push the boxes from on top of him. Some people in the crowd gather to watch the scene. I give him my arm to hold on to, as I lift him up from the ground.

"I'm sorry, I'm so sorry! I was walking up, and the water was on the floor, and… Here, let me help you, sir!" I say to him as I pick him up.

He isn't too happy with the situation. I help him fix his suit and apologize once again. As I go to pick up the box of beer, I can see him brush himself off, and I also notice a couple of people laugh at the whole incident. The entire time I think, *please don't tell my boss!* Please! I notice that he is staring at me. I pack the cases back on my arm, kind of nod at him, and go about my business. As I turn my back, he grabs my arm. In an English accent, he says, "Hey kid, what are you doing here?"

"What? What do you mean? I work here."

"No, I mean what are you doing working in a bar?" he asks with a serious tone.

"Well… I just moved here from Virginia, and this was the set of cards that was handed to me," I respond, as I readjust my grip on the boxes.

"Very well. Now I'm gonna deal you some spades!" he says. At this point, I think he is one of the unknown managers that are never around, except for once in a while to see how things are going. The first thought that comes to me is that this will be my last night here.

"What do you mean?" I ask, gesturing my eyebrows as I ponder.

"Do you have any idea of who I am?" he queries. I immediately think to myself, be as polite as you can, because from my first impression, he seems like someone very important.

"I-I-I don't believe I know you!" I stutter. He looks at me for a while, as if giving me time to think about it. My mind struggles to figure out who this man is.

When he realizes that I have no idea who he is, he decides to break the ice by introducing himself. "My name is Lyons, Patrick Lyons. I'm an agent. I work for the most respected modeling agency in New York City. I want you to be in my photo shoot next month," he explains. I am quite confused. I don't know what to say. I am still kind of shaken by the whole situation.

After registering what he said, I came to my senses. Wait a minute, what is he saying? He wants to take pictures of me? "Thanks, I appreciate that, but I came here to be a writer," I responded.

He takes a step closer to me, and offers the same proposition, but this time his eyes are fixed more intensely. "I can offer you a lot more than what you see here. I can give you a modeling career. Think about it. You are beautiful. You are tall. Your eyes are a piercing blue. You have a gorgeous body and an innocent look in your eyes. You don't want to end up being just another starving artist who slaves themselves to get by," he says, as if he had met many like me. I am quite shocked. I can't tell if he's insulting me, or just using a salesman's tactic.

"Thank you, but where I come from, there's something more than just having a gorgeous body, and an innocent face. I proudly hold my morals and values very close to me," I say, responding to what feels like an insult to me.

"Well, suit yourself, but if you change your mind, here's my card. Just give me a call when you need, and I'll be available," he replies. He adjusts his suit and maneuvers his way into the crowd toward the exit.

His proposal elicits my curiosity, but I don't want to take a chance. I'm comfortable with this job. I take the card and continue doing my job. I can't help but think about what had just happened. As I think more and more about it, I become increasingly incredulous. I mean, if he really thought that I would be able to make him money as a model, I believe he would have been a little bit more persistent. But then again, he said he was the top guy in the business. He is not going to beg. Now that he offered me this opportunity, it's going to linger in my mind for a long time.

The night ends, and I made my way back home. Along the way, I take the card out of my pocket, and examine it for a bit. I begin daydreaming about that lifestyle; how great it would be to be known, to have your face on a billboard, or on a magazine representing Calvin Klein. Or perhaps Versace. I open the door to my apartment. The lights are off. Shane must be in bed. I walk to my room, sit on the bed, and take out the card to look at it again. I end up paying no mind to it. I throw it on the desk, on top of some stacked paper, and lay down to sleep.

TWENTY-SEVEN

Liam

I WAKE UP in the late in the morning with the sun shining through my window, and laughter coming from the kitchen. I get up, still sleepy eyed and in my underwear, and enter the kitchen. Kyle and Shane have breakfast on the counter.

"Good morning, sunshine!" Shane says to me, as he carries the coffee pot to the counter.

"Good morning," I say.

"Hey, we made extra French toast for you, Liam," Shane offers. "Oh, thank you."

I pull up a chair, and sit with them to have breakfast. "So, how's it going with your bar gig?" Shane asks.

I pour myself some coffee. "It's going all right, I guess," I answer. "Have you met a lot of interesting people yet?" he asks.

Before answering Shane, I think about it, because I'm a bit of an introvert. I don't really like sharing too many details about my life. Even with close friends, I tend to keep to myself. Maybe I have an issue with trust, but then again, he is my childhood friend. "Well, yesterday I kind of met this guy by accident, who offered me a job as a model," I say, not so enthusiastic about it.

His eye brows shoot up. "So what happened?" he asks eagerly, while he stuffs his mouth with bread.

"I don't know. He told me that he worked with Calvin Klein, Armani, and that they are looking for new faces," I reply, thinking I've said too much. Shane motions toward his ear, making the sign of a phone.

"So are you gonna call him?" he asks. Kyle and Shane pause from their breakfast to look at me eagerly for an answer.

"Hum…" I pause to think about it. "I don't think so, Shane. I mean, being a model wasn't something that I came here for, you know?" I say, as I lower my eyes onto my French toast.

"What was his name?"

"It was, uh… I don't really remember." I pause for a moment, searching my mind for the name. "Oh yeah! It was Lyons. Patrick Lyons," I say, while taking a bite of my French toast.

"Whaaaat? You met Patrick Lyons?" he asks, almost choking on a piece of bread.

"He's the top guy in the business right now, and you said no to him?" Shane asks, running his fingers through his hair in disbelief.

"Well, I didn't meet him the way you are probably thinking. I ran into him with some beer boxes," I reply, trying to avoid explaining the whole incident.

"Oh, so he didn't approach you specifically?" he asks.

"No, not really. It sort of happened that I was rushing through the bar with some beer cases, and I slipped on a puddle of water. The boxes flew in the air and landed on him," I clarify. Shane and Kyle immediately laugh and slam their fists on the table.

"You mean that you almost killed him with the boxes?" Shane asks, laughing while putting his hand on Kyle's shoulder. He laughs as well.

I knew I shouldn't have told them, because now I have to explain, in detail, what happened. It wouldn't be a problem if the story wasn't so comical. "Yeah, I knocked him to the ground. I helped him up, and while I was picking the boxes, he looked at me up and down, then offered me an opportunity to work for his company," I explain, as I take another bite of my French toast.

"Oh my God! You just got an offer that many people have struggled to get. Look at Kyle. He's been modeling since he was eighteen, and still hasn't caught a break like that," he replies. I don't believe him. Kyle looks at me and nods, agreeing to what Shane says. He doesn't speak much. He just sits back and lets Shane do all the talking for him.

"Who knows, Shane?"

"I don't know what's going to happen, but until then, I can't forget why I came here. To publish my book." I remind him.

When Shane realizes that I chose not to take the offer, he does not approve of my decision. "It's funny how some people work so hard for something, and some people get those things handed to them, but they won't take it," Shane replies, and shakes his head in disagreement.

I take a bite of my French toast, ignoring Shane's disapproval, and ask him, "How was your night?"

"What?"

"Your night, how was it?" I ask again, noticing he's a little anxious. "Oh, it was okay. Kyle and I stayed home working on a transaction for a client," he stammers. He avoids eye contact. For a moment I get the impression that he's hiding something from me. I begin to wonder if he has a hidden agenda.

I don't know how Shane understands the investors and those numbers on the Dow Jones. I've seen those stock brokers on TV, and to me it looks like mayhem, because everyone is yelling over each other. Some of them gesture angrily as if they were in some sort of confrontation. Well, I guess they all understand each other, so I came to a conclusion; it's like your room.

It might be a mess, but since it's your mess, you know where everything is. Even though I come to this theory, it's still all Greek to me.

We all help clean up the breakfast table, and Shane and Kyle go back to work on their computer. Their computer isn't like a regular one; it has three screens, and each screen displays different settings. I begin to wonder if the computer is legal. I've seen that computer before, but only in banks, security offices, and government offices. I get a little suspicious about Shane's source of income.

During the week, he leaves home at 9 AM. and returns around 2 PM. If he lived a modest lifestyle, it wouldn't raise questions. Since he is a high spender, and is always blowing money. It keeps me second guessing. Another factor that intrigues me is this apartment. Its value is very high, and it's located in one of the most expensive neighborhoods in Manhattan. Every time he goes to Raven, he manages to spend four thousand dollars on the VIP section, entertaining his friends with bottles of Crystal. There's something that Shane is hiding from me, and I hope it's not something illegal.

I head to my room, sitting down and begin to write a few chapters of my book. Here we go. I'm writing the second act of this love story. Are the two main characters going to proclaim their love for each other? Or are they going to give in to their insecurities and close the page on their love? I know this book will touch the innermost sensitive parts of people's hearts, because we all have, in one way or another, been dishonest to ourselves and to others.

We sometimes don't take chances because there is always a risk of pain and rejection. Instead, we choose to stay on the side of illusions, dreams, and fantasies. Some live this way because it's safe from harm, it's safe from rejection, it's safe from anxiety. It's safe from true happiness. I have come to realize that sometimes it's not loneliness that keeps us from following our dreams, it's happiness itself. Some people are afraid of being happy, because they've been insecure and lonely for so long that they've forgotten how it feels to be loved. God didn't create us to be unsatisfied. He made us to be more than conquerors, to live happy and satisfied lives.

As I finish writing more chapters of my novel, I wish that my story with Bia would be like one great romance novel. I wish, down the road, that I would have the heart to tell her how magnificent she is, how beautiful her smile is to me. How her presence makes me feel like a hero, and how when she stares into my eyes, my life becomes so peaceful. Like the sound of the ocean waves during a morning sunrise.

I feel really lonely. I'm on my own in a new city. I've made friends here and there, but nothing fulfilling. Friends in New York are a dime a dozen. You meet one today, and they're gone tomorrow. I feel that, in New York City, the people's hearts have grown cold. They just don't have that warmth that I experienced from people back home.

Money is a major factor on people's hearts. Their obsession over their ambitions makes their time limited, and distances them from what really matters in life. The true fulfillment and satisfaction in life can be found in a smile, a gentle gesture, and a tight hug, a kiss on the cheek, an encouraging word, a simple gift, a phone call, and a relationship with God.

Often, I daydream, reminiscing of old stories from when I was just a little boy. I would wait for my father to come home. Every Friday, Daddy would bring me chocolate yogurt. That simple gesture had a predominant effect in my life. I know that no matter where I go, my family cares for me. A simple, kind act can alter someone's value about themselves.

These values are important to me, but I'm looking for someone that I can talk to. Someone to share my life with, someone to laugh at my jokes (even the not so funny ones), someone with whom I can be affectionate with. Someone tangible, someone whose eyes I can stare into, and say, "I love you."

The truth is that I don't see myself falling in love with anyone else but Bia. I know I have to let her go and move on. I don't even know what her feelings are toward me now. Time has marched on. Am I a prisoner of my own love for her? How do I conquer this fear? Uncertainty.

Should I pick up the phone, be bold, and confess my passionate love for her again? I've always been meticulous in the aspect of love. I don't want my story to end up in a broken-hearted romance novel. You know, those novels where the protagonist is in love, but to their dismay, they find out that the other character is in love with someone phenomenally good looking, and has a bank account fit for a Hollywood star? Oh, and to top it all off, it's their best friend? After all this revelation, the wounded character gets into their car, crying frantically. As soon as you hear the sound of the ignition, torrential downpour hits the window.

The character takes off into the rainy night doing 70 mph on a 25. They cry their heart out like it's an Oscar winning performance, but they make one fatal mistake. While closing their eyes to reminisce about a romantic moment, they miss the sign that reads "Dead End." The next day, their picture makes the front cover of the city's paper with a headline that reads, "A Dead End to Love." That's not how I want to go.

I want my story to be legendary! Not necessarily Romeo and Juliet, but more of a Rapunzel. Where I would ride through the night with my white horse, and reach her castle, where loneliness has been holding her hostage. As I get closer to the castle, I could see her looking out the window, waiting for her sword wielding knight to break those chains that's been holding her back from happiness. Then, when I reach the castle, she would smile as I extend my hand to her. She would climb down from her window onto my horse, and we would ride away through the night.

For some reason, people all over the world are intrigued by stories of romance, true love, and a hero to take them into a place beyond their dreams. Perhaps this infatuation comes from a yearning to know that there is someone out there for everyone, and that one day those persons will meet, and realize that they were meant for one another. It's a question that remains unanswered.

Many poets tried to figure out an equation to solve the problem. Many writers tell fascinating tales of love and happy endings. I've come to learn through many prayers that love can only be found in one place. That place is God. Learn to love him, and obey him, and he will send you that someone you have been dreaming about. Maybe I'm a dreamer?

All I need is patience. It's one of my virtues, but I have to stretch it some more. Maybe all this time I'm spending on my own can help me reassess my goal. Help me build a career. Am I starting to think like a Yankee? Or is it healthy to think like this?

Whether I like it or not, I am, in a way, driven by ambition. That's part of the reason why I'm here in the city, but there's a line in the sand that has to be drawn. I came to the conclusion that to have no ambition is to eat something dry with no refreshment. To have just an ambition is to drown yourself in the refreshment. To balance your ambition is to eat and drink smoothly. It's healthy to have balance in life, and it's healthy to manage these issues in harmony.

Now that I have seventy percent of my novel complete, I decide to visit some publishing companies around New York City to pitch them my idea. I go to every company that I know of, but they are hesitant about signing new authors. Although I don't get many positive results, I keep believing that maybe the next door will be the door of success.

It's the third day that I'm out here, hustling to get a book deal, but still no positive outcome. It's already evening as I'm walking home. I decide to stop and get something to drink, just to end my journey. I walk into a bar/café on Houston Street, where at this time, the regular evening crowds were gathering.

The inside looks like every hip New York style café. They have brown loveseats, couches, and little round tables. The walls are decorated with purple, soft, leather wallpaper. It makes the ambience very comfortable and relaxed.

I ask the bartender for a martini. I've never had one before. The bartender gives me a thumbs up, confirms my order, and begins to make the drink. "Hey, what's the occasion?" he asks.

This bartender was young, probably in his early 30s. He had a well- built body, with spiky black hair that matched his dark eyes.

"Hum… Nothing really. Just my first evening drinking a martini!" I answer, adjusting myself on the bar stool. The bartender looks at me through the corner of his eyes with wonder while he makes my drink.

"You're not from around here, are you?" he asks curiously, while handing me the martini.

"No, I'm not. I'm from a small town in Virginia," I reply, sipping my drink. Boy, did it taste strong.

"How long have you been in the city?" the bartender asks.

"I've been here for about ten months now," I reply, taking another sip of my martini.

He begins to clean the countertop, and asks, "So, how do you like it so far?"

"Well, can't complain. I got a job the first day I arrived. I just finished writing my book, and now I'm working on getting a book deal," I summarize.

"You're a writer? I like to read. What is your genre?" he asks, motioning his eyebrow.

"I mostly write about romance and love stories," I explain.

"What is the theme of your novel? he asks. Without giving away too many details, I give him a preview of the story, in as dramatic fashion as I can.

"Well, it's about this young man who falls in love with his best friend as an adolescent, and as years go by, he never tells her how he feels. Then, one night, he decides that he has to let her know about his fondness toward her. So he gets on his motorcycle and heads down the narrow road, but he sees a truck headed his way. He attempts to swerve out of the truck's way, but the road was too narrow, and by the time he glances at the truck, it's too late. He never makes it to his destination," I say slowly, using a low baritone whisper. The bartender stares at me, leaning against the balcony, intrigued by the story. After he snaps out of his daze, he stands.

"Wow, that was deep. I mean kind of tragic, don't you think?" he asks. "Yeah, it is. But life sometimes can also be tragic," I respond.

"Man, that was really good. How did you come up with that story?" he asks, putting his hand on the balcony, as he awaits my reply.

"Well, I didn't plan this story. It just happened. It came to me in a dream, and it was so real that when I got up in the middle of the night, I started to write about him. For some reason I tried to remember his face, but I just couldn't see it." For a second, my mind wonders why I couldn't see the character's face.

"So, that was the story that inspired you to become a writer?" he asks. "Yeah. I guess it was, but I used to write as a hobby. I've written poetry, lyrics, and short stories before, but never thought about writing professionally until I became inspired to write this story," I say.

"What about you? Did you always want to be a bartender?" I ask. "Um… not really. I came here to be an actor. I moved here when I was about your age—21 to 22 years old. I was full of dreams back then, but after many failed attempts, I walked into a bar one night and asked for a martini. I was trying to forget my life for a little while. As I sipped that drink, the bartender started asking me questions about my life. I told him how I was going nowhere with this acting career. He offered to teach me how to bartend.

At the time, I wasn't interested in becoming a bartender, but I gave it a shot because life was getting tough for me financially. So, almost ten years later, here I am. Giving the same speech that was given to me while I was drowning my sorrow in a martini. But you are different. You have that spark in your eyes that's very seldom seen on people.

You see, I gave up on my quest, but from the looks of it you seem like you are focused on your goal. The vibe that I get from you is that you know what you want, and you seem to be the kind of person that has something to believe in. In other words, you are a go-getter," he says, encouraging me.

Wow, I don't know where that encouraging speech came from, but it makes me feel good. Maybe I am a go-getter. I could very well be all that he said, but I do have my weaknesses.

"Well, in some aspects, you are right. But there is one thing that I'm scared to conquer!"

"Hey, we all have our insecurities, but you just have to face them if you want to be successful," he says.

"I think that there's a reason for everything. Don't you?" I ask.

He just smiles at me, and moves on to serve another customer. I look at the time. It was about 11 PM at night. I pay my bill with the bartender, and put my backpack over my shoulder. I leave the bar to go home, and I start thinking about what he had said. How some people will never live their dream. As I turn the corner, I see this homeless man sleeping by the side of a building. He lays on a flattened cardboard box, and uses his dirty backpack as a pillow. His stained and torn pants seem two sizes too small. His beard and his hair haven't been trimmed for quite a while.

My heart aches to see this man in such a situation. What could have caused him to come to such a fate? With much compassion, I begin wondering if this man once had a family, a home, or a dream, but one day he probably got dealt the wrong set of cards, or maybe he just made a bad decision.

Maybe someone he loved left him, and no one else told him how important he was. Could his heart be broken? Now, all that was left was this lifeless man who's been broken by the world. By a society too self-absorbed to even notice their victims as they lay on the streets of the city of opportunity!

TWENTY-EIGHT

Liam

I WALK AWAY from the homeless man and make my way to my apartment. I climb up the steps very tiredly. I open the door, and to my surprise, I see Shane and Kyle with two suitcases full of money. I stand there for a moment in shock, looking at them counting all the money in the suitcase. I take a couple of steps in, and they spot me, and immediately they try to hide the suitcase from me.

They realize that I have already seen what is going on. I close the door and begin to make my way to my room, trying to avoid eye contact. What did I just witness? My instinct tells me that something is very wrong. What should I do now? Should I ignore it and be nonchalant about it, or should I get involved and ask for a clarification? Shane looks at Kyle in confusion, then he gets up and says, "Liam, wait!" He motions his hand for me to stop. He slowly stands up from the couch.

"I know you are wondering what we are doing with all this money, but I can explain," he stammers. He walks closer to me, and I stop and turn to him. One can almost grip the tension in the air.

"Liam, I know what you're thinking. How did I get all this money? Well, let me explain," he begins, clearing his throat. "Kyle and I work in Wall Street, and we know a man who is an insider of the Trade Department. A while back, Kyle and I had invested a lot of money on some shares and stocks. Everything was running smoothly until a week ago, when I got a call from my friend, from the Trade Department. He told me that the market was going to crash, which means our investment was going to take a hit, so he advised us to pull our money out before that happened. That's what we did!" he explains, trying to clear things up. He's like a child who's been caught doing something he's not supposed to.

"I appreciate you telling me this, but isn't that illegal? Getting tips from an insider?" I ask suspiciously.

Shane turns to Kyle. He runs his fingers through his hair to relieve some tension. He takes a deep breath.

"Well, if you look at it that way, it is illegal, but try to look at it as I do. I look at it like this: Say your friend was in a fight because he hooked up with someone else's girlfriend. The girl's boyfriend found out, and decided that he was going to fight him. Would you take the side of the girl's boyfriend, or would you protect your friend?" he asks, looking into my eyes.

"Actually, they are both wrong. One is wrong for hooking up with someone else's girlfriend, and the other is wrong because he is resolving the matter in a violent way. But to answer your question, I would choose to protect my friend," I answer, knowing exactly where he was going with this. "You see! You would have done the same thing. He is a friend and he didn't want to see us lose money," he replies, pleading his case.

"Shane, what are you saying? This is different. You are dealing with money, businesses, and even the government. What you did is a felony, maybe worse. Look at what happened to Martha Stewart and Bernie Madoff," I tell them, trying to convince them that what they are doing is wrong.

"Liam, you're overreacting. It's not that serious. How do you think I get to live this kind of lifestyle? All the partying, limos, these expensive clothes, and this apartment? Look, we've been doing this for a while now, and nothing has happened. Hey, to live a good life in this city doesn't necessarily mean that you're a hard worker. You just have to be smart, that's all!" he says, not backing down.

"You know what? Do whatever you want, just don't get me involved. That's all I ask," I declare. I give them a convincing look for a couple of seconds, then turn away, making my way to my room.

When I open the door, Shane speaks up and says, "Hey, don't worry about it. It's going to turn out alright. It always has."

I glance at them, analyzing the whole situation, and for a moment I can feel that Shane knows that I am disappointed with him.

"Good night," I say, and go into my room. I go to bed and try to forget what had just happened.

In the morning, I get up and go to the living room to call my mother back home. I grab the phone and dial. I want to know how my family is doing back home. In a way, I kind of miss the life that I had back home. I just want to hear a voice that is familiar to me. The phone rings a third time, and I hear the soothing sound of my mother's voice.

"Hello," she says.

"Mama, how are you?" I ask. By the sound of her voice, I can feel that she's glad to know it's me.

"Hi, my angel! How are you? I've missed you so much. The house has been so quiet without you here."

"I'm good, Mom. I've just been working, trying to get my book published," I answer.

"Oh darling. I've been missing you so much! I always go to your room to remember how it was when you were here," she says in a morose tone.

"Yeah, I miss you too, but I've been so busy trying to get my dream to come true and working, it's been kind of hectic," I say, trying not to get emotional.

"Liam, let me ask you, how's Shane doing?" she asks.

I hesitate for a second, contemplating whether or not to tell her about his scheme.

"Hum… Shane. He's good, actually. He's doing very well," I reply. Mom and I talk for a while. We talk about old times, and many memories we share back home. Anyway, our conversation always ends with the usual. Mom cries, urges for me to come home, but I tell her that this is something that I have to do.

Friday rolls around. I get up to go to work. I did the usual things that I would normally do. I fix my room, make a few calls, and leave the house around six o'clock. A couple of blocks from my house, I see an ambulance pass by. Then, after a few blocks, I see two more ambulances pass, followed by a couple of police cars. I begin to get curious, because they are headed toward the street that I am going to.

I pick up my pace, and as I turn the block, I hear a loud explosion. For a second, I stand back with fright. I run closer to the scene, and I see Donny sitting on the sidewalk. His hand is on his head while the firefighters vigorously fight the flames with water hoses. I run toward Donny and reach down to him.

"Donny, are you okay? What happened?" I ask, worriedly.

I look at his hands. They are shaking. His face is white as milk.

"I don't know. I was… I… was cleaning the bar, getting ready for tonight, and they were testing out the lights. That's when, all of a sudden, we saw some sparks, and the next thing I know, the roof was on fire! So I ran out as fast as I could, and that's when the fire reached the gas pipes. The moment everyone stepped outside, that's when the explosion occurred. I couldn't believe how powerful the explosion was. It threw everyone to the floor. Now, the firefighters are trying to put out the flames. I just thank God that no one was hurt," he says in disbelief.

I try to console Donny, but he is still in shock about the whole situation.

I encourage him, trying to abate the moment, but everything seems like it just isn't real.

I can't believe what I am seeing. It feels like a movie. That club was somebody's dream, somebody's way of life, and so many people's memories. Now, it is all up in flames. The result of years of work is turning to ashes. I stand there in disbelief as firefighters put out the flames. I look up, and thank God that everyone is okay.

The firefighters tell everyone to leave the scene, because the investigator is coming to search for clues as to what could have happened. I turn around, and begin to walk home. I'm in disbelief. What am I going to do, now that my job is gone? How am I going to pay my rent?

I can't go back home to Virginia, because when I left that town, I made a vow to myself that I would never look back, or go back, without first making it in New York City. To me, it feels like the sun had just gone down on me. I don't know what to do. I keep walking. I look over my shoulder a few times, to see the smoke rising from what used to be the place that I worked.

Suddenly a feeling of loneliness rushes through me like a flood. My face is downcast, looking at the sidewalk as I stroll home. Many thoughts are running through my mind, but none are positive nor productive. I take a deep breath and exhale to relieve a bit of my anxiety.

When I reach West 4th Street, to my dismay, I see two police cars with the front door open, and the flashing lights on. I didn't think much of it, as I rode the elevator to my apartment. When I reach my floor, I can hear shouting and stomping. I notice that my apartment door is open, and that the noise is coming from within. I take a couple of steps stealthily toward my door.

When I reach the trim of the door, I look carefully inside. That's when a man, standing behind the door, reveals himself while pointing a 9mm to my face. He shouts, "Put your hands behind your head! Now!"

I slowly put my hands on my head. This is so surreal. I feel like I'm in a movie, or part of a big prank. My body becomes weak, as I stare into the barrel of the 9mm.

"What's going on? Who are you?" I ask frantically.

"We're the FBI, and you're under arrest for grand larceny, and money laundering!" he declares, pushing me against the wall. When I hear the accusation, my heart drops. Still pictures of my life play inside my mind. How can they accuse me of such things, when I'm not even involved?

"I'm a bartender, I think you got the wrong guy!" I plead. Then I look to the living room, and I see Shane and Kyle in handcuffs, standing by the wall. Shane spots me and yells out.

"Hey, let him go! He has nothing to do with this!"

"Shut your mouth, you scumbag. Who gave you the right to speak?" the officer demands, while pushing Shane against the wall.

"He's just a roommate. He has nothing to do with this. Let him go," Shane demands right back.

The officer looks at me suspiciously. "Who are you?" he asks.

"I-I-I... My name is Liam," I say, stuttering.

The officer looks at me, up and down. "Let me see some ID."

I reach into my back pocket, and show him my wallet. He takes the wallet from me, pulls out my ID, and examines it for a few seconds.

"Do you know who you are living with?" he asks.

I was so nervous that I couldn't even put a whole sentence together. "Well I... They are my..."

"These guys have been under our radar for quite some time now. They are wanted for larceny. They stole over one hundred million dollars from the investors," he explains, pointing to them. "Did you know what was going on?" he asks.

"Officer, Shane is a friend of mine, but I tend to stay away from his personal life. We've known each other since we were kids. I moved here from Virginia a while ago. Shane offered me a room to stay while I'm in the city, but I don't really know what goes on in his life! I tend not to ask."

The officer stares at me for a moment and then says, "You're still going to have to come down to the station for questioning."

With that, all three of us are escorted down to the back seat of the cop car and driven to the police station.

After four grueling hours of questioning the officers finally let me go. As I am walking out, I see two officers pick up Shane and Kyle, and escort them, still in handcuffs, to the jail cells. As Shane passes by me, he whispers, "Liam, man, I'm sorry. I didn't intend for you to see this."

His eyes are remorseful, as they escort him to the elevator. I just look at him, as he is taken away by custody. What else can I do? I can't do anything to help.

I get back home to find that the apartment has been ransacked. All the evidence that they needed was found. The officers came back and took the computers and a few hard drives were gone from the shelves.

I collapse on the couch in exhaustion. I lay there for a while, staring at the ceiling. I am emotionally drained. My thoughts are too numerous to decipher. If there was ever a bad day in my life, this one is it. Thoughts of insecurities consume me to the point of wanting to throw everything to the wind and go back home to Virginia.

What am I going to do now? How am I going to survive? What am I going to tell people back home, when they pick up a newspaper and realize that I have been living with criminals all this time? Where do I go from here? It seems that today my dreams, my friends, my entire life all fell apart.

I fall asleep, right where I am. I wake up in the morning. It's 8:15 AM, and I realize that I had been asleep since 11PM the night before. I am well-rested, and still trying to comprehend what had happened yesterday. I get up, and make myself some breakfast.

Soon after, I get myself ready to look for another job. I can't stay home, wallowing in self-pity, because that doesn't get you very far. Here I am, thinking only of myself, when my friends are in jail. Shock still grips me from the incident last night. My hands are tied; I can't even defend them in court, because the police found all the evidence needed to convict them. I want to help, but I can't.

Even though all of this is going on, I can't sit back and be passive about it. I have to take a stand, even though nothing is going right. Sometimes you have to just step out in faith, and keep on going.

I make a list of bars and restaurants that I know, and go to them to see if they are hiring. I go to interview after interview, and still no one is hiring. Some even say that I don't have enough experience to work as a bartender. I become a little discouraged, but in my situation, I have no option but to keep going.

Later that day I try to go and visit Shane and Kyle in jail, but the lady at reception tells me that they are not allowed to have any visitors. With my shoulders slumped, I start walking out of the police station.

"Hey," the officer behind the desk says just before I step out, "if you want, you can attend your friend's hearing which is in an hour at the courthouse. You can see them then." I thank her and leave.

Exactly an hour later, I sit at the back of the courthouse and watch as the judge sentences my friends. As the guard is escorting him out, Kyle spots me and smiles weakly. He looks terrible in his orange jumpsuit. I can't stand seeing him in those chains so I get up and walk out with my head hung low.

It's been about four days in which I've been looking for work, with no break at all. Besides having to stop to tie my sneakers every two blocks, I am doing all right. It is already 2 PM, and I am still going from place to place. I don't even stop to eat. I keep going for the rest of the afternoon.

I can't call my family. They are barely making ends meet. Plus, they will ask me to come back home. *Failure! How embarrassing that would be!*

No. I have to make it. There's no turning back or other options. For me, it is either victory or death.

Nightfall is just around the corner, and still I am exploring all the caves of this jungle. I am trying not to let this situation get to me, but when I think about the rent that I have to pay, and the situation that my friends are in, it drains the energy out of me.

As I am nearing Houston Street, I decide to stop in, and get a drink. I walk in, and the place is kind of full. I take a chair near the corner of the bar. To my surprise, it is the same bartender as last time I was there. He walks toward me.

"Let me guess. A dirty martini," the bartender guesses.

"Make me a filthy martini this time!" I say, while adjusting myself on the stool.

"Wow, what's the occasion? Wait, let me guess. Hum… You just lost your job. Am I wrong?" he asks, while making my drink.

"No, not really," I say, not wanting him to know the truth. On the other hand, I have no one else to talk to. "You're right on the money! How did you guess that?" I ask. I am a little bit puzzled that he knows what is going on.

"I've been a bartender for many years, and dealt with so many faces, that when I look at someone's eyes, I can tell a thing or two about their lives," he replies.

"So, you're like a psychic bartender, huh?" I reply with a smirk. "Yeah… something like that!" He hands my drink, returning my smirk. Squinting a grin I say, "Dude, I just lost my job because the building I was working in went up in smoke. To top it all off, I just spent a whole day going through every bar and café in the city, but none hiring, or so they say," I say, while taking a sip of my filthy hard hitting martini. I squint a grin.

"This city could give you anything that you want, but at the same time, it could take it all back, anytime it wants too," the bartender says with a mystical tone to his voice.

"With so many businesses in this place, it's hard to believe that no one is hiring!" I take another sip of my filthy martini.

"One thing I've learned in this city is that you can never put your head down, because once one door closes, two other doors will open. The key to those doors is persistency!" He gives me this advice, and walks away to attend to a customer. I sit there, drinking my martini, while thinking about what he said to me.

You know, tomorrow is another day. I have faith in God; He would never hand me a situation that I wouldn't be able to handle. Life is simple. Just put your trust in God, and leave the rest to your intuition. It will take you in the right direction. You know, I'm not going to stay home dwelling on my situation. If I stay home, I'm going to fall into that trap of self-pity, and once you're in that zone, it's very difficult to come out.

Just about an hour later, I leave the bar. On my way home, I begin evaluating my life. I'm trying to decipher my next step. Human beings, by nature, always want to have control over the situations in their lives. I constantly battle with myself about it, but I have to remind myself that I already gave my life to God. So why am I still trying to push with such force? I come to a conclusion. I'll do the best that I can, and leave God to do the supernatural.

I walk into my apartment, and lay down on the couch. I stare at the ceiling for a little bit, and think to myself. Since I've been here, I haven't really gone out to see the city. It's a Thursday night, what could be going on? They say this is the city that never sleeps! I think I'm going to go to that club that I passed by today. It seems like a cool place to hang out.

After a few minutes, still laying there, I look at my watch. It's about ten to eleven. I make my decision: I'm going out. I get myself ready and head downstairs. I get a cab, and ask the cabbie if he knows where the club 'Exit' is. He takes me there, and to my surprise, there are signs all over the wall stating tonight's special event.

They are having Lenny Kravitz's album release party. So, I stand in line for about a half-hour. The bouncers are being very selective about the guests.

When I reach the door, the bouncer approaches me. As I reach for my ID, he looks at me and says, "What are you doing waiting in line? You are on the guest list?"

He moves aside, and tells me to go to the next bouncer, down the corridor. I walk down the corridor, not understanding what's happening. I approach the next line, and when it comes to my turn, the bouncer says, "Your name?"

I don't know what to say, because I know my name isn't on the list.

Then again, I'm not going to lie and say someone else's name.

"Liam. Liam D'Fiori," I say, and wait for him to find out that I am not on the guest list. To have him kick me out for trying to get in VIP.

"Huh… I don't see any Liam here," he says, checking the list again. "Well, that other guy told me to come here," I point at the first bouncer.

Now I'm frightened, because my name is not on the list, and both of the bouncers are triple my size. The second bouncer's physique is so wide and muscular that it makes his head look small. At this moment, I recognize David's courage when he fought Goliath.

"Yo! Ajax! Who is this guy?" bouncer number two shouts to bouncer number one.

"Let him in, he's with the modeling crew," bouncer number one shouts back.

"I'm sorry. I didn't know you were with the modeling party," he says, showing me the way to the dance floor. I stand there, looking at him, trying to figure out what just happened. What's going on? Why are they referring to me as a model? It could be that they are just confused due to the overcrowding at the door.

I walk in, and I was inside the VIP section of the club, facing the stage. I scout the place curiously, and it is packed. There are so many celebrities that I think I am in a movie.

Upon scanning the scene, I proceed to the bar. The bar is made of white marble with a blue neon light reflecting on it, giving off a very mellow effect. I ask the bartender for a Coca-Cola on the rocks. As I take the first sip, the band takes the stage. The crowd goes wild with shouts and screams of excitement! I approach the balcony of the VIP section to watch the band perform. Like usual, the hits come first, to make the crowd roar in excitement.

Halfway through the set, I go to the bar to get another coke. After receiving my drink, I turn my back against the counter of the bar, and lean on it, simply observing the crowd. In the midst of all the people surrounding me, I feel completely alone. It's an empty feeling, because I am in a crowd of people, but I feel estranged.

Everyone around me is having fun, but as I watch them laughing, hugging, and enjoying each other's company, it makes me wonder about my life. I drift miles away in loneliness. I don't understand why I am this way, nor feel the way I do. This is a side of myself that I'd eliminate if I could. I never had any lasting friendships. I always tend to just be a spectator, while everyone else is involved in life.

While I am having my pity party in my mind, I notice someone staring at me from the other side of the room. I turn to her, gazing straight at her. She returns my gesture with a smile. Her smile stirs something inside me, and courage begins to rise inside me. Her look intrigues me, as I make my way through the crowd.

The closer I get to her, the more beautiful she becomes. My heart pounds, and I begin to feel my body get warmer and warmer. She stands a couple of feet from me, dancing with her friends. As she dances, her long brown hair moves about her profile.

Her tender olive skin shines with glitter. I am a couple of feet from her, when her beautiful brown eyes make contact with mine. I am consumed by her beauty. This is the first time that I have laid eyes on her, but it feels like we were lovers all our lives. As the revolving lights hit her eyes, they shine like honey on a comb.

She begins to take notice of me, and I can see that her friends are also taking turns glancing my way. I think that maybe there is someone behind me that the girls are looking for. But now she glances at me more fiercely, and also throws me a smile now and then. I keep my composure, and stand there glancing back flirtatiously.

When she receives my smile, she starts to make her way toward me. She moves slowly, while dancing, to get to me. With my heart still racing, she grabs me by my hips, and pulls me toward her. We begin to dance to the swinging sound of the music. I put my arm around her to feel her whole body next to mine.

For a brief moment time stops, and it is only the two of us. As she moves, I could smell the sweet scent of her hair.

Without hesitation, our lips meet. We feel the softness of our tongues rolling over each other. Her kiss mesmerizes me the way she presses her soft lips on mine. From that moment on, we can't keep away from each other.

TWENTY-NINE

Liam

TWO DAYS HAVE PASSED since my heart melted. We keep the phone to our ears until it is time to go to bed. Michelle! How could a name be so exciting? How could just a name trigger my heart to beat faster?

Without knowing if this feeling is good or bad, I wonder where it will lead me. I guess I just hold on to my guns, and ride this crazy horse. I mean, how far can wild horses drag you away?

I feel so alive today that I get up around 8 AM to make myself some breakfast, and get ready to go meet Michelle at Central Park. I asked her to spend the day with me, so she took a personal day off work. I start to head to Central Park, and on the way, I call her to hear her sweet, soothing voice. We make plans to meet there at 10:30 AM. On the way, I pick up some French pastry with chocolate fillings. I arrive at 10:15 AM, and she's already waiting at the entrance by the park wall.

I pick up my pace, smiling as she spots me. She runs toward me with that glowing smile, and her hair blows in the wind. She jumps into my arms, crossing her legs around my waist. She kisses my neck and the side of my face.

"Hi, sweetheart! How good it is to see you!" she says between kisses.

"Look what I bought you." I show her the box of pastries. She smiles, thanking me. The day is sunny and bright. It has the beginning of the essence of summer. We start to walk in the park, while eating the chocolate pastries. I stare at her, while she takes every bite, and I am dazzled by her charming beauty.

We stroll around for a couple of minutes, and begin to comment on our surroundings. I take notice that she is very detail-oriented, by the way she uses her words to express what she thinks is interesting. She also has a confidence that I admire. As she expresses her view on life, she tends to focus her eyes deeply into mine. I stare right back at hers, losing myself in them. It feels so good to have her with me, sharing this time together.

The conversation goes on, and we approach a hot dog stand. I buy us some hot dogs and a soda. We sit at a wooden bench nearby, and while we eat, we begin to discuss personal subjects within our lives. I take a sip of the soda we share, and say, "You have a soothing, southern drawl, which most southern people I meet don't have."

"Well, I'm from Texas, and as you know, Texan girls are the sweetest giiirls arooound," she says, embellishing her southern drawl even more. I laugh.

"Yeah, I agree they are sweet," I say, looking into her eyes. "You think I'm pretty, don't you?" she asks, lifting her eyebrows. "Yep," I reply with a wink.

"You think I'm sexy?"

"Hum, let me see." I look at her from head to toes, and gaze back into her eyes.

"Yep."

"You think I'm the most sweetest, charming, lovely, intelligent woman in the entire world?" she asks, twirling her finger through her hair. I look into her eyes.

Puckering my lips in pondering mode, I say, "Well you could be, but you see that girl right there?" I point to a beautiful woman in her thirties, with her friends, feeding some pigeons popcorn.

"Well, that woman contains all that quality," I say sarcastically. Michelle glances at her, turns to me, and slaps my arm.

"But how can she be all these things, being a blonde?" she asks, laughing.

"Simple. She's a true blonde, not bleached," I say, defending all blonds from the stereotype that society lays upon them.

Michelle gives me a smirk, and says, "Well, I guess I'm gonna have to dye my hair blonde." We both laugh and begin walking again.

Further into the park, we approach a water fountain that gushes with water. The outer rim is made of marble, as is the middle where the columns are stacked, from the larger piece at the bottom, and as they stack higher, it becomes smaller. The top piece pours out water into the basins below, making a cascade effect. We approach it to count the pennies on the bottom.

As we watch the sparkling water, I ask her, "We have been together for a couple of days now, and I don't even know why you are here in the city?"

She stares at the water as she answers. "Well, I don't know really! It's always been a dream of mine to come to a big city."

I push my hands into my pockets and ask, "What drove you to do this? Any dreams to fulfill?"

She looks at me, and turns to the fountain. "The main reason I came here was to have a career as a model. It's been my life's dream to be a professional model. Since I was a little girl, I was fascinated with photography. I used to look at magazines just to see the new poses of the models. I would even imitate those poses in front of the mirror when I was by myself in my room. As I got older, I decided that I wanted to pursue modeling as a career. I always thought I could be a great role model for young women, just as the models I admired were when I was growing up."

"So, is that what you do? You model?" I ask, throwing a penny into the fountain without making a wish.

"No, not really. I work as a secretary in a consulting company uptown," she answers with a tone of dissatisfaction.

"Are you pursuing that dream?"

"I am. I've been in a couple of ads, but nothing serious. I haven't yet been approached by any big-time firm," she says, running her fingers through her hair.

There is a sudden silence between the both of us. After a couple of minutes of reflection, I lean toward her, grabbing her hand. She approves my gesture by tightening her grip. We walked back through the park. It is now about late afternoon. The wind gains a little momentum, and her hair is like the ocean waves, as they flow from side to side.

On the way back, we don't say much. I am just enjoying her presence, and I think she is enjoying mine, because we look at each other's eyes and smile. Her eyes are so serene, and her face has an angelic look. It makes me feel safe and content. We keep walking along until we reach an exit of the park, near a subway station.

I stand there facing her, figuring out what to do next. I didn't want to go home, but then again, I have to get ready for tomorrow. I still don't have a job. Before I can say anything, she turns to me coyly, licks her lips, and utters, "Liam, if you want, we can go to my apartment? We could order some food, and then watch a movie."

I am glad that she broke the ice, but I am feeling a bit nervous. She makes me feel so secure that I can't let this go.

"I would love to spend the evening with you," I reply with a smile. She leads me by the hand into the subway station.

"You are going to love it. There is this Chinese food restaurant that makes the most delicious food you've ever tasted, and also, I have this movie that would make you cry," she says excitedly, as we head down the steps to the subway station.

"Cry," I repeat. "Cry. I don't cry from movies." I stand my ground, defending my macho ego.

"Come on, don't lie. Yes, you do! Every man cries," she responds with a smirk.

"Yeah, but I'm not like every man. I don't cry. Instead, I work out. I play soccer, I-I-I… I do other things," I insist, trying to cover up my emotional side.

"Oh, you've got to see the look on your face! You look soooo cute, trying to neglect your sensitive side!" She pinches both of my cheeks, and then kisses me with those soft lips. At that moment, the E train arrives, and we make our way to her apartment.

Upon arriving at her apartment, I notice it is a studio. It is fairly big, with an L-shaped leather couch sitting on a 6 x 4 foot Arabian carpet. A glass rectangular table sits in the middle, and in the corner of the room, near the window, is her full-size bed. It faces a flat screen TV, hanging on different colored walls. I walk in and sit on a bar stool by the kitchen counter.

"So, what's your choice of Chinese?" she asks, holding the phone. "I'll have whatever you are," I reply.

She makes the order, and then reaches under the counter where she keeps a bottle of wine. She grabs two glasses, opens the bottle, and pours the wine into each cup. She makes her way to the couch, where I follow her. We sit there, close to each other, admiring one another. About twenty minutes later, the food arrives. I help her set the table, and we eat.

As we eat, we talk to each other, asking a few more questions. We want to know more about each other's lives. I romantically feed her, to make up for my stupid remarks about being macho. As we finish, I helped her clean up and put things in order.

The evening winds down, and I get anxious. I know that I have to get to bed early, so that I can get up tomorrow to search for work. I can see her setting up the DVD, and removing some of the pillows from her bed. After she sets up the movie, she looks at me.

"Come lay here beside me so we can watch the movie!" she says. I approach the bed, remove my shoes, and lay beside her. The wind picks up, and the curtains from the windows sway like wheat in a field. The weather had changed from sunny to murky, darkened rain clouds. She closes the window, leaving just an inch open to keep the room brisk, and then she climbs back into bed. She pulls the bed covers over us.

The movie plays. It's called *Titanic*. It's the story of a couple Jack and Rose who find themselves on the grandest ship in the world, from two opposite backgrounds, and fall in love. Then the ships hit an iceberg and sank. Jack dies. In my view there was definitely room on that door for both of them. Spoiler Alert!!! Poor Jack didn't make it.

As the movie goes on, I can hear the raindrops hit the window, like the sounds of pebbles being thrown into a puddle. I can feel her warm body inch closer to mine. The movie proceeds to its conclusion, and I'm touched by the ending quite a bit. Unintentionally, a tear escapes my eyes. Michelle glances at me.

"Baby, are you crying?" she asks.

I wipe that one small, tiny tear away and stammer, "No, I'm not crying."

"Oh. How sweet," she says, leaning toward me with a kiss. The rain comes down more intensely, but as its droplets hit the window, it makes a gentle soothing sound. We fall into each other's arms, and melt in our warmth.

THIRTY

Liam

I WOKE UP in the morning and the rain had stopped, but flowing in from the window I can smell the scent of roses after a cold rain. I turn over to find Michelle getting ready for work. She looks so beautiful walking around back and forth organizing her things, bushing her long brown hair in the process. It's Wednesday morning, so I decide to get myself ready for the day ahead of me. I push the cover off me and reach for my pants.

As Michelle passes by, she gives me a good morning kiss and asks where I am going. I hesitate, not wanting to tell her that I am unemployed. I try to think of an excuse and say, "I'm going back home to make a few phone calls to some publishing agencies."

We head down the elevator together and I walk her to the bus station. We kiss each other goodbye and I proceed to the other side of the block to catch my bus home. When I arrive home, I lay on my bed, daydreaming about her and the night we've spent together.

My ecstasy didn't last very long before Bia's face pops into my head. I close my eyes and picture her beautiful smile. I day dream for a couple of minutes before catching myself. I have to stop thinking about her now that

I'm with someone else. Michelle is real and tangible, and Bia… well, I don't even know if she feels what I feel for her anymore. I have come to the realization that I have to stop living in a delusion. I have to stop hiding behind my comfort zone. This is my reality right now. Michelle is my reality now.

I get up from my bed and begin to look for the papers with the club listing address. While I'm searching through the stack of paper on my desk, a card falls on my shoes. I reach down and pick it up. To my surprise, it is Patrick Lyons' card, the model agent guy.

I take it and sit on my bed, looking at it and thinking. This is not something I want to do. It's not why I came to this city. Then I begin to analyze my current situation. It's not looking too good. Rent is coming up, all the bars and clubs I've been to are not giving me the time of day. My money is running out and I don't want Michelle to find out that I'm a step away from becoming homeless. My options are limited. I have no choice but to give it a try.

I stand up and put the card in my pocket. I decide to go ahead and give it a try. I'm not even sure that Patrick will remember me. He must see new faces every day, why would my face be any different. I make my way down the elevator to get myself a cab. After an expensive $30 taxi ride, I found the building on Park Avenue. After clearing security, I take the elevator to the top floor. The elevator door opens and I approach the secretary.

"Hi. I'm here to see Patrick Lyons."

"Do you have an appointment?" she replies with a serious tone.

"No, I don't, but he gave me this card and told me that I could stop by and see him anytime," I tell her as I reach into my pocket to show her the card. She studies the card and asks in a doubting tone, "Patrick Lyons personally gave this to you?"

"Yeah, we met one day at Raven and he told me to call, but I never did. Instead I decided to come here in person," I say, assuring her that I know him personally.

"Do you have a portfolio with you?" she questions. "Excuse me, a portfolio?" I ask confusedly.

"Yeah! A portfolio is a group of selected photos taken professionally by a photographer to present your work," she says sarcastically.

"No, I don't have one," I say disappointedly.

She looks at me quietly for a second. "Wait here while I'll talk to Mr. Lyons."

I stand there in the lobby with my hand in my pocket. I look around the room, noticing all the pictures on the wall of the models that have worked with them. There are many pictures of Patrick Lyons at different events that he'd attended, many pictures with celebrities and fashion designers.

After analyzing the awards on the wall I began to think, what am I doing here? I'm not a celebrity. I'm just a small-town country boy and to top it all, I'm shy. I can't even imagine being noticed by everyone. Everywhere you go people know who you are. You get to go to the hippest parties. You get to meet other celebrities. You get privileges that regular people don't get. Basically you live a life full of excess.

At that thought, I spot the secretary walking down the corridor. She calls my name and motions with her index finger to follow her. She walks me into Mr. Lyons' office where he is sitting behind his desk writing on what seems to be his agenda.

The secretary leaves discreetly, closing the door behind her. I sit on the right chair in front of his desk. I scan the room to find more and more plaques of Mr. Lyons' successful career. Mr. Lyons breaks the silence.

"What brought you here?"

"Well," I shift in my seat. "I lost my job and my friend/roommate got in trouble with the law so here I am trying to pay rent." I give him a brief summary of my situation. "I remembered your offer to me that night in Raven and found your card so I decided to see if you are still interested in hiring me," I finish, stammering just a bit. For some reason, I get nervous in situations such as this where I have to ask someone for something.

He puts his hand down, sits up on his chair and, with a smirk, he fixes his eyes on mine.

"It was a matter of time, I knew you would come," he says as if he had anticipated my arrival.

"What do you mean?" I ask, a puzzled frown crinkling my eyebrows. "I watch the news… I know what happened. I believe that things happen for a reason. That's why you're here," he says as he leans back on his black leather chair.

"Mr. Lyons, I'm going to be honest with you. I didn't come here to become a supermodel or a celebrity. I came here to see if I can earn some money, so that I can publish my book and put some bread on the table," I tell him. He smiles, scratching his chin.

"Liam, you need me and I want you. So we are going to find a middle ground here. You know why you came to New York City. You want to be known. You want to do something that people will remember you for. That is why everyone is here. They want to be known. You want to be known as a writer, but I have a different proposition for you. I'm going to make you be known for your exuberating beauty."

While I don't know about that last bit, I know that he is right—I came to New York because I want to be known. Mr. Lyons is a good businessman. He seems to know the exact words to say and when to say it. As I think about his proposition, I know deep inside why I came here. I want to impress Bia.

The reason is because her family disapproves of me for monetary reasons. I want her to find a reason to be with me, because no matter the distance between us, it seems that my feelings for her stay close to me. I want to show her that I am more than just another country boy. I want to feel special. I want to show her that I am ambitious. I want Bia to admire me, the way I admire her.

I can see that Mr. Lyons in some ways needs me, business wise. So I decide to play hard to get, even though I'm in a dire straits financial situation. I cross my legs, look up at Mr. Lyons, and boldly ask, "Other than 'being known,' what's in it for me?"

Mr. Lyons gives me a dog sly smile and says, "If you sign this contract and work for me, I will make you rich and famous beyond your wildest dreams." He hands me a contract and I look over it.

"How much money are we talking here?"

"Well, how much do you need?" he returns my question.

"Well, my rent is due in two weeks and I need at least ten thousand dollars to add up to what I already have saved."

"I'll tell you what Liam, you do this one fashion show this Saturday and I guarantee that you won't be disappointed," he says, staring into my eyes. I let my mind drift, thinking about the fame, the money, and all the excess that comes with being famous. For some reason, this fuels my curiosity.

"What do I have to do?"

"It's simple, just sign the contract and meet me at the lobby on Saturday at 6 PM," he says with confidence. I take a pen from his desk and scan the contract briefly. After reading some of the larger print, I sign at the bottom. "Liam D'Fiori." I hand him the contract knowing that I made a viable decision. He looks over it and stretches his arm toward me. I shake his hand.

"Welcome aboard, Liam! This will be a ride that many don't get, but you did, so enjoy it."

I leave his office and go home. After the excitement fades away, I realize that I just signed a contract without really understanding the terms. It makes me a bit nervous not fully knowing what I signed. I call my mother and tell her everything that has happened. She sounds happy that my life is coming along, but she is also worried that I'll run into the wrong crowd.

I comfort my mother by telling her that she raised a level headed son with moral and values.

My parents gave their all to raise me and my sisters in a respectful manner. They were always affectionate toward us. And they never hesitated to discipline us when they thought it was needed (or when the neighbors thought it was needed!). But what stands out the most in my mind is their love for us. I know that no matter what I do in life, they'll take me back with great love and arms wide open.

Evening approaches with a beautifully full moon. The night is cool and fresh. I call Michelle to invite her for dinner to share my surprising victory.

At eight o'clock, we meet at Sushi Samba on 7th Avenue by Christopher Street. It's a nice trendy restaurant decorated with bamboo tables and soothing lights.

Michelle called me earlier saying she would be a little late for dinner due to some problems at the firm. So I go ahead and order some drinks and appetizers. Just a few minutes after the appetizers arrive, she walks in the door. She greets me with a sweet kiss and a vibrant smile. She sits down and we begin to talk and take some bites of our food. The night goes on; we laugh at each other's jokes and share stories about our lives.

Little by little, I'm beginning to let Bia go. I feel good around Michelle; she helps me let go of my insecurities. With her I don't have to hide. I can express my feelings; I can just let them flow. I love her characteristics: she's funny, intellectual, gorgeous, pleasant to be around, lively, and I love when she talks because she tends to pantomime every word as she expresses herself.

The night carries on as the crowd goes in and out of the restaurant. I prepare myself to tell her about my new job. She dips her spoon into her chocolate mousse and brings it to her lips to taste it. She samples half the spoon and says, "Liam, I have known you for a many weeks now, but you always neglect to answer when I ask you what kind of work you do?"

"I used to work at Raven, the night club," I say. "Raven, the club that burned down?"

"Yeah," I reaffirm.

"Really?! I used to go there all the time but I don't think I ever saw you there!" she exclaims. Not that I am ashamed of being a bar-back, but I feel reluctant to tell her what I did. It's not as exciting as being a bartender. "I was always running around helping the bartender," I say, avoiding my title.

"Oh, so you were a bar-back," she corrects me.

"Yeah, I was a bar-back," I confirm. Her expression becomes more serious. "So what are you doing now that the club is shut down?"

"Well, for the past two weeks I've been job hunting all over the city," I say.

"And did you find any? Are you employed?" she asks.

"Yeah, I got a job today actually, but it's not related to what I was doing before," I say, smiling with excitement. I know she's going to be happy when I tell her that I'm going to be a model.

"While I was working at Raven, I ran into someone who gave me an offer to work for him in a modeling agency, but since I was comfortable where I was, I didn't give it any second thought, until Raven burned down.

Then one day I was home searching for the paper where I had written the club's listings. As I was going through a stack of paper, a card fell on my shoes. It was the card of that man that I had met a couple of months before the club burned down. Since I was running out of money and my friend Shane was not around, I decided to go to the agency. When I got there, I got the opportunity to talk to the CEO of the agency!" I pause. Michelle's eyes open wide in suspense.

"Well, what happened?" Michelle asks excitedly.

"Well," I say, drawing it out, "we talked about a lot of things, the business, our goals, our visions, etc. And guess what…" I pause. "He offered me a contract to model for his company," I say enthusiastically, leaning back in my chair with a big smile.

"Wow, that's great! I can't believe it. So now you are going to model. And what is your agent's name?" she asks.

"Patrick Lyons, and he works with all of the big clothing lines in the world. He has work for me for this Saturday already," I say. After saying his name, I notice that Michelle's facial expression changes from cheerful to sad. I don't know what happened and I am afraid to ask. What could have upset her so much?

We finish our desserts and leave the restaurant. We take a cab to Michelle's apartment where I'm going to spend the night. On the way home, I notice that Michelle is still bothered by something. She stares out the window with an empty look on her face. I ask her what it is, but she persists in saying that everything is fine. By the expression of her face, I could see that she is contemplating something. Her mood changed right after I broke my good news.

For a second, I flash back and remember what she said in the park. She told me that her dream was to be a professional model. I had totally forgotten about that. Now I know why she's reacting this way. I should've been more considerate, but then again, I had forgotten what she told me that day.

Slowly, I put my hand on top of hers and I squeeze my fingers gently between hers. I want to ask her what's wrong, but if she answers me, I don't know what to say. I keep my hand on top of hers and pretend that everything is fine.

THIRTY-ONE

Beatrice

IT HAS BEEN TWO months since I sent in my application to study law at Virginia State University. Every Tuesday and Thursday at around 2 PM, I find myself pacing the front lawn beside the post box, waiting to scan through the mail that the mailman drops in.

Once the mailman walks away, I yank the letters out and flip through them at lightning-fast speed to see if any are addressed to me. Previously, none of the letters have been for me, but I have a feeling that today is the day. Slicking my long hair back in a high ponytail, I rush downstairs and fling open the front door. From where I am standing, I can see that the mailman hasn't come yet.

So, I go outside to 'casually' peruse around the garden. With every car that goes by, my head anxiously shoots up to check if it is the postman. Five minutes turn into ten and after what feels like an eternity, I finally hear the all too familiar splutter of the postal van as it struggles to climb up our hill. My adrenaline spikes and my palms instantly become drenched.

Trying to act casual, I walk over to the post box nonchalantly. Striding through the grass like I have no care in the world. The postman notices me and waves, I return his wave and he is on his way. As soon as he turns his back, I book it to the postbox and yank the letters out.

The stack is thicker than usual. I notice a few of the regulars, two letters from the bank, a few invitations for my parents and then my heart stops. Everything becomes eerily silent and I actually have to rub my eyes to ensure that I am seeing correctly.

In my hand I hold a stark white envelope with my name printed on it in bold, black writing and the Virginia State University letterhead at the very top of the right-hand corner.

It is finally here… I don't know if I can open it.

Standing on my lawn, I stare at the envelope as my thoughts race a thousand miles per minute. I have waited so long for this letter and now that I have it, I cannot seem to bring myself to open it. A gust of wind blows and sends shivers down my spine. I place the envelope on top of the rest, clutching the stack to my chest, I make my way back inside.

As I walk through the doors, I place all of the letters down on the little table in the foyer, all except one. I take the letter from V S U and head to the kitchen where I know that I will find Di. As expected, she is busy putting away some dishes when I walk in.

"Are you hungry?" she asks as she closes the cupboard door after putting away some plates. "I made waffles."

"Nope," I say as I sit at one on one of the high stools by the counter.

Di stops what she is doing and turns around to look at me. "What is the matter?"

I place the envelope on the kitchen counter and stare at it. Di walks over and stands beside me in silence for a few moments. We are both just frozen.

Eventually, she asks, "Well, aren't you going to open it?" I nod my head and slowly reach out to pick up the letter.

Di places her hands on my shoulders, which feels comforting. I rip open the letter and have my eyes shut tight as I say a little prayer. Before I can even open my eyes to read what the letter says I hear Di shout with glee. Quickly, I open my eyes and scan the words in front of me.

My ears start to ring and I jump off the stool, flinging my arms around Di.

I GOT IN!

Di and I dance around the kitchen in joy. I cannot believe that they actually accepted me.

"What is all this racket about?" my mother asks as she walks into the kitchen lugging two huge shopping bags behind her.

I shove the letter in her face.

"Congratulations!" she yells and gives me a hug.

Di is now pacing up and down the kitchen. "We have to celebrate. If I start now, I should be able to whip up a delicious roast dinner and maybe even some apple pie."

My mother smiles and says, "That won't be necessary. In fact, Di, you can have the night off because we are not going to be home."

"We aren't?" I ask, looking at my mother quizzically.

She shakes her head and hands me one of the huge shopping bags that she lugged in just a few moments ago.

"No. We are attending a charity auction and ball at the country club. I can't think of a better way to celebrate this momentous occasion. Who doesn't love giving to charity and having fun while you raise awareness," my mother says.

I roll my eyes and smile. "Sure," I say with a chuckle.

My mother smiles and points at the shopping bag saying, "Well, go try it on."

I nod and head upstairs. The name on the front of the shopping bag is from the high end, designer boutique in town. So, I know that whatever is in this bag had to have cost a pretty penny. Placing the bag on my bed, I push away the paper to reveal the most breathtaking dress that I have ever seen.

It is a floor-length iridescent lavender silk gown. The sweetheart neckline and flowy skirt give the dress a magical, fairy princess aesthetic. I kick off my sneakers and yank off the rest of my clothing excitedly. I have never owned such a beautiful dress.

As soon as I pull it over my head, without even having to look at my reflection in the mirror, I know that it is going to be breathtaking. The way it fits my body makes it seem as if the dress had been tailor made just for me.

There is a knock on the door and my mother peaks her head in. She gasps as soon as she lays eyes on me. "The moment I saw that dress, I knew it would be perfect for you. Beatrice, you look absolutely stunning."

"Thanks, Mom," I say as I look at my reflection in the mirror.

My mother wipes away a lone tear from her face before sniffling and saying, "Marc will be here to fetch us in an hour. I will come and help you do your hair shortly."

I nod and she walks away, shutting my door behind her. Admiring my reflection in the mirror, the only thought that is on my mind at the moment is that I wish Liam could see me now.

What is he doing? Does he even think about me? As soon as I got the acceptance letter, the first person that I wanted to tell the good news to was him, but I stopped myself when I remembered how he left me behind a few years ago. We have rather brief conversations every now and then. I try to be overly friendly so that my friendliness hides the stabbing pain that I am going through every time I hear his voice.

Sighing, I do as my mother said and head to the shower to freshen up and get ready for the event. Standing under the hot water feels somewhat cathartic as it washes away my pain and tension. When I step out, I feel better, almost excited even.

Tonight is going to be fun. You are going to enjoy yourself because you deserve to be happy.

I towel dry my hair and sit down at my dressing table to get started on my makeup while waiting for my mother.

Exactly 40 minutes later, my mother pins the final butterfly on my hair and steps back.

"All done," she says as she admires her handiwork.

It has been years since my mother last did my hair. I smile at her in the mirror and look at my hair feeling impressed with what she was able to do.

On either side of my face were springy curls that accentuated my roundish facial structure. The rest of my hair was curled and pulled back being held in place by what felt like 2,000 bobby pins sticking into my scalp.

One final touch up and some hairspray before we were out the door and on our way to the country club. During the drive there, all I can think about is me not being able to remember the last time I felt this genuinely happy and beautiful.

My mother is wearing an equally elegant yellow gold evening gown and her signature red lipstick. She places her palm on my hand as we sit together in the backseat of the car. A few moments later, we pull up to the country club where my father is waiting to meet us in a black tuxedo.

He gasps when he sees us and says, "Both my girls look radiant tonight and congratulations, my darling Beatrice, on being accepted at Virginia State University. We will celebrate in style tonight."

With that he leads us up the stairs to the country club entrance.

THIRTY-TWO

Beatrice

WALKING INTO THE COUNTRY club ballroom, I see that the ceiling is decorated with so many twinkling fairy lights. It looks so magical.

"The theme for this year's charity auction is 'A starry night,'" my mother says over the cool toned jazz music that the band is playing.

I nod and smile. My mother and father go to mingle with their friends in the crowded room. My tummy begins to grumble and I decide to make my way over to the snack table set up on the other side of the room.

They absolutely nailed the theme.

There are little stars twinkling everywhere as well as some dark, midnight blue draping and sparkly gold stars hanging from the ceiling. In this lighting, my dress looks even more iridescent than it did at home. I walk through the rows of chairs that have been set up for the auction and get to the snack table which has an impressive spread. I grab a napkin and help myself to a few of the bite sized treats, most of which I have no idea what I am eating but it is delicious.

"Try the smoked salmon canapés. You won't be disappointed," a familiar voice says behind me.

I turn around to see none other than John standing behind me. I quickly try to swallow whatever I just stuffed my mouth with and say, "Oh my goodness. Hi!"

He looks even more dashing and suave than I remember. John has definitely grown a few inches taller and his shoulders are sleeker and toned now. He is wearing a well-tailored royal blue suit and his shaggy, blond hair barely covers his ears.

"How are you?" John asks as he flashes me his kilowatt smile.

My stomach flutters. This could be because of all the canapés I have just gobbled down or it could be due to the fact that this gorgeous man is standing here and talking to me.

"I am good, very good actually. How are you?" I ask.

"Doing much better now that you are here," John says. His voice is as smooth as silk. Previously, I would have found that comment extremely sleazy, but now it actually makes me blush a little.

"Would you like a drink?" John asks. "I would love one. Thank you," I reply.

What is going on here? Maybe my previous judgment of John's character was a bit harsh. I also know that my judgment was a bit biased and could have been clouded by the fact that I was so in love with Liam at the time. When compared to how I felt about him, any man would never live up to that.

As these thoughts run through my head, I feel the need to turn and run. Fighting off the urge, I try my best to silence my inner voice.

No! I deserve to be here and have fun. Liam is probably out at a club, having drinks with his friends or in some supermodels bed right now. So, there is no reason for me to feel guilty for talking to an old friend. Yes, he is just an old friend. Nothing more, for now anyway…

As I am waiting for John to get our drinks, my mother comes up to me. "So, I see you and John are getting along," she teases.

I chuckle and say, "He is just a friend I haven't seen in a while. That's all."

"Whatever you say, but he is a good boy with a bright future," my mother says cheekily before popping a canapé into her mouth and walking away.

John comes back holding two glasses of sparkling wine. He hands me one and asks, "So, what have you been up to?"

Clutching my glass, I tell him about my acceptance to Virginia State University. John is so proud and supportive.

"You know I graduated this year, but I still have some buddies at the university if you ever need help with anything," John says as he takes a sip of his drink.

"Thank you. I am such a nervous wreck. There is no doubt in my mind that I am going to need all of the help that I can get," I say sincerely. John brushes the air in front of him and says, "Don't worry about a thing. They are going to love you. I mean, look at you, how could they not?" The heat rises in my cheeks and I am certain that my olive skin is bright red at the moment. I look at the floor shyly because I don't want John to know that he is having this effect on me. Just then, I hear someone scream in a high-pitched voice, "No freaking way. Is that you, Bia?"

I turn around to see a jolly, red faced, redhead stampeding toward me. Opening my arms, I welcome Mary's embrace despite the fact that she almost knocks me off my feet.

"What are you doing here?" Mary gasps.

I shrug and say, "I don't know. Just felt like getting out of the house I guess."

"Good for you," Mary says with a huge, toothy smile before turning to John who is now standing there awkwardly. "Oh, hey John," she says dismissively and turns her attention back to me saying, "You look absolutely beautiful, Bia."

"She really does," John says as he looks at me from head to toe.

A small part of me feels a bit awkward and uncomfortable because of the way that he is looking at me, but I ignore it and thank them both.

"Ladies and gentleman, please take your seats. The auction is about to begin," a man in a black and white suit announces from the podium.

"I would love to catch up with you more. What do you think about joining me for coffee tomorrow?" John asks.

Whoa! I was not expecting that, but it is just coffee. There is nothing wrong with having coffee and catching up with an old friend.

I try to convince myself that what I am doing is perfectly okay. "Yeah, coffee sounds great," I say with a smile.

"Perfect. I will see you tomorrow then. Enjoy the auction, ladies," John says as he bows his head a little and then walks away.

Mary pinches my arm as soon as he is too far away from us to overhear the conversation.

I yelp and rub the spot where she just pinched me, "What was that for?" "Did you just say yes to going on a date with John Winston? Who are you and what have you done with my best friend?" Mary says dramatically.

Rolling my eyes, I tell her, "It isn't a date. Anyways, I have more important news to tell you."

"More important than your date with John?" Mary says as she eyes me curiously.

Sighing, I reply, "It isn't a date and yes, more important than that. Come to my house at noon tomorrow?"

"I'll be there. In fact, I have some news to share with you as well," Mary says with a smile before prancing away in her flowy orange dress to her seat.

As I weave my way through the crowd, I feel like there are a pair of eyes on me and no matter how hard I try to shake the feeling, it just doesn't go away. When I finally find my parents and sit down, I scan the room and make eye contact with Liam's sister.

She is wearing a white shirt and a black waistcoat. Based on her appearance, she must be working as a cocktail waitress at this event. She maintains eye contact for a few minutes before looking away and disappearing behind one of the draping curtains.

Did she see me talking to John? Will she tell Liam? Does he even ask his family about me?

"Hey, turn around, the auction is about to start. Apparently, they have some exquisite pieces this year so feel free to bid on whatever you like," my mother says excitedly.

The host starts the auction, but my mind is elsewhere.

By the end of the night, my parents purchased some vases and a few art pieces. Overall, the night was okay, but I headed home feeling exhausted.

My parents suggest that we go for ice-cream before heading home but I decline the offer. The only thing that I want now is to shower and get into my bed. They decide to go out by themselves and Marc takes me home.

The house is quiet and empty when I get there since my mother gave Di the night off. I trod up to my room with my heels in my hand. When I open my room door, I find a cling-wrapped plate and a little note on my bed.

Congratulations, my beautiful girl. Now the world can see the shining star that I have always known you to be. I hope you enjoyed your night out.

Love, Di

Tears stream down my face and fall onto the little cling filmed brownie as my heart swells up with joy and emotion at the sweet and thoughtful gesture. This is without a doubt the highlight of my night.

THIRTY-THREE

Beatrice

THE NEXT MORNING, I wake up to the sounds of the hummingbirds flirting with the flowers in the garden below, the rays of the sun gloriously shining through the tiny gap in my curtain and the smell of cinnamon French toast.

My eyes are barely open as I get out of bed and make my way to the bathroom to wash up.

"Oh, you're awake," Di says, popping her head around the corner of the bathroom door. I smile and nod my head as I brush my teeth. She goes back downstairs to finish getting breakfast ready. It is a miracle that I do not weigh 5,000 tons because of all the delicious food that Di cooks.

I pull on my sneakers and decide to go and visit my baby Snowie before I sit down for breakfast. As I walk into the kitchen, I see Di flipping a slice of French toast in the skillet.

"Breakfast will be ready soon," she says.

I walk toward the two-door silver fridge and pull it open, scanning the contents for some carrots. When I find them, I grab a few and say, "No rush. I want to go and visit Snowball anyway."

Di smiles and continues with her breakfast preparations as she chops up some fruit. When I get to the back door, I turn around and say, "Oh and Di, thank you so much for the surprise you left me. I love you too."

Her facial expression instantly softens and her eyes become watery. She nods and quickly gets back to her task. I walk outside. The grass is wet with dew from the previous night, the air is chilly and crisp as I take deep breaths.

This morning, it feels like the weight of the world has been lifted off my shoulders. I am no longer carrying around a burden and I have this rejuvenating feeling of relief and hope. These are things that I thought I lost when Liam left.

As I make my way to the stables, I hear Snowie neighing happily.

He gives me a huge grin and gobbles up the carrots that I carried out for him. I brush his stark white coat and decide to take him for a quick ride to the stream. It has been a while since I rode him and I honestly feel guilty for not visiting as often as I probably should have.

Snowie and I go for a leisurely ride down to the stream. When we get back, I hurry back to the house and freshen up before sitting at the breakfast table.

Di places a plate of cinnamon French toast and a fresh fruit salad in front of me.

"Hmm, this smells yummy," I say.

Di smiles. I know that one of the best compliments you could give her is about her food. She has told me that preparing food is sort of her love language.

"Did you enjoy your ride?" Di asks as she pours me a cup of coffee.

I nod and stuff my mouth with a huge bite of the cinnamon French toast smothered in syrup.

After breakfast, I decide to do some yoga and meditation in the backyard before showering and getting ready for my lunch with Mary.

I just finish applying a coat of mascara when Di lets me know that Mary is here. Walking down the stairs, I make my way to the dining room where she's waiting.

"Hey you," Mary says chirpily.

She is always so bubbly and full of positive energy. At first, her infectious grin and high energy spirit used to grate on my nerves slightly, but I have grown to love it over time.

"Hi, are you hungry? Di made her famous chili," I say.

Mary smiles and smacks her lips playfully. "I'm absolutely famished."

Di walks in carrying two steaming bowls of chili and places them down in front of us.

"I will be back with the cornbread," she says and walks out. "So, are you excited for your date?" Mary asks.

At that exact moment, my mother walks into the dining room and hears her question.

"What date?" my mother asks.

I wish that the ground would open up and swallow me whole at this moment.

"It isn't a date," I whine as I shoot Mary a warning glare before continuing, "I am just going for coffee with John."

My mother's face lights up and she says, "John? Like John Winston?" I nod.

"You should invite him for dinner tonight," my mother says as she grabs her coat and heads toward the door.

She wants me to invite him for dinner? I cannot even believe what I am hearing. This means that my parents actually approve of John. Then again, why wouldn't they? He is a university graduate with his own business and his family is absolutely loaded.

"Mom, no," I groan.

My mother turns around and looks at me seriously before saying, "Beatrice, the Winstons are one of the most influential families in Virginia. You want people like them on your side, especially if you want to become the best lawyer in the state. You will invite him to dinner."

With that she walks out of the room before I can even protest.

"Wait, did your mother just say that you want to become a lawyer?" Mary asks.

Oh right. This is the whole reason I invited Mary for lunch!

"Yes, that is what I wanted to tell you. I applied to V.S.U. and got accepted. I am starting in the fall semester," I say.

Mary yelps with glee and jumps out of her seat to hug me. I was expecting her to be excited, but not this excited.

She takes a step back from me and says, "I cannot believe it." Okay, now I am confused.

"You can't believe what?" I ask.

"Bia. I also applied to V.S.U. to study law and I got my acceptance letter in the mail yesterday. That is the big news that I wanted to tell you," Mary says.

I jump up in joy.

Mary and I grab each other's hands and start chanting, "Virginia State University, V.S.U," together as we jump around the dining room.

"What is going on in here?" Di asks as she comes in carrying a plate of cornbread and a pitcher of sweet tea.

"Di, Mary and I are both going to study law at Virginia State University!" I yell with joy.

She smiles and says, "Well, I guess that means we are having ice-cream sandwiches for dessert to celebrate. Congratulations, my lovely girls."

I cannot believe my luck. Not only was I pursuing my dream, but now I have my best friend coming along on this journey with me.

Life is good.

Once Mary and I settle down, we polish off our bowls of chili and basically inhale Di's chocolate chip cookie ice-cream sandwiches.

"Oh my goodness, I have never been so full in my life," Mary groans as she throws herself on my bed and rubs her belly.

I sprawl out on the bed beside her and weakly say, "Me too."

Mary and I stare at the ceiling above us as we try to recover from our food coma and fantasize about what the future holds.

Before I know it, it is almost time for me to meet John.

"Ugh, do you think that I should cancel?" I ask Mary as I roll over to my side so that I can face her.

She has her eyes closed as she asks, "Why?"

"I don't know. I feel kind of guilty for moving on from Liam," I say meekly.

This is the first time that I actually admitted it to myself and said those words out loud.

"Is that the only reason?" Mary asks. "Yeah, I guess it is," I reply.

Mary sits up. "Well then, I think you should wear your cutest dress, go out, and have fun with John. You deserve to be happy, Bia. Liam did what he did for his own happiness, you owe yourself this."

Just like that all of my doubts and reservations about meeting John disappear and I do exactly what Mary says. I scour through my closet and find a cute, knee high, pastel pink floral dress. I pair these with white kitten heels and Mary does my hair and makeup.

"You look beautiful, Bia. Now go and enjoy your date," Mary says as she practically pushes me into the backseat of the car. Marc drives me to the café that John said we should meet at. The entire time, I sit in the backseat clutching the strap of my handbag.

Why are you so nervous? Calm down.

"Who is the lucky guy?" Marc asks as he drives.

I am grateful for the question because it distracts me from my own crazy thoughts.

"Oh, he is just a friend from school," I reply. Marc smiles, never taking his eyes off the road.

"I am glad to see you going out and living your life," Marc says.

We pull up to the café and I thank Marc before jumping out of the car.

THIRTY-FOUR

Liam

I SPENT THE TWO DAYS before the fashion show going to publishing agencies to see if they are interested in my book idea. Finally, yesterday afternoon, I had a breakthrough. I visited with the editor of Penguin Publishing House and presented my idea. After he evaluated the brief query letter that I presented, he got very excited to work with me.

He decided to pursue publishing my book once I have completed it and asked me to bring whatever I had of my manuscript back in about six months, because at the present time he was in the middle of a project that was turning one of his author's books into a movie.

Still, riding that high, I'm just a couple of hours away from my first day working as a model. I have no idea what's going to happen. I don't know what to expect from a fashion show. My mind drifts as I get dressed and prepare to leave the house. I think about the catastrophic events that have happened in less than two months in my life.

First, the place where I worked caught fire, then I came home to find that my best friend/roommate was involved in a big scandal in the Wall Street money market, and then I was left to pay for the rent that Shane left me. At the same time, I had to find a new job. This has been a whirlwind that I never want to go through again. Anxiety has plagued me for the past two weeks. With no job and no money, I felt useless. As I think about it, this is what drove me to sign a contract with Mr. Lyons. It was survival.

After getting ready, I hop in a taxi to Mr. Lyons' office on Park Avenue.

I approach the lobby and tell the attendant why I am there. "Are you Liam D'Fiori?" he asks.

"Yes," I respond.

"Mr. Lyons asked if you would wait by that limo outside. He'll be right down," he says, pointing outside past the revolving door to a white limo.

At precisely six o'clock, Mr. Lyons appears in the lobby with his assistant, a young woman in her early twenties. We greet each other and step into the limo to head for the fashion show. On the way, Mr. Lyons explains to me everything that is going to happen behind the scenes during the show, and at the after party. I listen very carefully to everything he says and try to contain all my excitement. He warns me that tonight's fashion show is going to be big.

The world's top designer will be there. The event will be broadcasted throughout the world, live. The whole event is the pinnacle of the fashion industry. And to make the butterflies in my stomach even more agitated, he says, "This night could make a model's career soar high like an eagle, or it could break its wings." As we turn around the block on Madison Avenue, I can see from afar a white marquee; under it, there is a red carpet that stretches from the building entrance to the end of the sidewalk, and two white velvet ropes separate the photographers from the carpet.

Upon arriving, the limo stops right in front with my side of the door facing the red carpet. My stomach drops, I'm so nervous. I've only seen this kind of event on TV, on Oscar night or some other celebrity related event. I look out the tinted window and see, on both sides of the carpet, many hungry photographers pushing their way to take the first picture.

I can see many others standing around with paper and a pen, hoping to get an autograph I suppose. I don't know what to do—if I get out of the car, they are going to laugh at me. They don't know who I am. I sit there and look at Mr. Lyons to see if he is going to get out first. Instead, he looks at me, gives me a wink, and says, "Let's roll."

I open the door and take my first step out, and for a moment, I swear there is total silence. All eyes are on me. The photographers and the bystanders stand there without saying anything or snapping their flashes. This is the definition of an awkward moment.

I give them a smile and a wave 'Hi.' A few seconds that feel like an eternity later, the assistant steps out of the limo to the same reaction. When they see Mr. Lyons step out of the car though, they immediately start snapping their flashes, the hands are stretched with a pen and paper, and the journalists start their interrogations.

I let Mr. Lyons go ahead of me and as we walk up to the entrance, I hear the curiosity of the journalists: "Who's this new guy? Is he part of the show?" "Is this the surprise protégé that you promised?" I can't hear if Mr. Lyons replies.

After he signs a couple of autographs and answers some of their questions, we head inside. Walking back and forth, staff members try to keep their composure while coordinating the event. I spot many celebrities, musicians, movie stars, and socialites.

We head down a corridor to a door that reads 'Backstage.' I am stunned by how many beautiful people are running around, getting ready for the show.

"You are going to have to stay here and get ready while I go upstairs and take my place by the runway," says Mr. Lyons.

"Wait, you are just going to leave me here? I don't know what to do. I mean I've never done this before," I say, slightly frantic but trying to keep my cool.

"Junior, relax, you were born for this." He taps my face with his hand and walks out of the room. For a moment, I simply stand there, in shock. I'm a writer, not a pretty boy who takes his shirt off.

Well, Mr. Lyons got me this far, so I guess I'm going to have to figure this one out on my own. I walk to the side of the room where there are various clothes on hangers. I begin to pick out something that I like. There is one black leather jacket that looks really good to me so I tried it on. As I'm pulling on a pair of ripped, distressed jeans, I hear a loud whistle.

I look up and see a girl walking my way. She looks like a model, tall with a stunningly lean figure. She's wearing red leather pants, black high heels, and a ripped Rock'N'Roll t-shirt. Her long hair is blonde at the roots with a pink, blue, and light green braid coyly framing the left side of her face. Her hips sway from side to side as she nears me.

She stops in front of me and juts her hip to the right. "What's up! I'm your stylist, Roxy. Are you ready?" she says with a Rock'N'Roll attitude.

"Hello, I'm Liam… Hum, I don't know if Mr. Lyons told you, but I've never done this before."

Rolling her gum from one side of her cheek to the other, Roxy contemplates me. "First off, he does not like to be called Mr. Lyons, he likes to be called Patrick. Secondly, yes, I've been notified that you haven't done this before. So are you ready?" she says.

"I… hum… I guess… hum," I stutter. I wasn't ready for this attitude; she makes me a bit nervous.

"Let's Rock'N'Roll," Roxy says while taking me by the hand and pulling me into a walk-in fitting room full of other models.

"Wait a minute, don't I get a private room?" I say. Roxy looks at me with a smirk.

"Who are you, Madonna? Come on, stop being a punk and get changed!" Roxy stands there watching me, chewing her gum with her mouth open.

This is not a common situation for me. I'm not used to changing in front of other people, with not only men but also women around.

I look around and notice that the other models don't seem to be having such problems. I get changed very slowly, making sure to pull clothes off and on while everyone's attention is elsewhere. Roxy hands me an outfit that makes me look like a country Rock'N'Roller. Not very different from what I had picked up at the door myself, I now wear ripped up Levi's blue jeans, a black t-shirt, a red leather jacket, and a cowboy hat. My hands, wrists, and neck are covered with any and all the accessories that Roxy can find.

She takes me to the side of the stage where there are a couple of steps going up to the stage. I start to get nervous again. I don't know how to model! I look up to the ceiling and say "God, you got to help me on this one." As I look back down, I see Roxy walking away. I shout after her.

"Roxy, where are you going, what do I do now?!" She looks back at me, gives me a smile, and in a sexy tone of voice, says "Rock'N'Roll." I feel like an idiot as I stand there, watching her walk away.

The show starts. The music is loud backstage, and I can hear applause every time the announcer says a celebrity's or a fashion designer's name. I stand by the stage peeking through the curtains. The place is packed.

Photographers are setting themselves up with the proper angle to take their photos. The waiters are serving drinks to the elites. Everything out front is nice and calm, but backstage is another story. Everyone here is running around taking the last few minutes to fix themselves in front of a mirror. I, on the other hand, have only one outfit to wear, so I don't have to run around.

The director busts through the door with both of his assistants behind him as close as ticks on a dog. He shouts, "Alright boys and girls, the show starts in two minutes. The curtain is on the left. You will walk in through the left of the stage and come out through the right, got it? Everyone remembers to walk tall, walk in style, and give them some 'I don't care attitude.'"

His speech doesn't cheer me up. In fact, it gives me the jitters. Now that time is running out, we can hear the MC announcing the show. When the models start to take to the stage, I examine every step they take, and every gesture that the models make. I try to focus on the details. It didn't seem so hard to just walk tall, look straight, and act like you don't have a worry in the world. I has been one hour and I'm still standing here waiting to be called.

I can feel eyes on me and sense that some of the models aren't happy that I'm here. Though some smile at me as they pass, you can cut the jealous tension with a knife. My hands begin to sweat, my knees are trembling, and the butterflies in my stomach are having the time of their lives. I keep watching as the models pass by me to the stage. The program director approaches me, taps on my shoulder, and says "Cheer up! You are next!"

My heart starts pounding so fast that I think it may fly straight out of my chest! Then all of a sudden, I hear, "Now we reached the highlight of the night. The big surprise Mr. Patrick Lyons has promised us!" Hold on a second, a big surprise?! What surprise is this? Oh God, I hope he's not talking about me. "Here he is, Mr. Lyons' very own protégé… Liam D'Fiori!" I guess that's the cue for me to go on. I take my first step on stage, facing the runway.

The spot light is on me, the cameras are flashing. I stand still for a couple of seconds, orienting myself to the spectacle. For a split second, my mind freezes. Out of the corner of my eye, I can see Mr. Lyons and Roxy sitting by each other, giving me encouraging looks.

Right. Rock'N'Roll. This is what I signed up for. It's this or nothing. I take a deep breath to suppress my fear and start walking to the end of the runway, trying to strut with the best attitude that I have in me. With every step, I can hear a metaphorical clock ticking very slowly.

I try to look into the crowd, but the blinding flashes don't allow me to see the crowd. I try to make my face blank. At the end of the runway, I make a U-turn and walk back. *Liam, hold on for just a couple of steps. This is almost over.* I tell myself.

When I get to the back of the stage, I stop one more time and face the crowd. Then, in what I hope is a very smooth way, I exit the stage and walk back into the backstage area. Just like that, it is over. Bright side, I didn't fall flat on my face!

I feel like I just got off a roller coaster ride. My adrenaline is in full throttle. I can hear the crowd still applauding and cheering. The announcer says, "Thank you for coming out and goodnight." The program director comes up to me and says, "Man, good job." None of the other models approach me.

Then, after a couple of minutes, Roxy walks in and congratulates me on my first walk. She grabs me by the hand and walks me out to meet with Mr. Lyons. He stands by the bar in the ballroom where they've set up a banquet for the guests. "Liam, congratulations on your first walk," he says, giving me a quick and awkward hug.

"How did I do?" I ask with enthusiasm.

"You were great. Everyone from all over the world is here. From designers to movie stars, business men to producers, and etc. They were all on their feet and amazed by your charisma," Mr. Lyon says. He hands me a folded piece of paper. "Let's start off with this." I put the check in my pocket without scanning the amount.

"Roxy, do you mind waiting for one second while I go put these clothes back? I'll be right back," I say.

"Liam, don't worry about it, the outfit is yours," she straightens out my jacket.

I stay at the party for a little while longer, but soon feel the excitement of the day catch up with me. I say my goodbyes and grab a taxi home. I sit in the back seat, gaze out of the window, and start counting the street signs. I smile slightly as thoughts of tonight flash through my mind.

My situation has officially changed. A week ago, I was hopeless, almost ready to throw in the towel and head home. But now I'm filled with the contentment knowing that I belong. I do have a place in the world. Tonight marks a new chapter in my life and from now on I recognize that my life had changed.

For better or worse, I don't know yet, but it indeed has changed. Upon entering my apartment, I go straight to bed. I am so tired that I don't even take the time to call Michelle.

The morning sunshine beams on my eyelids from the window. I reach for my pants and find the check that Mr. Lyons gave me last night. I look at it, and can't believe it; I am stunned by the amount of money. I made twenty thousand dollars by walking a couple of yards down a runway for less than two minutes.

I am so blown away that I jump up on my bed and start to celebrate like a child does the night before his birthday. I am so fired up that I call Michelle. I dial so fast I worry for a moment that it won't go through, but nothing can stop me from my goofy dance of excitement. After three rings, Michelle picks up.

"Good morning, sunshine. How are you this beautiful Sunday morning?" I say in a deep, and what I hope is a sexy tone.

"What?! How am I doing? What do you mean? Yesterday you hung me out to dry without even a phone call. Who were you with? Are you seeing somebody else? Cuz if you are I'll…"

I cut her off.

"Sweetheart… bring it down… first of all, again, good morning," I say flirtatiously with a slight hint of sarcasm.

Refusing to bend, Michelle responds. "Where were you yesterday… huh… I was waiting for your call!"

"I was too busy showing off my stuff," I say just to get a rise out of her. "You were WHAT?! How dare you call me to say you were showing off

your stuff? Who do you think you are?" she says angrily.

I again cut her off to tell her the news.

"Hey, hey, hey, sweet cakes. I was too busy on the runway showing off my stuff to all those photographers and people from the fashion industry on Madison Avenue," I tell her with excitement.

"Hold on, you are telling me that you were down on Madison Avenue doing a fashion show? One with Patrick Lyons?" she asks me calmly, curiously.

"Hum… I guess this massive check in my hands means I was!" I say. "Oh baby, I can't believe it. I've been trying to model for Patrick Lyons since I was eighteen." I can't tell if she is pleased or angry.

"I was on the runway for two minutes and made twenty thousand dollars!" I continue in excitement.

"Oh my God, I'm so proud of you," she says with a softer tone of voice. "Thanks, babe!" I pop my hips, still dancing to the beat of my excitement.

"Babe, I have to be honest. I've been in this city for five years and I tried so hard to model for Patrick Lyons, but he never gave me the time of day… and now you get an opportunity that many models are struggling for. You got it without even trying," she says in disbelief.

Because I still don't really understand why he chose me, I change the subject. I can feel that Michelle is happy for me, but then again, the jealousy is now palpable.

"Hey, get ready, I'm going to take you out tonight and we are going to the best restaurant in town. I'll be there around six to pick you up, alright?"

After a reluctant agreement, we hang up the phone. Later, I get ready to take my princess to dinner. I pick her up and we go out to some fancy restaurant Michelle had said she wanted to try. The whole time we eat, she asks me about the modeling show. I tell her everything she wants to know. I don't really understand why she never got her big break.

She has every quality a model should have: she is tall and beautiful and graceful. Perhaps modeling is just not her call? Who knows, maybe God sent her here to do something else. Either way, I let her live her dream through me for an hour or two. After I pay the tab from the restaurant, we take a cab home. We spend the night together for the first time in my apartment.

I wake up in the morning to find myself hugging the pillow. Where's Michelle? I get up and go into the kitchen. On the counter there is a note:

Good morning,
I made you some French toast and some coffee. They're in the kitchen.
I'm on my way to work. Hope you have a good day!

Love, Princess

My favorite! I eat my breakfast rather quickly so that I have enough time to organize and prepare myself for a meeting with Patrick. Today, he said that we are going to decide on my next step.

I arrived at the office at 9:45 AM for my ten o'clock appointment. As I talk to the secretary, I notice that she seems more polite and courteous than the other day. A few minutes later, she walks me into Patrick Lyons' office. I take the chair on the right again and greet him with a hand shake. He sits there smiling and nodding his head.

"Liam," he begins, "you have what it takes. You got charisma, you have charm, and a face that everyone is hypnotized by. I've decided on a deal for you. A great deal if you're willing to take it."

"And that is?" I ask.

"Well, the deal we originally made was for one time only, but after Saturday, I'm willing to give a five-year contract." He pauses and looks at me. "For the amount of twenty million dollars. So, are you interested?" he crosses his arms and leans back.

I'm amazed he just offered me twenty million dollars. How can it be that one day I have nothing, and the next I can have anything I want? I don't really understand, but I know that this is my shot. This is my time to shine and I won't let it go past me.

I look around the room thinking about my life so far. How did I get to this point? So many others strive in life to get to where I'm about to go, and I got here by sheer coincidence. I have nothing to complain about.

Even if it is not my dream to model, I can't turn away this chance. There is nothing left to say, except that in some strange way, this could be my destiny. Well, if this is part of my destiny the only thing left that I can say is, "Where do I sign?"

Patrick hands me the paper. I skim, sign it, and give it back to him.

I stare at the paper as he looks over it, and for a moment, I am inclined to revise my decision. I came to New York for one thing, and that was to be a writer. That is my dream, that is my goal. But it seems that the world has somehow conspired against me. I didn't make this decision on my own, but my circumstances had led to me having to make a choice. At this moment, it seems as if my dream of becoming a writer is drifting away from me.

Patrick closes the contract. "Now we're in business. Excuse me while I make a few calls."

I sit back and try not to think while he whispers into the phone. "Okay, right in front of the lobby is a limo waiting for you. The driver will take you to your next job."

I leave the office and take the elevator downstairs.

After only about a ten-minute ride, I arrive at the job. I spot Roxy standing in the lobby. I step out of the car and head toward her. Without any greeting, she orders me to follow her.

"Roxy, what are you doing here?" I ask.

"Patrick promoted me. I am now your personal assistant," she says, walking quickly to what looks like a photo shoot.

"You know, I think that this is probably not what you wanted, but your life will never be the same," Roxy throws that statement in the air. I don't respond, but that comment lingers in my consciousness.

She is right. This isn't something I wanted, but it was handed to me. It seems as if I was destined to do this. For a while, it felt like I wasn't in control of my future. I worked so hard on trying to be a writer, but that didn't get me far. But now, at least I feel in control.

Roxy takes me to a room where there is a studio setup with other male and female models. We will be shooting next year's summer calendar. Roxy points to some outfits in the style of the 50s. I feel so uncomfortable; not only because I'm camera shy, but also because of the vibe between the models.

By this point, the gossip mill has succeeded and they've all heard my story, about how I got discovered and immediately signed. Some of them are bitter about my success because they've been in the business for some time. To top it all off, the photographer keeps favoring me, and on every new pose, he deliberately puts me in the center.

At the edge of the set, I can see Roxy chewing on a piece of gum with her mouth open, nonchalantly observing the scene. Occasionally she calls the photographer and expresses a few suggestions. She has a very intense charisma; a characteristic seldom seen in others. She is also attractive and mellow. Her strong personality lets off an authoritative vibe that makes everyone around her listen respectfully to every suggestion she makes.

The photo session lasts about two hours. After, Roxy calls for a company car to chauffeur me home. It's been a tiresome day.

You'd think that posing for a photo is easy, but in truth, I can tell you it's not! As time passes, you become emotionally drained. After the first hour, I began to stare into the distance and picture Bia's beautiful smile, her deep mysterious eyes looking deeply into mine.

I smile to myself just imagining what it would be like to have her in my arms, to feel her warm embrace, to even taste her sweet lips against mine once again. Oh, how great I will feel if one day I return to her, so that we can be together to the end of time.

THIRTY-FIVE

Liam

5 YEARS LATER ...

A FEW YEARS have passed since my first photo shoot, and my career couldn't be better. I've been on TV commercials, magazine covers, and I've even made a few television appearances. I am now living the life I used to think was only for successful and talented people. A life that never seemed possible for someone from my background.

Michelle and I continue to see each other, even though our conflicting schedules get in the way a little bit. I've grown very close to her, but I'm afraid to call it love. I seem to run away from the word 'love.' Every time I hear the word, my stomach drops and insecurity seems to dominate my emotions.

When I see a couple that's in love, I tend to doubt their motives. In my mind, I think one of them is in that relationship with an ulterior motive, or with some thought of self-gratification. I can now recognize that what I had with Bia was sincere and maybe once in a lifetime. The rejection from her parents always held me back and the fact that they were right and she was way out of my league. I was just holding her back.

But with Michelle, I don't want this to be so. I see it in her eyes that her feelings for me are genuine. I have to take a step by faith now, and allow my true sentiments to be shown.

Today, I have a surprise for Michelle. In addition to the twenty- million-dollar contract I signed with Patrick, I get a kick back from the appearances I make, and a bonus for increase in sales. I also make money with sponsorship. So I just bought a new apartment on 5th Avenue, right across from Central Park. I plan to take Michelle out to dinner and then surprise her by bringing her to see the place. I call her and make plans to meet at a fancy restaurant near midtown at seven-thirty.

When she arrives, I spot her across the room, and like always when I see her, I am overcome by how her beauty lights up a space. I realize in that moment how far I've fallen for her. She makes me feel alive. Special. I smile at the sound of her voice. She gives me a hug followed by a sweet kiss.

The warmth of the candlelight makes the ambiance even more romantic. After our second glass of wine, we share dessert and declare our most intimate thoughts. Our eyes never leave the others, and our smiles never fade. After our meal, we walk hand in hand to my driver, who has been waiting for us out front.

"Where are you taking me, Liam?" she giggles. I gaze into her eyes and whisper that it is a surprise.

When we arrive at my new apartment, we climb out of the car and I escort her through the lobby and into the elevator, to the penthouse suite. Michelle is so excited that she's jumping with joy and laughter. I open the big wooden double doors to reveal the inside of the apartment. Michelle's mouth falls wide open when she scans the apartment. She takes a couple of steps inside very slowly.

Each room has been specially decorated by a designer. Everything was made with the best quality materials. The living room is decorated in white.

The three-piece white couch sits in the middle of the room behind a glass table and an Arabian style carpet. The living room opens into the kitchen, and there is a wooden western countertop in the middle of the room, with pans and utensils hanging overhead. The appliances are all made of stainless steel.

Michelle jumps on me with a hug. Her legs cross behind me as I spin her around. She covers me with kisses and then runs around the house, curious to see how each room is decorated. As she tours around, Michelle makes suggestion after suggestion as to where her things would go and the best place to place her flowers. I push my hands into my pockets as I follow her through the apartment.

It feels so good to watch her excitement about the house. Seeing her filled with such joy makes me feel content. As she continues to move from room to room, she sways her hips from side to side and delicately motions her hands to express her decorative ideas. She is so attractive and seductive. So vibrant and alive.

It seems that life is all coming together for me now. Every sweet smile from Michelle confirms to me that she may be the one. She could be the woman that I marry. The woman that can bring joy to my heart for the rest of my life. The thought of growing old with her seems very soothing for me at this point in my life.

The tour ends in the main bedroom. The room is decorated in a more modern style with a queen bed against the furthest wall. On the four corners of the bed, there are poles from which hang silk white drapes. I grab Michelle's hand in front of the bedroom window, and have her face the closed curtains.

"Close your eyes and open when I say so."

She does as I ask. She closes her eyes. I open the curtain to a splendid view of Central Park. "Can I open my eyes now?" she asks eagerly. I stand by her side as she opens her eyes. After she catches a glimpse of the view, she is breathless. The moon is full and bright tonight, shining on the tree tops and on the grass below, giving it a hazy gray glow. The wind is still and the night is quiet. All of Central Park can be seen from this height.

"Sweetie, it's beautiful," she says.

I gently turn her to me and softly say, "For you deserve the stars and the moon and everything else unreachable." I lean toward her and kiss her. We tumble onto bed and I can feel her heart beating alongside mine in excitement.

All night i toss and turn, trying not to wake Michelle. i shift to face her and watch her sleeping. Her face remains still and peaceful. My mind begins to drift. I am suddenly carried away by the feeling that something is not right.

My stomach begins to twist anxiously. I turn to the window to watch the moon and I take a deep breath and am amazed at how magnificently it shines. How it has no shadow and shines so proudly.

I want to shine like that moon. I want to glow as intensely as it does. But the moon is nothing without its source of light. It cannot light up the night, it cannot guide the steps of those who travel in the dark. Nothing can thrive without the light. I am starting to understand my life. As much as I care for, and even love, Michelle, I need Bia to make my heart complete.

Very carefully, I leave the bed, making every move gentle so that I will not wake Michelle. I go over to the desk near the window. I open one of the drawers and grab a notebook. I take a pen and look over my shoulder to see if Michelle is still sleeping. She lays there safe and sound. I take one more look at the moon. I have to shine like it does, for I don't want to fade away. I put the pen to the paper and begin to express my innermost thoughts to the source of my inspiration.

My Dear Bia,

All of the world's most beautiful words can't express what I felt when I first saw you. You instantly stirred something inside me. You brought to life something that I was searching for. And my life hasn't been the same since. I traveled to a distant land to try to forget about you, but really, I have been trying to reach you by achieving success and impressing you. I am writing a book in the hope that someday you will read it and realize that the love story is about you and I. Know that my life has taken such a turn, I don't know if you're ever going to read it. I don't know if anyone will. Life has kept me from publishing it. The one thing that I've realized lately is that sincerity and love are not about all the things that the world considers to be important. The worlds way of expressing love is through what you have, through what you've achieved, and through what you can physically give. I've chased all these things and found them all to be of no virtue. Empty. Without my love for you, all the riches and all the achievements that I've conquered mount to nothing. I thought that if I could achieve all these things, you would be impressed. Your family would approve. I realized now, deep within my heart, that I truly love you and care for you. I'm writing you this letter to proclaim my love for you once more, my sincere love. Please let me know if you miss me as much as I miss you.

Love, Liam

A sudden wave of emotion comes over me as I sign the letter. I closed my eyes as I put the pen down. My heart is torn like a fork on the road. Everything I thought I wanted in a relationship, I already have right here in front of me.

Michelle provides me with everything a man needs. She's caring, fun, loving, intelligent, affectionate, hard-working and to top it all off, she loves me. And it feels really good, but as much as I try to forget Bia, and get closer to Michelle, it seems that I find myself comparing one with the other. I don't want to lie to Michelle any longer. I want to be honest with her. But if I tell her the truth, I'm scared that she'll leave me. I look over my shoulder once more to see if Michelle is still asleep.

She lies in the same position. I carefully rip out the letter and fold the pieces. I place the torn words inside the back pocket of my jeans on the floor beside the bed. I take one last look at the moon and wonder if my love for Bia is worth leaving this all behind.

The sun brightens the room as i look over the bed and find that Michelle has already left for work. I lay there for a couple of seconds, holding the pillow to my chest. The fragrance of the comforter makes me think of a spring morning. Spring: when everything seems beautiful, the beginning of life, the death of winter.

I hug the pillow tighter and close my eyes, pretending that the lump of feathers and cotton is Bia. I smile, fantasizing a day where she will lay beside me and share the early mornings with me. If she was here, I would make her feel like a queen. We would stay in bed cuddling with each other. I would tell her jokes and make her laugh. We would plan our lives together. Just to have her close and here, to feel her heart beating alongside mine. Just to feel the warmth of her body against mine. Just to call her mine again.

These fantasies are so common but I know that they don't help. I have to mail her this letter today. I can't keep procrastinating the truth. I get myself dressed and ready, and make my way down to the nearest post box. I approach the mailbox, open it, and freeze.

There is that feeling again. The feeling that I've been struggling with all my life. The feeling of insecurity. Why do I feel this way? Why am I scared? Could it be the fear of love? What about rejection? This fear has dominated me for so long that I don't know what it's like to live without it. Ever since

I set eyes on her, I've been consumed by this emotion. In a way, I like it because it keeps me safe. Sometimes I think that we as humans would rather live a lie than to be hurt by the truth. I have created so many illusions about her and I ever since we parted.

Before I left home, I gave her many hints and signs to let her know that she meant more to me than anyone else. But now that I look back, I didn't do anything out of the ordinary. I should have taken more chances. Been bolder maybe. Brave even.

I should have stayed and married her. Family. Sons and daughters. A true life.

I should have listened to Virgil, the Roman poet, when he wrote "Audentis Fortuna Iuvat." Fortunes Favors the Bold.

I should have told her how happy she made me feel. And how breathtaking her smile seemed to me. I could have mentioned the connection between us, picked the right moment to seize the day.

Coward.

If I had the power to turn back time, I would take her into my arms again, tell her how much I need her in my life, then without hesitation, I press my lips against hers. Oh how sweet, it is to fantasize about her, but this is not the reality I have created for myself. I have to snap out of it and face the present.

If I send her this letter, something will definitely change. For better or worse. It would change with Bia, and it would change with Michelle. It's a risk. Now I'm starting to understand that saying "the truth shall set you free."

What is truth?

Quickly, I rewrite the letter before I drop it in the mail and suddenly, a weight falls off my shoulder. Walking home, I feel refreshed, knowing that I have told the truth, finally. Knowing that she's going to have to write back with an answer. Whether the answer is positive or negative, I'll be glad because through it, I will find clarity.

I look at my watch and realize I only have one hours to get ready and go to work. Today, I have two photo shoots, an interview, and a meeting with a movie director who wants to cast me in his next movie. My career has picked up great momentum. These are things that I never thought I'd be doing.

My horizon, work wise, has opened up into a vast field. Many options and opportunities. All because of my modeling work. All because of Patrick Lyons. All because of Raven. It's amazing to think of how far I've come. I never planned this for my life; I just happened to be at the right place at the right time. Luck? Maybe.

This was all possible because I took a chance. I've risked it all. I sacrificed. I bought the ticket. I took the ride.

After a quick breakfast and shower, I make my way to the shoot. My driver, Ron, has to make a few illegal turns to get me to the job on time. Upon arrival, the set is all ready and the hired models are already there. They are all waiting for me.

Four hours later, I am finished. I walk over to my side of the dressing room to change, and Chaz Dawson, the photographer, comes over.

"Liam, listen, Sparks is throwing a party at the Exit and he told me to tell you that you and Michelle are on the list."

"Why didn't he call me?" I question while changing clothes.

"You know how he is always in the middle of filming scene," Chaz says, placing his camera gently into its bag.

"Chaz, I don't know if I can make it. I have an interview and after that I have a meeting with a movie director," I say.

"Interview with a movie director?! Are you going to drop modeling and be an actor like Sparks?" he asks, surprised. Sparks also started as a model in his early days but then he crossed over to acting and now he is a Hollywood heavy-weight.

"No, it's just a proposition. I don't even know what it's about," I say, walking with him to the nearest exit.

"Look, the party doesn't start until 10 o'clock. If by then you are done with this meeting, stop by. A whole lot of celebrities will be there. Oh yeah! It's a white party theme, so dress in white," he says as we part ways on the street.

I spend the rest of my day working. Unfortunately, I declined the movie role. In these past five years, as successful as I am, I've become more disillusioned with my life. I know how blessed I am. I have money, fame, and a beautiful girlfriend who loves me very much. But I feel estranged, as if there is some kind of a void. Many would die to be in my shoes. I have many friends that are struggling artists, musicians, entrepreneurs, businessmen, writers, models, etc. Yet they will never experience the victory and hollow feeling at peek of the mountain. They will never believe me that the journey is more rewarding then the trophy.

Furthermore, I have completely neglected the reason that I came to New York. I came here to publish my book, but it's still hidden away inside my drawer, just sitting there, collecting dust. I've been to a lot of different places all over the world. And after all this, I feel a void, an empty space inside that I can't seem to fill. My smiles are not as sincere as they once were. But I refuse to let my heart grow cold like some people do. They tend to give up on their happiness.

Some settle for a mediocre life, they say: "This is what I got and it's okay because if I take a chance, I might lose what I already have. Plus, it's comfortable where I am, trying new things makes me anxious. Leave life as it is and maybe something new will happen tomorrow!"

I don't want to have that attitude. I know that I'm made for more. I know I can contribute to humanity in other ways. I was made to conquer. Better yet, to be more than a conqueror. We are made to live a great life. We are made to leave an extraordinary legacy. An excellent contribution to humanity. You can never win until you're not afraid to lose. My life's journey has just begun. I have many plans and goal to accomplish.

I get in the car and tell Ron to take me home. On the way, I decide to call Michelle and invite her to the party. She agrees to go as I tell her about my day, but she is a little disappointed that I declined the movie offer because the story is a Romeo and Juliet type of story, and she loves romance.

"Hey Ron, can you pull over please?" I say as I spot the most beautiful engagement ring in the window of a boutique store.

Walking toward the store I stand on the sidewalk and look in.

This ring would look so beautiful on Michelle's dainty little fingers. It would make the perfect engagement ring.

I am slightly taken aback by this intrusive thought. That was not my intention when I walked up to the window, but the more that I think about it, it makes sense.

Carpe diem.

A few moments later, I walk out with a huge grin on my face and the most perfect engagement ring for my princess Michelle.

THIRTY-SIX

Liam

INSIDE THE CAR on the way to the party, I can't keep from gazing at her, she is so beautiful. In her tight white dress, she looks so peaceful, but as I stare at her profile, it seems nebulous. Her eyes stare out of the window without focusing on anything in particular. I sense that her mind is heavy, her thoughts are drifting into space, and I wonder if I am among her daydreams.

I've recently noticed that, for some reason, Michelle's been distancing herself from me emotionally. Perhaps for the past six months. Maybe it's because I've been so busy with work, going to different countries to do runway shows in Milan, Paris, and Geneva, among others. She only accompanied me to Milan and while there, I did everything I could to make her feel special.

We went out sightseeing. We had romantic dinners and spent many hours enjoying each other's company while walking around the city. Eventually, she had to come back home due to her work, but I told her that she didn't have to work; I would take care of her. Instead of going to work, she could go shopping with her friends, pick up a hobby of some sort, or she could keep me company as I travel to different locations around the world. A big part of it is that I miss her when she's not around. I miss her touch, her hugs, and her kisses. But she doesn't want that, she wants to make her own living.

Many times I arranged for her to meet modeling agents, but she always refused and rebuked me for doing so. She would say that if one day she did make it as a model, she wanted it to be because of her own talent, not because she dates someone that's in the business.

Perhaps she isn't unhappy though, it's just the impression that I got. Besides, she always says crazy things when she's stressed about something. After all, she could just be distracted. Anyway, here we are in front of the 'white' carpet. Before we climb out of the car, Michelle turns to me and gives me a vague smile.

I get out of the car first and extend my hand to her, as a real gentleman does to escort his madam. We hold hands as we walk down the carpet. The flashes of the photographers are overwhelming.

Inside, a young man approaches us and escorts us to the main ballroom. The ballroom has about two dozen circular tables with white dishes, white table cloths, and in the middle are white roses neatly arranged in vases. The ballroom is filled with high profile guests. There are movie stars, musicians, movie directors, businessmen, models, reality TV stars, and others part of the media.

Michelle and I sit down at our table after greeting some of the other guests. Even though we are late, they serve us top of the line French cuisine. The evening is quite pleasant, with many of our friends stopping by to converse. I look around the room and see Sparks talking to everyone and hugging every woman he passes by in his flamboyant, unique way. I notice Michelle also looking at Sparks. She shakes her head, disapproving his over-the-top style, and especially his exaggerated affection toward his friend's girlfriends.

"Liam, take a look… I can't believe that Sparks acts like that, he's so rude. I mean, why does he have to be the center of attention and look! Look at how he disrespects his friends. He hugs their girlfriends as if they were single," Michelle says, disapproving of Sparks' actions.

"I know what you are saying, Sparks can get a little out of hand," I agree with Michelle as we both watch Sparks from a distance.

"Don't get me wrong, Sparks is a nice guy, but I think he tries too hard to impress people. Especially now that he got those movie roles," Michelle says.

"Well, I like Sparks. He's always been like that. I don't think it's because he got a movie role. I have worked with him before, and that's just the way he is," I say in defense of Sparks.

Michelle and I keep talking until Sparks spots us and starts to head our way. As he walks to our table, he greets everyone along the way. Many people misunderstand Sparks. They think he's a show-off or arrogant, but I think he's just gregarious. I get up to greet him as he walks around the table to give me a hug. "Liam, man, how are you? I've missed you. Haven't seen you for about six months. How've you been?"

"Sparks! I've missed you, too… Well, I'm doing great. My career is going well and everything else is fine," I respond.

"Hey, Michelle," Sparks says, proceeding toward her to give her a hug. "What about you? How have you been?" he asks her.

"I've been good, doing well, great to see you," she says after he lets go of the hug. "Alright, so all is well, huh? Hey why don't you guys follow me to the bar and have some drinks?"

We all head to the bar. By this time, everyone has finished their meals. The DJ comes on and starts to blast music into the party. The guests all head to the dance floor as the music kicks in. I stay at the bar conversing with Sparks and Michelle. We chat for a while about our lives, career, and business. He tells us how his career just sky-rocketed when he decided to take on that movie role. I tell him that I'd gotten an offer to star in a movie, but confide that I declined the job. Sparks laughs.

"That was the stupidest thing someone could do!" he yells at me. I get it. In Sparks' mind, it was stupid. This is the kind of thing that made him famous. He is the kind of guy that craves attention, day and night. He does anything to be noticed. I, on the other hand, am more laid back and mellow. I don't need all the attention. I know who I am by this point. I don't need people to keep assuring me.

After the third martini, Sparks goes to entertain the other guests. Michelle and I stay in the bar, observing the party as bystanders. We make occasional comments to each other about the ambiance. On the fourth round, Michelle takes a break to the ladies room. Meanwhile, I stay there leaning on the counter gazing into my drink, then I feel a hand on my side. I turn around and it is Giselle, a friend of mine that I met in Milan while doing a runway show.

I haven't seen her for a while; she kisses me on my cheek and gives me a hug. I order her a drink and we get talking. We catch up on the events of our lives and reminisce about old stories. Giselle is one of a kind. She has such an expressive way of telling stories. With every verb she uses, she motions her hands and arms. Her facial expression is always filled with nuance.

While we are laughing, I spot Michelle through the corner of my eye, rushing toward us. When she is about two feet from me, she pushes my shoulders back and begins to yell.

"Who is this?" she says firmly. "I can't leave for two seconds and you go hit on somebody else!"

She pushes my shoulders back again, and this time my back smacks against the counter. Her sudden outburst surprises me. She has never acted this way before.

"Michelle, what's the matter with you? This is Giselle, my friend from Milan," I say.

"Just a friend… just a friend… I saw you two getting close to each other, whispering in each other's ears, and you tell me she's just a friend?!" she angrily shouts, gazing into my eyes to see if I am lying.

"Sweetheart, the music is loud. We couldn't hear each other. Why are you acting like this?" I say.

Seeing us arguing, with wide eyes, Giselle decides to explain what happened. "I'm sorry… Michelle, I think you got the wrong impression. Liam and I are friends from work and we haven't seen each other for a while. We were just catching up on things," Giselle says gently, trying to clarify.

By this point, people have begun to take notice and we are becoming a scene. It is clear that Giselle is uncomfortable about this situation. Michelle merely narrows her eyes, preparing to retaliate.

"Listen, don't tell me what I saw. I saw you two getting too close to be just friends," Michelle says, pointing her finger at Giselle.

Giselle doesn't take the finger pointing lightly. She furrows her eyebrow at Michelle, saying "Look, I don't even know you, but I know that you are Liam's girlfriend and I respect him, so I'm gonna pretend that you didn't raise your voice or point your finger in my face."

Turning herself toward the bar and avoiding eye contact with Michelle, Giselle goes quiet. But Giselle said some heavy words, and from the look on Michelle's face, it did not go down smoothly. Michelle steps forward and grabs Giselle's forearm. Now they stand face to face with each other.

"What! Who do you think you are talking to me like that?" Michelle gets in her face.

"Excuse me! Who do you think you are! Don't ever get in my face like that!" Giselle retaliates by pushing Michelle back. I stand there in disbelief as I watch them both argue. I try to ensure that they don't get too close to each other. Giselle has had enough of arguing at this point though. She shakes her arm off from Michelle's and begins to walk away.

But at this point, it's clear that Michelle is furious that Giselle turned her back on her. Michelle reaches and grabs Giselle's arm, making her face her again. Then with her other hand, she reaches to the counter, takes hold of a half full glass of martini, and splashes it into Giselle's face.

By now, everyone close by is watching, and after Michelle splashes Giselle with the drink, we all freeze, standing there in shock. I am in awe as I gaze at the martini dripping down from Giselle's forehead. Giselle takes a second to register what just happened.

Her eyes are fixed on the floor, and she slowly lifts her head until her eyes meet Michelle's. At that instant, she rushes at Michelle with both hands locking into her hair. Michelle grabs back. They shove each other, bouncing against the crowds with their backs. As they wrestle, Michelle slips on a puddle on the floor. They both go down. Some bystanders in the crowd are cheering them on while some look on with their mouths open in dismay.

I step in along with two other guys to break them up. I wrap my arms around Michelle's waist and pull her away. Still, she tries to kick away and reach Giselle. I carry her all the way to the exit door. Only when we get outside do let her go, signaling to Ron to get the car for us to leave. Michelle stands there, leaning at the exit door with tears running down her face.

I walk back and forth pacing with my hand running through my hair. I am so mad and angry that I don't even know what to say to her. She embarrassed me in front of the whole party. Not to mention that the press was there, taking pictures of the whole thing. Guess what's going to be in the headlines tomorrow?

I stand there with one hand resting on my head, looking at Michelle while she gazes into the distance, weeping.

"Why did you do that, Michelle?" I pause for a minute to let her answer. "What's wrong with you? I've never seen you like this. Did you really think that there was something going on?" I wait for an answer but she keeps quiet, still weeping. "Are you happy? Do you know what you just did? You embarrassed me in front of my friends, not to mention those executives who are here for business."

I wait there for an answer. After a few more minutes of weeping, she gains her composure, wipes her tears from her cheeks, and asks, "Do you love me?" The question lingers in the air until it vanishes, swallowed up by a silence that lasts too long.

"What?" I ask, trying to decipher her thoughts.

"Do you love me?" She turns until she faces me. Her eyes are fixed on mine. What am I to say? My feelings are very strong for her, but after what I just saw, I am hesitant to say it is now love.

"Look, this is not the time, okay?" I gesture to the party behind me. "It's a simple question, Liam, do you love me or not?" she asks yet again. Uncertainty grips me and my heart refuses to tell the truth.

"You know I love you." The arrow of the lie pierces my heart and now remorse is lurking within me, but if I tell her the truth, I might lose her.

"So then why don't you look at me the way you used to?" she asks, her eyes becoming teary again.

"Darling, I do look at you the same. Maybe it's just that I've been a little busy these past weeks with work. You know I've been offered a movie role, and that's a career change for me. So I've been a little reclusive trying to make a decision," I say, softening my voice, hiding my lie behind my excuse.

"No, Liam, you've changed. You are not the same person I met five years ago. You are not romantic anymore. You're always busy with your friends or working or somewhere I don't know about," as she speaks, her voice cracks and tears run down her face.

"Baby, don't cry. I'm sorry. I know I've been a little distant, but that doesn't change anything between us. I know I tend to get caught up with work, but I'm going to dedicate myself to us again," I answer, getting closer to her.

"Liam, you've changed, you don't look at me the same way that you once did. You don't write anymore. You don't sing to me at night. You've even forgotten the reason you came to New York. You told me you wanted to be a writer, but your book is still hidden out of sight," she argues.

"What do you want me to say? Sometimes life doesn't work the way we want it to." I shake my head.

"I see it in your eyes, Liam, your heart is somewhere else," she says, weeping.

I put my arms around her, hugging her tight. I have no more words, for she is right. I have changed. I'm not what I used to be. My heart still yearns for that feeling from years back. I don't feel complete here.

I should be mad at the predicament that she put me through tonight, but I know her pain. I know that she feels that I'm drifting away. What can I do? I can't change my heart. If I had a choice, I would definitely stay with Michelle because her love for me is real.

I wipe her tears and kiss her forehead. Ron pulls up; I open the door of the car for us. We get in and leave for home.

THIRTY-SEVEN

Liam

THE MORNING AFTER the party, I wake up with a splitting headache and somewhat of a revelation.

I cannot do this anymore. It feels like my soul is being sucked out of me and I fear if I stay here a moment longer, I will have a mental breakdown.

Picking up my phone, I call Roxy and let her know that for the next three weeks I will be unavailable. Michelle has already left for work now so I quickly scribble her a note to let her know that I need some space before dumping a few essentials, my passport, and my manuscript into my duffle bag and heading to the private airport.

I am not entirely sure where I am heading, but I do know that when I get to the airport, I will figure it out. Standing on the curbside, I haul a cab and ask the driver to take me to the private airport. Once I get there, I go up to one of the help desks and speak to the lady sitting behind the counter. "Good day, sir. How can I help you?" the lady behind the desk says with a friendly smile.

"Hi, how soon can you have my private jet ready?" I ask.

She frowns and starts clicking away at the keyboard in front of her before replying and saying, "Where will you be heading?"

I shrug and ask her if she has any suggestions. A few moments later, she is finalizing the details for my trip to Amsterdam and tells me that I can wait in the lounge while they get the jet ready.

Twenty-five minutes later I am sitting in a comfy seat and am on my way to Amsterdam. I watch a movie, take a nap and snack on some salted peanuts for the duration of the flight. When we finally touch down, the first thing I do once I have gotten off the plane is go to the help desk.

A tall man with bleach blond hair is behind it.

"Hello, sir. How can I help you?" he asks. His accent is thick and it takes me a moment to register what he is saying.

"Yes, can you please let me know which is the best hotel in the city and give me the address?" I ask.

The man nods his head and writes down the address to the Four Seasons hotel. I take the piece of paper and hand it to a taxi driver who is standing just outside the airport exit.

"Welcome to Amsterdam, sir," the driver says as he loads my duffle bag into the trunk and heads to the hotel.

We pull up and I somehow manage to get a room. After dropping off my stuff and quickly freshening up, I decide to go and explore the beautiful city.

Just a block away from my hotel, I see neon lights that say 'Coffee Shop'.

A coffee does sound delicious right now.

So, I go in. The entire menu is in a language that I do not understand so I just point to the picture of a flat white and the brownies that are in the glass display on the counter. The server nods and motions me to take a seat.

The décor in the coffee shop is pretty hip and there is a neon sign of weed on the wall but it is Amsterdam after all. I would assume that almost every place has something weed related in it.

A few moments later, the server comes over and places a steaming flat white and brownie in front of me.

"Is very good," he says in broken English as he places the brownie on the table. I nod and smile. The server turns around and goes back behind the counter.

Sitting there, I am rather enjoying the mellow vibe and soothing music that is playing. I take a bite of the brownie and it does taste a bit odd but it is still pretty delicious. After scarfing it all down, I sit back and slowly sip on my flat white.

I order a second flat white and as I am waiting for it, I begin to feel a bit weird.

Oh no. Did I just make such a rookie mistake?

Getting up, I slap some money on the table and rush back to my hotel. As I am walking down the streets, I notice that time seems to have slowed down and everything around me is moving so slowly. The colorful buildings are so bright and vivid. It feels like the colors are jumping out at me as I walk past. As I keep walking, I hear some all too familiar shrieks. I've been spotted.

"Look, it's Liam D'Fiori," one of them yells. Then a group of girls flock up to me and ask if they can take pictures with me. I nod my head and try my best not to look high.

After they are satisfied, I walk down the block and make it to my room just in time. Sprawling on my body, I lay there paralyzed as the room around me begins to spin and the colors around me start to talk.

I ride out my trip and pass out.

The next morning, I wake up feeling as fresh as a daisy. I laugh at myself for making such a dumb error and accidentally eating a space brownie in Amsterdam. I order some room service and decide that it is time for me to leave and see what crazy adventure the next leg of my journey has in store for me.

As I am sitting there eating my pan au chocolat, an ad for vodka comes up on the screen and just like that a lightbulb goes off in my head. I know which country I am going to visit next. The news comes on and I find myself laughing at the weather report that I don't even fully understand. I chalk down my ridiculous outburst to the possibility that I am still high from my escapades of the previous day.

After eating, I call the front desk and ask them to get me a cab to the airport. Just like that, in a few hours, I am on a flight heading to Russia.

When I land it is night time. I ask the lady at the front desk of my hotel, "Where is the best place to go on a Tuesday night?"

She smiles and tells me to come down in half an hour. Intrigued by her unexpected and somewhat mysterious response, I agree. In my hotel room, I quickly shower and change into my jeans.

Tomorrow I need to do some shopping.

I help myself to a packet of chips from the minibar and eat that while walking back down to the lobby. When I get there, I see the woman and there is a man standing beside. They both smile when they see me.

This is a bit unsettling. Am I about to be kidnapped?

"Hello," the man says in a distinctive South Carolina country accent.

"Hey, you're from America?" I say in shock.

The man chuckles and nods his head, "So my sister told me that you were looking for something to do tonight."

"Yeah, I am only in town for a short while and I want to make the most of it," I reply with a shrug.

The man holds up his hands and says, "Say no more. Follow me."

He walks out the door and waves goodbye to his sister. When we are outside, he turns to me and says, "I am Bobby, by the way."

"Nice to meet you, Bobby. I am Liam," I say as I outstretch my hand.

"That is a mighty string handshake you got there. Let me guess, Virginia," Bobby says as he points his finger at me.

Bobby is a little bit shorter than me with dark brown hair and the physique of a bodybuilder. His appearance is a bit comical because he looks kind of like a jacked up little garden gnome.

"So, what brings you to Russia?" Bobby asks as we walk around a corner.

"Well, I just needed to get away for a bit and you?" I ask.

Bobby shrugs and says, "I am here to visit my sister. She has been bugging me about coming to see her and my nephew for years now, so I finally gave in and here I am. Well, I have been here for the past two months now. Everything is just so lovely and I work online anyway so there is no need for me to rush back."

"That's cool," I say.

Bobby stops in front of a random, unmarked door and knocks on it three times.

"Password," a gruff voice says.

Bobby clears his throat and says, "Gray goose."

I hear some rattling, the sound of chains clinking and then the door opens.

The large man nods and lets us in.

"Trust me, this is the best spot in town," Bobby says. I follow him down a narrow passage and down two flights of stairs to the basement.

I hear the hum of music playing just beyond a door that has the word 'Entrance' above it in neon letters.

"Are you ready?" Bobby asks excitedly.

I have no idea what I am about to walk into, but it is exciting. Bobby pushes open the door to reveal a lively club. The dance floor is packed and there are girls dancing in cages.

"Whoa!" I say as I follow him to the bar.

Bobby orders us two vodkas and we party the night away. At one point we somehow manage to get into a brawl at the bar. One second I am sipping on some vodka and the next thing I know there is a fist flying at my face. Bobby and I beat down a bunch of thugs and are about to treat ourselves to a victory drink before the bouncers throw us out. We wobble our way out of the club and go on celebrating the night.

The next morning, I wake up on a couch, in a room that I do not recognize. I have a splitting headache and the taste of vodka still lingers on my tongue. Groaning, I try to sit up and figure out where I am. The room around me is dark but I can make out some cream couches and an old box television.

Bobby enters and says, "Hey, man," a little too loudly. "Shh," I scowl.

He lowers his tone and tries again, "Hey, man. Are you okay? That bruise on your face looks violent."

"Where am I?" I ask groggily.

Bobby chuckles and says, "Well, you were too drunk to get back to your hotel last night and since my sister's place is closer, I brought you here."

"Thanks, man." I say as I finally manage to push myself up. I touch my face and wince with pain as the memories of our bar fight slowly come back to me.

Bobby opens the curtains and the sun pours into the room. I clutch my head I pain and reach for the ridiculous pair of sunglasses on the little table besides the couch.

"Oh sorry," Bobby says as he shuffles to the kitchen and pours me a glass of orange juice and some tablets. "Here, take these. They will help."

I do as he says and after a few moments of agony feel a slight sense of relief. Bobby hands me an ice pack for my face and switches on the television. I see my drunken face on the screen and headlines that read "Liam D'Fiori, The Bad Boy of the Fashion World."

I laugh and ice my sore cheek. To be honest I have no idea how we even got involved in that fight in the first place, but it was rather thrilling.

"So, I have a few meetings lined up, but if you aren't busy later, I would love to take you somewhere cool," Bobby says with a huge smile.

I nod. "Sounds great. I am going to get some breakfast and sleep off this hangover. You know where to find me."

Leaving his sister's apartment, I do exactly what I said I was going to.

A few hours later, Bobby knocks on my hotel room door.

"Are you ready?" he asks. I nod and follow him outside. We walk a few blocks and he takes me to a dirt track.

"Hold on. Are we doing what I think we are?" I ask excitedly. Bobby smiles and rents us two motorcycles from the store.

"Have you ever ridden one before?" he asks.

I shake my head and say, "No, but I have always wanted to."

Bobby spends the rest of the day teaching me how to ride and by the end I am able to make it around the track by myself without stalling. Heading back to my hotel, I am certain that I have gotten everything that I needed from this place and I am certain that it is time to move on. My only rule for this trip is that I do not stay in one place for too long and despite the fact that I am going to miss Bobby, I know that it is time to leave.

THIRTY-EIGHT

Liam

THE NEXT MORNING, I wake up and long to be someplace warm. I pack my duffle bag and write a little note to thank Bobby for the wonderful time. On my way out, I leave the note with Bobby's sister at the front desk and head to the airport. When I get back home, I am certain that I am going to get myself a motorbike.

At the private airport, I take my private jet to Mykonos, which only leaves in two hours so I make myself comfortable at one of the lounges while I wait. As I am sitting on one of the couches, I see my cell phone at the very top of my duffle bag. I suppose at some point I should turn it back on, but I am not ready for whatever is waiting for me once I do.

Eventually, the jet is ready and I board. The jet-lag is catching up to me now so I sleep through the majority of the flight. We land in the early hours of the morning and I book one of those beach side villas for myself.

Laying outside on the terrace, I look up at the midnight blue sky above me, the gentle sounds of the ocean as the water swooshes below me and the cool breeze blows against my skin sending shivers throughout my body. The city is quiet as everyone rests, I know that come morning it will be alive and bustling.

For now, I lay here enjoying the peace and tranquility that the night offers. My mind begins to wander.

Did Bia receive my letter? I hope she did. I wonder if she is looking up at the stars right now. She and I are both under the same sky and when we look up, we see the same thing. This reminds me of the first time we made love by the fire. I remember how the twinkle in her eyes outshone that of the stars above. Oh how things have changed since then. I feel like I have lost my way and become a shell of who and what I once was. I feel as though I am an imposter living a life that is not my own and one that I do not even want. Nothing seems to make me happy. If I am being honest, nothing has made me truly happy since I left my heart behind in Virginia. What is the purpose of living? I seem to have lost my way and I don't know how to get back to the man I once was.

I bolt upright and rush inside. Rummaging through my duffle bag, I grab my manuscript and feel the sudden urge to write. This is it, the only thing that connects me to my past, to the man I came to New York to be. I want this manuscript to be the beginning of my legacy.

With adrenaline surging through my veins, I sit on the rooftop terrace of my villa and the words begin to flow. It has been a while since I have felt this passionate about wanting to write, but this serenity, grappling with my identity and the thoughts of Bia have rekindled my flame and made me feel the need to complete my manuscript.

I spend the next two days just writing. Here there are no distractions and I have the freedom to work at my own pace and more importantly on my own schedule. I don't have to put down my pen because I need to attend a photoshoot, meeting, or some other ridiculous event that Patrick needs me to attend. Here, I don't have to worry that I am not giving Michele enough attention or think about whether or not I put the toilet seat down.

In this villa, I can just be myself and enjoy the solidarity that comes with being on my own.

For the first time in my life I am well and truly by myself. Except for the short period where I was left stranded in New York by Kyle and Shane, I don't ever remember a time where I was by myself. This time is different. I am not carrying the burden and worries of how to come up with the rent or having to get to bed because I need to wake up in a few hours and get back to work. This is what freedom and independence feel like and I am absolutely loving it.

When I do get tired or feel like the words just aren't flowing and I need some motivation, I get up and take a walk on the private beach behind my villa. The sun is always warm and welcoming as I walk on the white, sandy beaches. Everything is so still and tranquil. I even dip my toes into the crystal-clear blue waters.

Taking a leisurely stroll back to my villa, I decide to get back to work. I sit at the desk, working on my manuscript until the sun starts to set. As I write down the final word to conclude my manuscript, a tear rolls down my eye.

Wow. I actually did it. My manuscript is almost complete. There are a few final touches that I need to make, but other than that, it is almost done.

This is a momentous occasion and I decide to celebrate by going to the nearby town and having drinks at one of the local bars. Everyone is so friendly and welcoming. One Pina Colada turns into five and before I know it, I am buying a round of drinks for everyone at the bar. I party through the night with some of the locals and stagger my way back to the villa in the early parts of the morning.

As I walk along the cobblestone roads, humming the tune of *Three Little Birds* by Bob Marley that was playing back at the bar, I can't help but wonder what my Bia is doing. As much as I am loving this newfound freedom of mine, I do feel a bit lonely. Especially at times like these where I wish I had someone to celebrate this huge accomplishment with me.

At the bar, there were a number of slightly intoxicated women basically throwing themselves at me, but in my tipsy state, I have a revelation. I know where my heart belongs and it is not at some bar in Mykonos. So I leave and when I get to my villa, I sit outside listening to the sounds of nature. Until I get a bright idea. It consumes my thoughts and I hurry down to the beach below and strip off all my clothes.

I have never gone skinny dipping before and what better place to do it than on a private beach in freaking Mykonos!

Before I can talk myself out of this wonderful idea, I mute my thoughts and charge toward the water yelling at the top of my lungs. As soon as my body makes contact with the icy water, shivers go tingling down my spine and all through my body. It is pitch dark out and the only source of light is the moon above me. I float around in the for a bit feeling the way the current moves, the way the water rises and crashes. It feels so natural that I almost become one with the water.

A gust of wind brings me back to my senses and I snap out of the trance-like state that I was in, realizing that I have drifted quite a distance from the shore. My survival instincts kick in and I plow my way through the water. When I get to the shore, I collapse on my back and try to catch my breath.

Now, I am stone cold sober and the realization of what just happened sets in. I have never been a reckless person, but what I just did was pretty reckless. A hearty laugh escapes my throat. I laugh and laugh, rolling around in the wet sand until my stomach hurts and laughter becomes tears. If someone had seen me right now, they would probably think that I lost my mind, but I do not care. My inhibitions feel like they have been released, but I also have come to the realization that freedom is not all that it is chalked up to be.

If we do not have an anchor to keep us from drifting away on the ocean that is life, we will definitely lose ourselves and find that we have landed ourselves in rather dangerous situations. My anchor is love. The love that I have for my family, for my writing, for my friends, and for Bia.

It is the only thing that keeps me from drifting away and losing myself completely. While lying under the moonlit sky, on a wet, sandy beach in Mykonos, it becomes clear as day to me that the only thing of real value in this life is the driving force that is love. It helps to keep us on track and reminds us of who we are. If I hold on to love and stay true to myself, I know that I will never feel lost again. The epiphany of falling in love with your life, that is truly romance.

With that, I grab my clothes and head back to the villa. After a long, hot shower, I pass out in bed.

THIRTY-NINE

Beatrice

AS I SIT IN MY TINY OFFICE cubicle at Dawson & Sons Inc. I swivel around in my chair and take in the fact that this is now my reality. I am currently doing my articles at one of the most prestigious law firms in Virginia and things have been going really well with John.

Looking at the framed picture on my desk of him from our vacation in Egypt last year puts a smile on my face. He is kind, charming, suave, and my parents approve. When I am with him, I feel safe and content. I wouldn't say that I am completely happy or satisfied, sometimes I feel like there is something missing when I find myself comparing my relationship with John to the one that I had with Liam.

My coworker pops her head around my office door and says, "You have a call on line one."

I nod and pick up the receiver.

"Hey, girl," Mary says.

I instantly recognize her voice. Mary and I spent all of our time together at university and graduated at the top of our class. She chose to go into property law while I opted for civil. Mary now works at the most exclusive real estate company in Virginia and is engaged to Tommy.

"Hi, Mary. Are we still meeting for lunch at our usual spot?" I ask. We try our best to meet each other for lunch at least every two weeks, but with our hectic work schedules, it is a mission.

"Yes. That is what I was calling about. So I have a viewing that might run a little later than expected, but I am definitely coming for lunch. I might just be a few minutes late if that is okay?" Mary says apologetically over the phone.

"That is perfectly okay. It means that I will have more time alone with those delicious chocolate chip pancakes," I say with a chuckle.

Mary laughs and says, "Don't have too much fun without me. See you in a bit. Toddles."

The line goes dead and I place down the receiver. It is almost time for lunch, so I grab my bag and head out of the office letting one of my coworkers know where I am going to be in case of an emergency on my way out.

The café is just down the road and the weather is nice today. Above me the sky is a beautiful light blue with white cotton candy clouds speckled across its vast expanse. The sun is out, but it isn't too strong so I decide to take a nice, leisurely stroll.

I watch as people hurry by getting on with their tasks, cell phones stuck to their ears and wonder if we have all forgotten how to live in the moment. It is a sad state of affairs in my opinion. Thinking back, I long for the days where the town square was filled with farmers selling their produce, kids playing by the fountain, and everyone having a good time socializing with each other.

Now, things are so different. Our little town has undergone so much 'development' and seems to have lost the sense of community that was once a vital part of the society. My parents are somewhat to blame for this change, they encouraged and pushed for the developments, such as the factory being built on the outskirts of the town. While these did provide a sizable injection into the economic flow, we seem to have lost the sense of community that we once had which is invaluable.

Walking into the café, I smile as it is one of the few places in town that hasn't undergone any major changes. The delicious aroma of freshly ground coffee beans wafts through the air, inviting any passerby in.

"Hello, what can I get for you today?" Mrs. D'Fiori asks without looking up.

I clear my throat and say, "Just a stack of your delicious chocolate chip pancakes and two flat whites please."

Her head shoots up as soon as I speak and her eyes widen. She smiles at me and says, "Oh hello, Bia. How are you, my dear?"

"I am well thanks and you?" I say sweetly.

Over the past few years, I have visited this café frequently and in doing so have somewhat formed a cordial relationship with Liam's mother. We generally make small talk and speak about everything besides Liam.

"Oh, same old, you know," she says with a sigh.

I look at her and see that some worry lines have formed on her once perfectly smooth skin. She even has dark circles around her eyes now which is something that she never has. For her age, Mrs. D'Fiori is normally one of the most fresh-faced and brightest people that I have ever met.

"What's the matter? If you don't mind me asking," I say.

Mrs. D'Fiori forces a smile and says, "It is nothing to worry yourself about, my dear. Have a seat and I will bring your order to you shortly."

It is about him. I know it is. It has to be. This is the only thing that she would hesitate to tell me about.

"Is Liam okay?" I ask as panic begins to set in. The words burst out of my mouth before I can stop them.

Mrs. D'Fiori tries to keep her facial expression neutral and replies saying, "I sure he is. We got a call from his agent that he is supposed to attend some huge campaign for Dolce and Gabbana this weekend, but they can't seem to get a hold of him."

I frown and say, "Dolce and Gabbana? What is he doing for them?" My curiosity gets the better of me and I need answers.

She smiles and pulls out a magazine cut out. She hands it to me and says, "Liam is a big-time model now. Just a few months ago he was on every runway for New York fashion week."

I look at the cutout and see my Liam standing in a fancy suit. The top button on his collar is open and his hair is long and shaggy. He looks so sexy.

Dolce and Gabbana? Trust Liam to be so modest. During our very brief exchanges over the years, he did tell me that he was in the fashion industry, but I had no idea that he was walking runways for some of the biggest names in the business!

Behind me the café door opens and Mary walks in announcing her presence loudly.

I quickly hand the cut out back to Mrs. D'Fiori says, "I am sure that Liam is okay," before backing away from the counter and going to sit down at the table that Mary just dropped her bag on.

"I ordered you a flat white," I say to Mary as I take my seat opposite her. "Thank you. You are such a darling, but did I just hear you say Liam?"

Mary says as she raises her brow suspiciously.

She really doesn't miss a thing.

I nod and fill her in.

Mrs. D'Fiori brings our order and Mary and I catch up while we share the stack of pancakes.

"Wait, isn't it your 5-year anniversary with John today?" Mary asks.

I take a sip of my flat white and say, "It is. We are going to dinner at that new, fancy sushi place to celebrate."

Mary squeals with glee and says, "Do you think that he is going to pop the question?"

I frown and reply, "I don't know."

Sighing, I take another bite of my pancake. "What's wrong?" Mary asks.

"It's just that sometimes I find myself comparing my relationship with Liam to my relationship with John and I don't know. It feels like there is something missing," I say as I sit back.

Mary says, "I have a question to ask you. Does John make you happy?" I take a moment to think about it before answering her.

"Yeah, I guess he does," I say.

He actually does make me happy. John is so thoughtful and he helped me to put myself back together after Liam left.

"That is all that matters. The truth is that no one ever really gets over their first true love. Liam was your first true love and he will always have a special place in your heart, but are you going to keep holding on to the past or move on and look to the future?" Mary says.

I take a deep breath and let the weight of Mary's words sink in.

Everything that she said made sense.

So, later that afternoon as I am getting ready for my anniversary dinner with John, I give myself a little pep talk.

It is time to stop looking over your shoulder and focusing on the past. Do what Mary said and keep looking straight ahead to the future. That is clearly what Liam is doing so stop holding yourself back.

I swipe on some red lipstick and adjust my black sequin dress before grabbing my little clutch bag and heading downstairs. John is standing at the bottom of the staircase and smiles at me as I walk down.

"You look absolutely breathtaking," he says and he slides his arm around my waist before gently kissing me on the cheek.

He is wearing a sleek gray suit and a crisp white shirt, his hair is slicked back and he looks pretty good himself.

"So do you," I say as I lean into the comfort of his warmth. John leads me toward the dining room and I frown.

"Where are we going? I thought we had a reservation at the sushi restaurant?" I ask.

John smiles and says, "We are, but I want to give you something first." Every cell in my body tingles and I know what is about to happen.

We walk into the dining room which is filled with my friends and our family members. Tears well up in my eyes and I see Mary smiling at me.

John gets down on one knee and says, "Will you marry me?"

I look at the eager smile on my parents face and nod yes even though my heart isn't really in it.

FORTY

Beatrice

I WAKE UP BRIGHT and early the next morning and decide to leave for the office. There are a few old case files that I need to read in the firm's archive room. Plus, getting an early start is never a bad thing.

I'm not sure if I am trying to convince myself that it is totally okay to creep out of bed while your new fiancé is still asleep so that you don't have to be here when he gets up the morning after your engagement.

Regardless, I get ready for work as quietly as possible and grab my bag before heading to the office. As I drive, I cannot seem to get over the way the ring looks on my finger as my hand is wrapped around my black, leather steering wheel. It feels… odd.

I try to swallow my discomfort and blast my stereo to distract me as I drive to work. When I get to my office, I greet a few colleagues before shutting the door behind me. There is a stack of letters on my desk and I decide that before tackling them I need a strong cup of coffee.

Heading to the office kitchen, I pour myself a hot cup of filter coffee and head back. Seated at my desk, I slowly begin to go through the letters. Most of them are the usual invites, bills, and a few thank you letters from my previous clients. Then I get to an odd one. I spit the sip of coffee out of my mouth when I see the postage stamp. Hot coffee sprays all over my desk and I grab a tissue as I quickly try to clean up my mess.

"Good morning. Is everything okay?" my coworker says from the doorway.

I nod and smile. "Yes, everything is fine. After years of working here, I am still surprised by how terrible the coffee is."

My coworker smiles and says that she will get us some flat whites from the café down the road. Thank her and she leaves.

Now, back to the letter I can tell by looking at the stamp that it is from New York.

This can only mean one thing. It can only be from one person. I know his handwriting.

Staring at the engagement ring on my finger, I am almost tempted to throw the letter in the trash without even opening it. However, against my better judgment, I cannot do it. I simply have to know what he wrote.

I take a deep breath and slowly open the letter. Holding the pages, I run my hand over them as I think that he recently held these very same pages. I feel close and connected to him again.

As I read the words that are scrolled on the pieces of paper, my eyes fill with tears.

Why now? How does he always know when to come back in and send me spiraling again? Just when my life is finally getting back on track and some normalcy is returning, he goes and does this. Why Liam?

Just then my phone rings and I get a shock. The pages fall from my hand and are spread all across the floor. John's number flashes on my screen. I pick up the phone and say, "Hello."

I hear a few muffled sounds, but get no response so I repeat myself saying, "Hello, John. Are you okay?"

Is this a pocket dial?

Just as I am about to hang up, I hear John's voice. Well, it kind of sounds like him. He moans saying, "Yes, Chelsea. Oh my God, yes!"

Chelsea? Like Chelsea the cheerleader? She is the only Chelsea that John and I know. He told me that they met up for lunch as friends a few times in the past.

I quickly hang up and try to make sense of what I just heard. The man just proposed to me the night before and now he is out cheating on me with Chelsea?

My eyes fill up with tears, but I unexpectedly feel an overwhelming sense of relief. I have always known that John and I were not meant to be, I just let the expectations and pressure from those around me get to me. With that in mind, it doesn't make being cheated on any less painful.

Bending down, I slowly pick up the pages of Liam's letter from the floor.

I guess even when you aren't around, you somehow always show up at the right time.

Sitting on my office floor, I yank the engagement ring off my finger and toss it in the trash before finishing Liam's letter. At the very bottom of the second page, he scribbled down his number.

Staring at the page, I try to figure out what I should do next. Do I call him? If I do, what should I say?

I decide to just go for it. Why not?

Picking up my phone I dial the number and wait nervously as it begins to ring.

One ring, two rings… by the fifth ring I am just about ready to hang up when suddenly the tone stops and a groggy sounding Liam says, "Hello. Who is this?"

"Liam. Hi, it's me, Bia," I say in a hushed tone. There is silence on the other side of the line.

"Did you get my letter?" he asks. I swallow and say, "Yes."

The line is very static and it is really difficult to hear him. "Liam, where are you?" I ask.

The connection is terrible and I can only hear every third word that he says.

"I… Austria… back… soon," he says in a jumble.

I take a deep breath and clutch the receiver in my sweaty palm before saying, "Liam, please come back. I miss you."

The line goes dead and I just hope that he heard what I said.

My coworker comes back carrying my coffee to find me still seated on the floor. I get up, dust myself off and thank her for the coffee before grabbing my stuff and letting her know that I am taking the day off.

I drive to my parents' house and knock on the door. Di opens and looks surprised to see me there.

"Hi, Bia. Aren't you supposed to be at work?" she asks, stepping aside to let me in.

I bounce past her and say, "I took the day off. Oh and my engagement to John is over."

As I am talking, I drop my bag down and pull on my riding boots. "Wait, what? Now where are you going?" Di asks. The confusion is plastered on her face.

I walk over and kiss her on the cheek before saying, "There is something that I need to do now. When I get back, I promise that I will explain everything."

This seems to pacify her enough momentarily and I make my way to the stable behind my house. I give my gorgeous Snowie a big hug and saddle him up.

I ride Snowball up the mountain to a patch of trees. This is where I saw my engagement ring from Liam land when I threw it off Lovers Mountains all those years ago. I silently pray that it is still here. Tying Snowball to a nearby tree, I spend the rest of my day searching for the ring.

The sun begins to set. I am now covered in dirt and cold to the bone. Just as I am about to give up and go back down the mountain I see a pile of leaves in the corner of my eye that I must have missed. I rummage through the leaves until I get to the very bottom and there wrapped in a leaf is my ring. It is just as beautiful as the first day I saw it. I brush away the dirt to uncover the diamond and smile to myself as I shove it in my pocket and ride down the mountain, feeling victorious on my white horse.

FORTY-ONE

Liam

ABOUT A MONTH has passed since the incident at the party and I am finally back in New York. After my whirlwind adventure around the world I have come to the realization that the only thing that matters in this life is love.

Recently, I've been trying to reassess my emotions. Michelle and I haven't been the same since that day. We are not as intimate as we once were. I don't look into her eyes like I used to. Her smiles aren't as bright as they once were. Deep inside, we know it's over, but neither one of us wants to face the truth. Sometimes the truth is so painful that we would rather live a lie so that we don't have to experience reality.

Why do some people settle for less? Why do I?

Why do we hide behind a mask of conformity?

This is my last photo shoot of the day. I'm tired, and choose to walk home from work. After reminiscing about my life in the city, it comes to me. What ever happened to that bartender at the café? I walk two more blocks and decide to pay him a visit. I hop into a cab and travel slowly down to Houston Street.

I walked in the café and took a seat in the corner of the balcony. I sit there observing the scenario; it hasn't changed one bit. There are still couches and coffee tables, with candles serving as the main decoration.

As I'm adjusting myself on the stool, I hear someone ask, "Good evening, sir. How may I help you?" I look up and reply, "Just a latté this time." He looks at me with an intense stare. Then, after recognizing me, he reaches out his hand to shake mine. "Liam, man. How've you been?"

"I've been good. I can't believe you remember me," I say, sort of surprised that he still works here.

"Yeah, man, how could I forget? You're the guy with the martini and now you're a celebrity!"

"Celebrity! I don't know about that," I reply, not wanting to talk about work or fame.

"Liam, man, you've made it! I've seen you on magazines, billboards, TV commercials, and even on some TV shows. I heard you're going to be doing a movie now too, is that right?" he asks with enthusiasm.

"No, I'm not. I've turned that down. I'm thinking about leaving the business and returning home," I say as he hands me the coffee.

"Are you serious? I thought this was what you wanted?" he asks. "Well, I came here to be a writer, and now I've become something totally different. It seems like I've drifted away from what I want, from who I am," I say quietly, taking a sip of my coffee.

"Hey, I know you came here to be a writer, but instead you became a model. Either way, you win because you made it! Many people don't get the chance that you got. Take me for example, I came here to become an actor, but instead I've ended up here bartending. It's not what I wanted, but the bills just kept on coming and someone's got to pay it!"

"It's not even about a career, it's about something else," I confess, wanting to express to someone the doubts that have been haunting my mind for years.

"I know it's not about a career, I see it in your eyes. It's about love, isn't it?" he says, leaning against the counter and looking into my eyes.

"How do you know?" I ask.

"Listen, let me tell you my story. I'm originally from Florida. I moved here almost a decade ago. Back in Florida, I fell in love with this girl that I met one summer. From my perspective, we fell in love immediately. We were inseparable, but we never verbally revealed our love for one another. As time went on, our lives changed. I decided to follow my dream and become an actor, so I moved to New York City. She stayed behind, studying to be a nurse. The whole time, I thought that if I could make it as an actor, it would impress her and she would fall in love with me. So time went on and I kept chasing my dream.

After a couple of years pursuing my career, I realized that for me, it was just a dream. I decided that I was going to go back to proclaim my love to her, but when I returned to see her after six years, she told me that she had gotten married and had a kid. I went ahead and revealed my feelings for her, and told her the reason I left. You want to know what she told me? She told me that she felt the same way, but she gave up on our love when I moved to New York.

She thought I was never going to return. So she moved on with her life, met some guy at school and married him. After that experience, here's what I got to say. Don't wait until tomorrow to tell the one you love that you love them. Follow your heart. Don't let opportunities get away. Don't be afraid of love, take a chance or you will never know what can be."

I sit there for a while trying to take in what he said. I realized that I'm not special; everyone's life is the same. We all search for the same things.

We all love the same way and we all fear the same way. The only thing that separates us is the fact that some people take a chance. They risk it all to lose it all or to have it all. I started to think about what Bia could be doing at this time in her life. She never returned the letter that I sent her. Maybe she moved on. I mean, after all these years, why would she wait for me?

Before I leave the café, the man asks me to sign an autograph for his daughter. I think after finding out the truth about his lost love, he has also moved on with his life. We part ways and I grab a cab home. At the present moment, my mind is racing at a million miles per hour. My stomach turns as the thought of Bia being with someone else.

Upon arriving at my apartment, I give the taxi driver a good tip, for I know how hard they work. In the elevator, I think about Bia. Anxiety sets in as I start to picture Bia's life at this moment. The thought of her being with another man is making my mind play through scenes of her life that might not even be real. The conversation I had with the bartender made me contemplate my current situation. I enter my apartment and Michelle is making dinner. I give her a kiss and go about my business.

An hour later, we have dinner, but while we are eating, I notice that Michelle is unusually quiet. I decide not to ask her why because sometimes people just want to be left alone. We finish dinner and I help her clean up. The whole time, she doesn't say a single word, so I make an attempt to let her know that I care.

"Baby, I've noticed that you're a little introverted today, what's on your mind?" I ask with a soft tone.

"Nothing, I'm just… I'm just a bit tired from work, that's all," she says while picking up the discarded silverware from the table. I stop washing the dishes, dry my hands, and look at her for a little bit while she goes back and forth between the table and the sink.

"Darling, I know you, and I also know that when you act like this there is something more than just work headaches. You seem sad. Look, sweetheart, you don't have to hide your emotions from me. I care about you whether you're happy or sad. That's why we are together. So tell me, what seems to be bothering you?" I ask, trying to sound comforting.

I stand there just observing her for about a minute or two to see if she will say anything. After a few minutes, she turns off the water, dries her hands, and stands by the sink, looking a bit coy. She tilts her head to the right and fixes her eyes on mine.

"Do you believe in true love?" she asks quietly. I stand there not knowing where she is going with this, but I decide to answer.

"Of course, of course I believe in true love."

"How do we know when we meet our true loves? Will we see it, feel it, just waltz into it?"

At this point in my life, I don't even know what to say. If I say I see it or feel it, I would be lying because I don't see and I can't feel my true love. I don't want to be a liar, but at the same time, what is true love? True love is unconditional love for someone. A love that surpasses all other emotions, all rationality. It has no boundaries and it doesn't always have to be mutual.

That's the love that the Greeks called Agape. Love is something that can be acquired through time and experience. It's a mutual feeling and a decision made by those involved.

I really don't have a response for her, but at this present time, I have to be rational. I don't want to hurt her any longer.

"Michelle, don't doubt my love for you. You know you're all I got. Besides you, I don't have anyone in this city that I love or who loves me the way you do," I respond truthfully, caressing her cheek. She smiles with confidence and throws the hand towel she holds onto the counter. She comes closer to me and gives me a tight, comforting hug.

After we finish cleaning the kitchen, we head to bed. It's about 2 AM and I can't sleep. All has been quiet for some time now and I still haven't heard from Bia. What could have happened? Did she get the letter? Did she read it and not want to answer back because she doesn't feel the same? Maybe it was never delivered! All I know is that I'm losing many nights of sleep over this. All I want is to know the truth, even if it opposes my desires.

I lay in bed, turned toward Michelle, watching her sleep. She's beautiful, her face peacefully dormant. I slowly run my fingers through her hair and as I gaze at her with admiration, my thoughts slowly drift, recapping all of our time together over the past five years.

She was with me when I traveled to Europe doing runway shows. We spent two weeks one winter vacation in a cabin on the northern part of the Pocono Mountains. That was one of the most romantic moments of our relationship. We spent all day drinking hot tea lying on an Indian style carpet watching the wood burn in the fireplace. Through the window, we watched snowfall delicately from the clouds, making the ambiance more and more intimate.

It was at that time that I realized that I could be falling in love with her. At that time, I thought Michelle was going to be the one to rearrange my theory on true love. As time progressed, my theory on love became more and more solid and my heart yearned to know the truth.

Now my heart's yearning has become a massive volcano about to erupt if it doesn't find the truth. That's why I waited so long for the truth. Even if I don't find the answer that my heart desires, at least I'll find some closure.

FORTY-TWO

Liam

THE SCENT OF THE EARLY summer's breeze flows through the half-opened window of my room. I lay in bed, stretching the duvet over me. I look over to the right of the bed, still yawning, to find that Michelle has already left for work. I stretch and yawn a few more times before getting out of bed. I look over my schedule to plan out my day, and notice that I have a photo shoot at 2 PM. It is now 9:36 AM and my stomach is so angry it keeps growling at me.

A blue pair of jeans and a white t-shirt will do for the day. I head to a café across from Central Park to have breakfast. At around 12:15 PM, I pay the tab and go for a walk in the park. The park seems so busy and alive, even though it's a Wednesday, but people are outside walking their dogs, playing with their kids, jogging, etc. I, on the other hand, love to look at the trees, the birds, and the beauty of nature. It reminds me a bit of home.

Through my walk, I can't get my mind off what Michelle asked me the night before. The thought of true love keeps popping up in my head over and over again. I try to make that thought visual, and every time an image comes to me, it is the profile of a 17-year-old Bia. Her smile keeps appearing to me every time I close my eyes.

To soften this anxious feeling, I decide to analyze my life. I came to the realization that I have not done what I came here to do. I have gotten so caught up in making money and living comfortably, that I have neglected the reason I came to New York City. My book manuscript is still in the drawer. I have forgotten about it. It's been a while since I've even thought of myself as a writer, the last time I looked at my manuscript was when I worked on it in Greece.

Is it the book that I'm concerned about, or is it her? I have to face it; the reason I'm here is because of her. My whole life so far has been of decisions made with her in my mind. I've been a fool for too long, and for a time, I got away with it, but now there is no getting around it. I have to know for better or for worse what she feels about me. I decide to go back home to Virginia to find the truth.

As I get into my apartment, I rush to my closet and grab a brown leather book bag. I start to pick through my closet for some clothes to take with me back home. I make up my mind that I'm going back. My heart is pounding fast and my breaths are getting shorter. The palms of my hands are moist and my body softly quivers.

My mind is as blank as sheets hanging to dry in the wind. My mind is trying to rationalize my decision, but I desperately avoid its condemnation. I pack all that can fit into the bag. I search the room for anything else that I might need. God, what is it that I'm missing? Yes, my manuscript. I search every corner of the house, but I can't find it.

Maybe it wasn't meant to be for me to be a writer. I've made many plans in my life, but most of them never came to pass. Life sometimes almost feels like destiny. I look around a few more times, but then give up looking.

I reach into the closet and put on my cowboy boots and my black leather jacket. I put on my backpack and leave the room. As I reach the kitchen, I look around the apartment, reminiscing about the time I've spent here. I open the counter drawer to find a piece of paper to write on. I know I'm a coward for leaving like this, but I cannot bear to look in her beautiful eyes and tell her that I don't love her the way she wants me to.

I take a pen from the corner of the counter and begin to write her a note:

Michelle (Princess),

I have decided to leave. Forgive me if I've hurt you in any way, it was not my intention. Don't cry, for those beautiful eyes weren't made for crying. With great remorse, I leave you this note. Life doesn't always give you what we want. For many things, it gives, but some we run after. I leave you this apartment because you deserve it. All the memories we'd shared here will get you through. Don't lose faith… keep on Believing. God has a good plan for your life. With this goodbye, I leave you a piece of my heart.

Love, Liam

I leave the note on top of the counter. I take a couple of steps toward the door and look around one last time before getting my black helmet from the lamp table. I close the door behind me and take the elevator to the garage. I can't hesitate or let my emotions get the best of me. Right now, my heart is wounded from leaving Michelle in such a way, but my heart would ache even more if I stayed here and lived a lie any longer.

Without consulting anyone, I hop on my motorcycle and point it toward the place where I left my heart. I roar the engine and leave the building. As I'm on the road, I look at the side mirror and watch Manhattan get smaller and smaller behind me.

While I'm riding, I can't help but have second thoughts about leaving Michelle. By now, she would have already found out and I hope that she doesn't overreact mawkishly. After all, I do love her and care about her. We have many memories together; not only in New York, but in other places that we've traveled together.

She was there with me from the beginning of my career. She saw me when I was broke, and she witnessed me take off into stardom. One thing that I can say is that I remained faithful to her all these years. In my line of work, this wasn't always easy, and it was generally looked down on by my colleagues. I had many opportunities to be unfaithful, but out of love and respect, I turned away. I figured out that loving someone is not only an emotion or a feeling, but it's also a decision.

The sun begins to appear in the East as I approach my parent's house. The wheat fields look so peaceful. The wind is calm and the wheat stands still. Sun ray's shimmer at the tips of the wheat, reflecting this beautiful yellow aura. I pull in the driveway and park my motorcycle next to the porch.

When I take off my helmet, the first thing I notice is the scent of freshness. I had missed it for so long. The air smells like pine and mist. I take a deep breath and close my eyes, remembering my childhood.

The grass in front of the house is sprinkled with dew. The brisk wind blows my tousled hair from side to side, and I feel so glad that I'm home again. I open my eyes to the screeching sound of the door. Then I see a face peaking between the edge of the door, suspiciously trying to figure out what was going on outside. By the color of her bright blue eyes, I knew that it was my mother.

I must have woken her up as I pulled in. As she realizes that it is me and that I am home, she walks down the steps to greet me. I step off of my bike eagerly and meet her half way with a giant hug.

"Oh Liam, darling, it's you. You're home," she says close to my ear. She takes a step back in disbelief, and puts both of her hands on my face, one hand on each cheek. She smiles.

"Yes, mama. I'm home," I say, returning her smile.

She takes me by the hand and we head inside the house where everyone is still sleeping. We head to my old bedroom, and as I'm walking up the stairs, I notice that the house is the same way as when I left it about five years ago.

She opens the door to my room, and at that moment, I feel comfort knowing that I am home. My room seems like no one has touched it since I left. Everything is in the same place as it always has been. I walk in and admire everything in it. It's been so long that I have forgotten what it looked like.

"Sweetheart, would you like some coffee?" Mama says, standing by the door.

"No thanks. I'm kind of tired and I was hoping to get some rest."

"I bet you are. Go to bed and we'll talk when you wake," Mom says, sending a kiss through the air as she closes the door. After she closes the door, I hit the bed without even taking my clothes off. I'm so tired from the ride here that it doesn't even bother me.

I woke up to the sound of a knock. After many knocks, I open my eyes. "Yes, who is it?"

"It's me, honey. Are you hungry? I've made chicken, some potatoes… oh yeah and your favorite French toast!" Mama says, slowly walking into the room.

"Mama, what time is it?"

"Well, it's about 1:20 PM and I've made us some brunch. Isn't that what you'd call it up there in New York?"

I laugh. "Great! I'm coming down." I say, yawning and still a little tired. After five minutes of yawning and stretching, I get out of bed and proceed down the stairs to have some breakfast. The aroma of the food makes my mouth water and my stomach growl with hunger. I step in the kitchen and I see both of my sisters there helping my mother set up the table, and as usual, my father finger picking the food to have a taste. "Good morning, everyone,"

I say with a higher tone to get their attention. Immediately my sisters rush to give me a hug. I can sense that they are very glad to see me because for the past year or so, they've only seen me in ad campaigns or on TV.

"Liam, so good to see you," they say, hugging and kissing my cheeks. "By the way, 'Good Afternoon!' you've been in bed for a while," Jennifer teases with a smile.

"I'm glad you're home." Rachel says as she walks past and ruffles my hair.

"Come, Liam. Sit, let's eat!" my younger sister Stephanie says, and proceeds to set up the table. My dad overhears the commotion and opens his arms to me. "Come here, boy. Give your father a hug!"

I rush to him with a great smile and hug him. It feels so good to be home; it seems as if I never left. My father gives me a tight hug with a couple of taps on my back, then he grabs me by my arms and says, "Son, I'm so glad you're home."

"So am I, Daddy, so am I."

We all sit down around the table to eat. I have a sense that everyone feels united and like a family again, complete for the first time in years. My family has never had someone leave town to live somewhere else; I was the only one who departed to live in another city. Everyone else before me has always lived in the same town, never moving more than walking distance from a previous home.

This experience was all new to them, and me too. That's how I know that they are overjoyed to see me back home. My father says a prayer before we eat and when he finishes, we start to serve ourselves. My sisters are so eager and excited that they can't help themselves. They begin to ask me questions right away.

"Liam, tell us, how was your life in New York City? Is it like what we see in the movies and in magazines?" Stephanie asks curiously.

"No, not really like the movies or magazines, but it is a lot more exciting than here," I say putting two spoons of vegetables on my plate.

"Wow! I can't wait till I go there and see all the glamor that is New York City!" she says with a smile.

"Excuse me, princess. Who says you're going to New York?" Mama says, raising her eyebrow in an authoritative expression.

"Well, Liam went and made it. I want to go to see what can happen!" she says, taking a bite of her toast.

"Steph, it's not really as glamorous or peaceful as you see on TV," I say, bursting her bubble.

"What do you mean? You've made it!"

"Yeah, I did make it, but I've seen many who are there and are struggling just to get by financially. Plus, many leave their families to go chase their dreams, and end up being lonely. Because of their loneliness, they make many bad choices to suppress that void that fills their hearts," I say, trying to convince her of the reality that TV and magazines don't show you.

"What kind of choices?" she asks, intrigued by what I said.

"Well, there are many things that are available in New York City and a lot of them are bad. It depends on the person's morals and values. Some people get depressed and become very reclusive, while others go out and lose themselves in many nights of partying," I explain.

"See, that's why I don't want you to go," Mama says to Steph. Stephanie takes a second to collect her thoughts and realizes that she is better off at her present state.

"Anyway, we got a lot of attention from the townspeople that saw you on TV and in the magazine ads. They were always saying 'there's that boy from down the street! Now he is a big star in New York. That boy done himself good.' After your ads, people all over town asked about you to see when you would come back home," Jennifer laughs.

"What about Bia?" I have to ask. I want to know if she was among the townspeople who asked about me.

"What about her?" Jennifer asks, raising her left eyebrow.

"Well, has she asked about me? How is she doing?" I put the question out there, pretending that it wasn't all that important to me, but it is. It's the main reason why I'm here. I'm here to settle that void in my heart.

"Oh, not too long ago I ran into her at the grocery store. She asked about you but nothing more," she answers nonchalantly.

"Just out of curiosity, is she with anyone? Or married?" I ask, wanting to know the answer, but also scared to find out that she's married. I mean, she's the reason why I'm here. My heart is starting to pound faster as my sister gathers her thoughts.

"Well, I heard she was dating someone, but from my last info, if I'm not mistaken, I think she is on her own now… wait a minute, why are you asking about her? Oh my God! Are you still into her?" my sister asks with a tone that seems like she caught on to my secret.

"Well, no… forget it."

"Come on Liam, come on… be honest tell us!"

At that moment the room gets really silent and everyone stops what they are doing and direct their eyes on me; even my father, who was reading— or pretending to read—a newspaper, lowers the paper below eye level to stare at me, also raising his eyebrow.

"Well… I…" I swallow. "… I kind of never got over her," I confess. "Ah ha! I always knew it. Every time you'd visit, it always seemed like you were looking for someone whenever we went out. Always scanning the crowd. Now I realize that you were looking for her," Jennifer says as if she just found the last piece of the puzzle.

I don't want to reveal the truth to them because then they will be very optimistic about my chances with Bia, and at this point I don't want to get their hopes up like I did the last time. They were almost as crushed as I was.

"Well, I'll be honest, I do still care about her and I would like to see her again. If only just to chat," I answer, hoping that my point gets across. "Liam, I can't believe that you would even want to speak to her after everything her family did to you. But hey, who am I to judge? The heart wants what it wants I guess," she says.

We finish our food and the conversation tempers off. We start to put the dishes away. I help my mother and my sisters rearrange the kitchen. We have so much fun talking, splashing water at each other, and tickling each other around the table. Meanwhile, my father goes out to his tool shed to work on some chairs that he is making for the town's library.

I pass the rest of the afternoon with my mother and sisters, just talking with them. When the sun sets, I look out the living room window and see the light in the tool shed still on. I make my way to the tool shed to help my father with his chair.

When I open the door of the shed, the scent of cedar wood fills my nose, just as it did many years ago. I look over to my father who is at the corner of the shed getting a hammer and some nails. He looks at me and gives me a warm smile, just like he used to when I used to help. Dad was never a talkative person; he mainly got his point across with facial expressions. I grab a hammer and begin to help him.

Time passes quickly and it is now a few minutes after ten. It is completely dark outside; the night sky is clear and full of stars. The wind is blowing softly. Mama calls Dad and I in for some hot chocolate, with bread and butter. It is a night snack that my family makes before going to sleep. We all eat together before going to bed.

As I look around at my family, I feel glad to be home. They are so full of love, and so compassionate toward each other. This is what I missed the most in New York City: it was the feeling that you get when you are around people that truly love you. I cannot express in words how blessed I am to have the family that I have.

The evening comes to a close. This is my first full day in five years that I have spent with my family. We finish our nighttime snack and give each other a kiss on the cheek before heading to bed.

I make my way up the stairs to my room, heading toward my bed to sleep. I'm still feeling tired from all the events that have occurred this weekend. I enter my room and began to change. Suddenly, the thought of Michelle appears in my mind. Even though I don't regret my decision to leave, I realize that I should have told her what was going on in my mind. Instead, I took the easy way out and copped out without facing the situation. I hope that her heart heals fast and that she'll move on with her life.

I put on my sleeping clothes and turn off the lights before lying down. I close my eyes trying to sleep. An hour goes by and I'm still awake in bed tossing and turning. My mind is running a million miles an hour with thoughts.

I take a deep breath, one after another, and still my mind cannot be stilled. My heart pounds faster every time I think that, at this exact moment, Bia is in this town with me. I'm just a couple of miles away from her. This is my chance; this is what drove me here.

Now I lay in bed without being able to sleep, overcome by fear and insecurities. I have to let these negative thoughts go. This is my time to do something about it. This is my time to discover the truth.

From my bed, I look outside at the moon and its brightness covers my face with light. I look over to the wooden clock on the wall and it's 11:11 PM. After a few seconds, I get up from my bed and reach for my desk. Suddenly, I feel inspired to write a poem expressing my sentiment for Bia. I get a pen and a piece of paper and write a poem:

To the skies above
To the angels who hold our hearts This moment so long I've waited With passion I wrote this to you My love melts into your heart
So that nothing could keep us apart
I Love You, Liam D'Fiori

After writing the poem, I lie back down on the bed. I somehow feel lighter, even relieved that I could put my feelings on paper. I will give her the poem tomorrow when I hopefully see her. Bia will read the poem, and she will know in her heart how much I have missed her and still care for her. Bia is truly my one and only. I fall asleep with a content heart.

The sky is dark, with gloomy storm clouds threatening to break into the first raindrops. It is eerily still, not even a breeze blowing, making the crisp air as sharp as the blade of a knife. I can see my family huddled together, staring at something before them. I am a few feet behind them, trying to see what they are looking at. A crow suddenly crows nearby, and I jump. I am confused about the situation. Where are we? And why does my family look like they are in mourning?

I call out to Mama, willing her to turn around and look at me. She doesn't seem to hear me. She just keeps looking straight ahead of her. I can hear my sisters crying woefully, grasping at each other for comfort. Daddy puts a hand around Mama's shoulders, and she rests her head on his chest, sobbing uncontrollably.

Something is horribly wrong. As if in slow motion, I finally take a few steps forward and reach them. I stop, searching their sad faces, trying to reach my hands out to them. I can't seem to touch them or feel them. Why can't they see me?

"Mama! Look at me! Why are you all in such a state of distress? What happened?" I turn to the thing they are looking at, and my heart comes to a standstill. This is not real. This cannot be. In disbelief, I stare at the grave in front of me. My grave.

"No!" I yell. I fall to my knees in exasperation. Suddenly, I feel tired, as if all the life has been drawn from my body. I read the scripture on the gray marble tombstone.

"Here lies Liam, our loving son and only brother. You were taken too early from us. Fly with the angels."

I begin to sob. How is it possible that I am dead? Mama comes forward, clutching a bouquet of white roses in her hands. She places the flowers on the fresh grave, and the petals instantly turn gray, then to ash. I watch in horror as the ashes are lifted by a sudden gust of wind, propelling the ashes high in the sky before disappearing.

FORTY-THREE

Liam

I WAKE UP SWEATING profusely and feeling out of breath. I am in a state of panic as to what I dreamed. It was just a nightmare. I lie back against the pillow and sigh in relief. The dream was so vivid, so realistic. I have never thought about death or what it would do to my family if I were to pass away.

My thoughts return to Bia. How would she react if I die? I shake the remaining thoughts from my head. This is not the way I wanted my day to start.

I wash up after getting out of bed. I put on my clothes. Downstairs, I can see my mother making chocolate chip pancakes for breakfast. I help her set the table, and we all sit to enjoy our pancakes. Mine is smothered in extra syrup.

"What are your plans for today, Liam?" Mom asks as she sips her coffee.

"I don't know yet," I reply between mouthfuls of pancake. "I might go and see Tommy today at his workplace. Other than that, I am still undecided."

My mother nods and finishes her breakfast. For once, my older sister doesn't mention Bia's name, and I am relieved. I am curious about how she has been these last couple of years, but I don't want to hear it from Jennifer. I help my mother clear the table and wash up. She hugs me tightly before I leave for the morning.

"You haven't changed as much as you think, Liam. You still help your old Mama around the house after being away for years. It's like you never left."

I smile at her, and rush to her with hugs, smothering her with many kisses. After saying goodbye, I ride my bike to Tommy's workplace.

I haven't seen Tommy in years, yet he still looks the same as when I left. Tommy is pleased to see me and gives me a big hug.

"Liam, my man! What are you doing back home? You've been a busy man these last couple of years! How's life treating you? How are you?"

I laugh at Tommy's enthusiasm and the fact that I cannot get a word in edgewise. "Slow down, Tommy! I can't keep up with all the questions you are throwing at me."

"Sorry. I am just so excited to see my old friend. I need to know everything there is to know about New York! I still can't believe you made it big time. And it's such a shame about Shane. Who would've thought that he would be part of masterminding a criminal Ponzi scheme? It sucks."

After catching up on my life in New York, I know the time has come for me to ask about Bia. I am nervous. If she has moved on with someone else, I am unsure how I will react to such news. I take a deep breath before asking.

"How's Bia?" I ask cautiously. Tommy goes quiet, and I search his face for any expression that might give me a clue as to what he is going to say. Tommy looks down before answering.

"Bia's good... I guess. I don't really see her other than when I run in to her in town. Bia and Mary are still best friends, but Mary usually meets at Bia's house. She rarely comes over to our house."

Tommy suddenly looks up.

"Bia is engaged, Liam. To John."

I can feel my heart come to a standstill as the shock sets in. *John?*

"As in John from high school?" I manage to utter.

"John from high school. I'm sorry to be the one to tell you, old friend."

I shake my head, still in disbelief over what Tommy is saying. "I don't understand. Bia hates John. Why would she be engaged to him?"

Tommy shrugs. "I honestly don't know what she sees in him, man. There was a rumor going around that John cheated on Bia, but it was never confirmed. I don't know if it happened or not. All I know is that I don't expect anything less of John. I don't know what she sees in him. Maybe she is only with him because her parents approve of him. You know, because he comes from money and whatnot."

I let Tommy's words sink in. I feel empty. Numb. Tommy clears his throat and looks at me with compassion. "You should talk to Bia, Liam. I hope you find closure."

Tommy is right. I must talk to her. Being engaged to John is probably the reason that she never responded to my letter. What if John saw the letter first and decided to get rid of it before Bia had a chance to read it?

I spend the rest of the day with Tommy, catching up on our lives. I realize it's getting late, and after saying goodbye to Tommy, I drive to Bia's office. I go to the entrance, only to realize that the office is closed. What now? I can't just show up at Bia's house. That would be too intrusive. I don't want Bia to feel uncomfortable in her own home.

Undecided about what to do next, I get back on my bike and drive. Cruising slowly, I end up on the main street. I see a familiar figure sitting outside one of the coffee shops, and my heart skips a beat. It's Bia. What are the odds? This must be fate. The fact that she is alone verifies the situation. This is my chance, and I need to take it. I might not get another opportunity.

I park my motorcycle across the street from the coffee shop. The sun has set behind the mountains, leaving the sky a dark orange. It will soon be dark. Streetlights come on one by one, blinking in twilight. Bia looks up and notices my bike. She watches as I switch off the ignition. I stand there for what feels like an eternity, uncertain how to proceed. Bia is still watching, unaware that it is me hiding underneath the helmet. It's now or never. I slowly remove the helmet. At the same time, Bia gets up from the table holding something in one hand. It's a piece of paper. I realize that the paper in Bia's hand is my letter. We lock eyes, and at that moment, I feel nostalgia for the first day I saw Bia in Miss Honey's class. I let the emotions wash over me, reveling in the moment.

We stare at each other as if frozen in time. Bia drops the letter. She has a look of disbelief on her beautiful face as if what she sees is unreal. Then we both run toward each other, meeting in the middle of the street. I pick her up and twirl her around in the air before she wraps her legs around my waist.

"I knew it was you," Bia says before passionately kissing me. The warmth of her mouth and the familiarity of her scent make me weak in the knees. Nothing else in this world matters. At this moment, I am home in the arms of my true love. My Beatrice. She is the one I have longed for and come back to.

Our lover's embrace is interrupted by the loud sound of people cheering and the honking of several car horns. I look around and realize we have caused a two-way traffic jam in the street. Embarrassed, we let go of each other.

"Would you like to join me for a cup of coffee?" Bia asks.

"Of course." I smile at her, and we head back to the coffee shop. I order a coffee and something to nibble on. Bia also orders another cup. While we wait for our order, we first sit in silence, just staring at each other. I can't believe I am finally with Bia after all these years.

"So, how have you been, Liam?" Bia asks. Her voice has a cautious tone, almost as if she doesn't really want the truth of how great of a life I have made for myself in New York. I take a deep breath.

"Do you really want to know, Bia?"

"I don't know. I don't know if I can bear hearing how you lived a life apart from me." Bia looks down at her hands in her lap.

"It wasn't always easy. You were always on my mind. What you were doing, who you were with. That was constantly replaying in my mind."

Bia looks up at me, anger building up in her beautiful green eyes. "Then why didn't you come back to me, Liam? I don't understand. Maybe if you came back for me, none of this would have happened." Bia goes quiet. I know what she is referring to—her engagement to John.

"Things could have been different for us… I know." I pause and look her directly in the eyes. "Why John, Bia? Why did you agree to marry John?"

We are interrupted by the waitress bringing our coffees. Bia still hasn't answered my question. Her eyes are cast down while she mindlessly stirs sugar into her coffee. Finally, she looks up at me. Her eyes are full of tears.

"It's the only way out for me, Liam."

"What do you mean by that?"

Bia sighs. "My parents approve of John. John might not be the one, but he is as close as I will ever get to loving anyone as I have loved you. John has money and can provide for me. He gives me a sense of security."

I scoff at the words. "Do you call cheating a sense of security?"

Bia's eyes flash. "Who told you that?" she demands.

"No one. Forget that I mentioned it. If you are happy with John, I will accept it." Bia says nothing in return. We finish our coffees, and I am just about to get up and leave when Bia takes me by the arm.

"Can we go for a walk?"

There is nothing in the world I would rather be doing, and I instantly agree. We walk up the main street, not having any destination in mind. Just being with Bia is enough for me. We hear music in the distance and follow the sound. About a mile ahead, we see that there is an outdoor music festival. A big crowd of people dance and sing to the live music on a makeshift stage. Bia and I look at each other with huge smiles on our faces.

"Shall we?" I ask as I take her hand and lead her into the crowd. We buy a couple of ice-cold beers and head to the stage area. The music is pumping, and it doesn't take long for us to begin to dance and sing along to the music.

One beer becomes two beers, and then three. I can't help but stare at Bia while she is dancing. Her beautiful long hair moves around her. Her eyes are closed, and she has a smile on her beautiful face—the girl of my dreams.

The music is too loud to hear the low rumble of thunder, and a sudden blinding light etches across the dark, clouded sky. The crowd shrieks in surprise as the sky lights up. The music is still playing as if there isn't a thunderstorm on the way. Bia looks at me. The sky suddenly opens, and rain pours in heavy, large drops. The rain is coming down hard, and the crowd runs for cover. I guess the festival is over. Bia doesn't seem to mind the rain. She grabs my hand, and we follow the last stragglers of the crowd.

"Where are we going?" I yell over the sound of the rain.

"I don't know," she says and laughs. We hold hands as we walk in the rain, singing and jumping into the puddles that have formed next to the road. We are soaked to the bone. Bia's dress clings to her perfect body, accentuating every beautiful curve. How could I have let her go?

We end up in front of the coffee shop. Bia looks at me, and my heart skips a beat. I smile at her.

"I should take you home," I say to her. I don't want to, but the storm is getting worse.

"I guess," she says. We walk over to where my motorcycle is parked. I hand her my helmet. She takes the helmet with a look of uncertainty on her face.

"I have never been on a motorcycle," she says. "But I know I will be safe with you. I am always safe with you."

Bia holds on tightly around my waist as we brave the rain. I drive slowly as I don't want the bike to slide, but also, I don't want this night to end. Too soon, we arrive at Bia and Johns' house. I park across the street. There is a light on in what seems to be the living room. Bia gets off behind me and hands me the helmet.

"Thank you for an unforgettable night," she says. Her eyes are shining brightly in the light of the streetlight.

"We should do it again soon," I say, winking at Bia. Suddenly, her face becomes grave, and she reaches her hand to my face. At the exact moment, the front door of Bia's house opens. I see John standing in the doorway. I can't make out his facial expression because of the heavy rain, but I can only imagine that he is furious with her. Bia pulls her hand back quickly, and before I can say anything, she runs across the street.

Before driving off, I hear John yelling at Bia before he slams the front door shut behind them. I drive off, feeling mixed emotions coursing through me. I pray that Bia will be okay.

FORTY-FOUR

Beatrice

"WHAT THE HELL, BIA?!" John yells as I run up the porch steps. Once inside, John slams the door shut and grabs me by the arm.

"Where were you, Bia? And who were you with?"

I try to release my arm from his grip, but John is holding on too tightly.

"You're hurting my arm, John. Let go of me!"

John loosens his grip, and I pull my arm free. I rub the tender spot and look at him defiantly. "Don't you ever touch me again, John Anderson," I say in a low voice. John looks surprised at my reaction, but then the anger returns to his voice.

"I am not going to ask you again. Who were you with on that motorcycle? I know it's some guy, obviously. Tell me who it is, this instant."

I laugh. "You have some nerve, asking me where and who I was with. How about we reverse the question, John? I know that you are still cheating on me. Chelsea was not the only one you betrayed me with. So now I ask you this. Who's the other woman in our lives, John?"

John is speechless after my accusation of him still cheating on me. I can see the truth in his eyes. John has always been a lousy liar.

"I'll make this easy for you. For us both." I take off my engagement ring and, without a glance, throw it in John's direction. "I'm not anyone's doormat, especially not yours. I don't care that my parents approved of you. They only approved because of your family's wealth and the fact that you can provide for me financially. Providing emotionally… now, that is another thing. It's over, John."

"You're going to regret this decision, Bia," John says as he walks to the front door. "Don't come crawling back to me." With those words, John leaves.

Relief washes over me as I get ready for bed. I doubt John will return now that everything is out in the open. My thoughts are of Liam as I drift off to sleep.

I wake up the next morning full of exhilaration. I remember the previous night and how Liam and I had such fun—how my feelings for Liam came rushing back the moment he took off his motorcycle helmet and stared at me with those piercing blue eyes. How I have missed him! It felt like old times. I really miss the old days when it was just me and Liam, our bright futures ahead of us, and the excitement of knowing that Liam and I were meant to be together forever. Those were simpler times. I smile and get out of bed.

I have a song in my heart as I shower and get dressed, all the while dancing and twirling to the beat of my heart. I am relieved to see that John has not returned and take it that he stayed at a motel last night. Either that or he stayed with his mistress. It doesn't matter, anyway. What matters is that I have broken off our engagement, and I am free from John.

I am excited for the day ahead and can't wait to see Liam again. In the meantime, I decided to meet with Di and Mary to share the good news. I have a lot to tell them. I call Mary first, asking her to meet me at my parent's house at noon. Mary happily agrees. Next, I call home. Di picks up the phone after the third ring.

"Hello?"

"Hi, Di. It's me."

"My darling Bia. What a pleasant surprise so early in the morning. I miss having you at home. How are you?"

"I have some exciting news, Di. Can I drop by at noon? Mary is meeting me there as well."

"Of course. It will be lovely to see you. I'll whip up a hearty lunch for you both. And dessert, of course."

I smile. "You are the best, Di. I will see you later."

After hanging up the phone, I grab a duffel bag from the closet and pack some clothes and other essentials. I plan to stay at my childhood home for the time being and will come back another day to collect the last of my things. I need a new start, which is the first step to a new beginning. My mind lingers on Liam and what he is doing right at this moment. I hope that he is thinking of me, too.

I arrive a couple of minutes before noon. Di is thrilled to see me and gives me a big hug.

"I miss having you here," she says. Mary is right on time, as enthusiastic as always.

"Bia! Di! It has been forever since I have seen the both of you. Being an adult is so much harder than I thought! I miss the carefree days of being a child, being able to do whatever we wanted when we wanted." Mary plops down on the sofa. She sniffs the air, the smell of Di's famous chili filling the air. "I'm famished! Just in time for your famous chili."

Mary and I sit at the dining table while Di fetches us a plate. I have missed Di's cooking so much. She has taken great care of me most of my life, and I will always appreciate her. She has been like a second mother to me. We eat in silence, scarfing our food like we haven't eaten in days. Di surprises us with ice cream sandwiches and piping hot coffee.

"So, what exciting news did you want to share?" Mary asks through mouthfuls of ice cream. I wait for Di to sit, and I clear my throat.

"I broke off my engagement with John. For good this time." I look at both of their expressions, trying to read their faces. It doesn't take long for them to react to the news. Di stands up and embraces me.

"It's about time. You deserve so much better than John. I am really happy for you, Bia." She looks at me with tenderness in her eyes, tears threatening to spill down her cheeks. "You were never meant for him, no matter that your parents approved of him." Di finally lets me go. Mary sits with the biggest smile on her face. She doesn't even have to say anything. Mary has been my shoulder to cry on, and she knows about John's previous affair. I see the disdain she feels toward John.

"I have another announcement to make," I say. Both look at me in surprise. I take a deep breath. "I saw Liam last night."

Mary's eyes get big. "And? Don't just sit there. Tell us what happened!"

I excitedly tell them about our spontaneous night, and I can see that they are excited for me.

"What happens now?" Di asks. "I am elated that Liam is back… But what does that mean for you, Bia? Is Liam here to stay?"

"I don't know yet. I haven't spoken to him today. All I know is that I want to be with him. He has always been the one, Di. You know how much I love Liam."

"Of course, I do. I just don't want to see you go through what you already have been when he left for New York. Seeing you in such a state again would break my heart."

I look at Di. "This time, it's different. I can feel it." She nods in agreement.

"You deserve all the happiness in the world, Bia. If Liam is the one to make you happy, I say you go for it!"

After my big news, Mary and I sit and enjoy each other's company for a few hours before Mary needs to go. We say our goodbyes. Mary gives me a final hug before she drives off. I walk back into the house with the thought of calling Liam, but at that moment, my parents pull up in the driveway.

Not wanting to deal with them now, I quickly head out the back door and sneak to my car. I drive back home, not really wanting to. I can grab some things there and then return to my parents' house later. I have a suspicion that they are not going to take the news of the engagement well.

The house is quiet. I sigh in relief. I was hoping that John would not be here. Just as I head to the bedroom, there is a knock on the door. I freeze. I wasn't expecting anyone today. Realizing it might be Liam, I run to the front door, swinging it wide open. Liam stands in front of me with a big grin on his face.

"Wow, it's almost as if you were expecting me," he says and laughs. I smile back at him, my eyes full of joy.

"I knew you would come," I say.

Liam points at the backpack on his back. "You want to go somewhere with me? I promise I will make it worth your while."

I nod without any hesitation. "There is one thing, though. If we are going where I think we are, can we please stop at my parents' house on the way? I would love to take Snowy up there with us."

We drive back to my parents' house.

Liam waits out front while I get Snowy. He fastens the backpack to Snowy's saddle. I again avoid my parents as Liam and I get on Snowy and ride to Lovers Mountain. I tilt my head upward as the wind blows my hair back. My arms are snugly around Liam's waist. We ride in silence, enjoying the closeness of each other. A feeling of nostalgia overtakes my body as we come to a stop.

Everything looks exactly like the first night we spent on the mountain. Liam sets up our tent and starts the campfire. Once Liam gets the fire going, we sit on a nearby log. Liam pulls me closer, and I let him. I take in his warmth, his familiar scent.

Liam reaches for his backpack and pulls out a bottle of wine and two plastic cups.

"Care for a drink?"

"Yes, please."

Liam pours wine into the two cups and hands one to me.

"Thank you."

"My mom packed us a meal," he says as he hands me a brown paper bag. We eat in silence, taking an occasional sip from our cups. The wine makes my stomach feel warm and fuzzy.

"How are things between you and John?" Liam suddenly asks. I am relieved that Liam is the one who brought it up, and I don't want to keep Liam in any more suspense than I have to.

"I broke off the engagement."

"Was it because of me?"

"Mainly, yes. But I wasn't happy with my life at all. John is still cheating on me after he made promises after the first time that I caught him."

"I knew that he was never good enough for you," Liam scoffs.

"I'm just glad the relationship is over." I take Liam's hand and say nothing further. It goes quiet for a while before Liam speaks up.

"What's wrong, Bia? You seem different than last night. Did something else happen that I should know of?"

I look at him, sadness filling me from the inside. "What are we doing, Liam? What is this between us?" I stand up, facing him. It is as if I lose all my inability to control my emotions as I stare him down.

"Why didn't you fight for me? Why did you give up so easily on our love?"

"Calm down, Bia. I—"

I don't give him time to finish. "You should have stayed!" I cry. "We could've had a life together. A family! Now look where we are. So much has happened in the time we were apart. I cried myself to sleep for months, hoping that you would come back to me."

Liam stands up, holding his arms out to me. "My beautiful Bia. Please hear me out. The only reason I left was so that I could make something of myself. To prove that I am worthy of you."

I turn around. "I found the ring."

"You mean…"

"Yes. The engagement ring that you proposed with." I take the ring out of my pocket, and I turn around to face Liam. "I went back to the spot where it landed when I threw it off the cliff. I searched the whole day until I found it." I toss the ring at Liam's chest, where it lands on the ground in front of him. Tears stream down my face. Liam bends down to pick up the ring, and when he looks at me, his eyes are full of tears.

"You don't understand how much I wanted to stay. I kept praying that you would beg me to stay, my Bia."

Liam then takes my hand and goes down on one knee.

"My beautiful Bia. I have made many mistakes in my life, but the biggest mistake of all would be to let you go a second time. You are my true love, Bia. There will never be a love like ours. Will you marry me?"

"Of course, I will marry you! That is the only thing that I am sure of. I want to spend the rest of my life with you."

Liam tenderly puts the ring on my finger, then pulls me down onto his lap. We kiss with fire burning in our eyes and desire coursing through our veins. We strip down to our underwear, and Liam picks me up with one swift movement and puts me down on the blanket under the starry night sky. We explore each other's bodies with the familiarity that lovers experience only with their one true love. Our love is insatiable and lasts into the early hours of the morning.

FORTY-FIVE

Liam

I WAKE UP EARLY the next morning. Bia is still asleep in my arms, and I carefully move away from her so as not to wake her. It's a beautiful, crisp morning. The birds are singing, and Snowy neighs when he sees me.

"Hello, boy," I say to him as I give him the carrot I took with our breakfast from the bag. The fire went out overnight, so I forage around for small pieces of wood and restart the fire. The aroma of freshly cooked oats must have woken Bia as she zips open the tent and inhales deeply. She stretches and sits next to me, kissing me on the cheek.

"Morning, beautiful," I say as I hand her a steaming cup of coffee.

"Morning, darling. Thank you for the coffee. Breakfast smells great!"

We eat in silence, enjoying our breakfast. Afterward, we walk to the cliff's edge, admiring the beautiful view.

"I have missed this view so much over the last five years," I say. I put my arms around Bia's waist and hug her tightly. She snuggles into my chest, and we stand as one. I will never let Bia go again. This is where she belongs. After a couple of minutes, Bia looks up at me with a smile.

"So, what do you think the future holds for us?" she asks.

"First, we are getting married. And this time, I am not waiting on your parents' approval of our love for one another."

"I want to travel the world with you, Liam. I want to experience everything that you have when you left for New York."

"I want to explore the world with you, my Bia. There is so much wonder out there. After our travels around the world, we will move into a big, beautiful house on the mountain and have lots of babies." Bia's eyes reflect my excitement as she imagines the life I want to give her.

"I want all of it. I love you so much." We kiss passionately, our love everlasting and the world at our feet.

We walk back to our camping spot and begin to pack up our things. As we ride Snowy back to Bia's house, I can't help but to think of what her parents will say about our engagement. Will they accept me after I went out into the world and made something of myself? I will marry Bia either way, but in the back of my mind, I long to be accepted by them.

Bia takes Snowy around the back while I wait for her in the front yard. Suddenly, the front door opens, and a familiar figure emerges from the house. Di runs toward me, her arms open wide.

"Liam!"

She embraces me in a big hug, not wanting to let me go. When she finally does, she looks up at me with tears in her eyes.

"Welcome home, Liam. We have missed you very much."

"I have missed you too, Di. Especially your cooking." I wink.

Di smiles. "You are such a darling boy, Liam. And handsome. I saw your picture in one of those magazines."

"Thank you, Di. I finally made something of myself."

Di pauses before speaking. "You were always good enough for our Bia, Liam. Love is all we need, and we all know that your love for Bia was exceptional."

Before I can answer, Bia comes through the front door. She smiles brilliantly as she holds out her hand for Di to see. Di starts crying, and she hugs Bia tightly.

"All is as it should be," she manages to say after a few minutes. Bia and I smile at each other. Di is right. Bia and I plan to meet later tonight to announce our engagement to her parents. They will be home much later tonight as they are attending some charity function. I kiss her goodbye and climb on my motorcycle. I need to break the good news to my family. They will be thrilled, especially Mama.

It's almost time to meet Bia and her parents at their house. I am nervous but determined to tell them about my love for their daughter. Bia has always been the one, and I hope they will see this after all this time. I suddenly remember the poem that I wrote for Bia. I never gave it to her. I rummage through the drawer of my bedside table until I find it. *Better late than never,* I think to myself. I put on my black leather jacket over my white t-shirt, my faded blue jeans and my cowboy boots. I fold the poem and place it in the inside pocket of my jacket.

I head down the stairs very softly, praying that the wood does not creak and wake anyone. I make it downstairs without waking anyone, and as I pass by the dining room, I notice a bouquet of roses. I decide to take the bouquet with me.

I take a sudden look at the clock it's 11:11 PM. I make my way out the door to my motorcycle. I put on my helmet that is hanging on the handles of the bike. I open the visor of my helmet and get a scent of the night's air. It is brisk with the scent of mist.

I hop on the motorcycle and place the bouquet of roses between my legs, leaning on top of the gas tank of the bike. Without wanting to wake my family with the noise of the bike, I roll it down the driveway until I hit the road. I close my helmet visor and turn on the motorcycle.

The humming of the bike begins to get louder as I travel down the road. I make a right turn on a country road that is very narrow with wheat fields on both sides. The wind hits my jacket, making it cold as I accelerate down the road. I look to both of my sides, noticing the moon light reflecting itself on the wheat field, making them appear gray as the wind swings them from side to side. It's a beautiful and peaceful night.

The sky is clear full of sparkling bright stars with not one trace of a cloud. My heart is racing and filled with joy. I focus my thoughts on the minute that I will come face-to-face with her. To see her smile and her eyes light up brings joy to my heart. To be close to her by her side again is all that I want at this moment. And here I am just minutes from her doorstep.

My emotions are overflowing and I can't control my smile. This is the moment I yearned for all these years. This is the reason I'm here. I concentrate my attention on the road again and in the distance, I see a dim light. It begins making its way towards me. Becoming bigger and brighter at a fast pace.

The light beam is way too bright so I signal to it by blinking my lights. I keep going at the same high velocity. I glance down at the bouquet of roses and witness them drying out before my very eyes. I look back up and am still blinded by the light's high beam. I signal my light again for it to turn off its high beams.

Behind the bright light blurring my eyes, I can see the fainted shape of the body of a truck.

Fear sets in as I glance down again at the bouquet of roses and I find that they are slowly becoming dry and gray. As I look up, my heart drops. I underestimated the distance between the light and I. Completely blinded by the light, I swerve left and right to get away from a head-on collision.

My arms are shaking as I lose control of my motorcycle. My hands lose grip from the handles of the bike as I desperately try to gain control.

A second before the collision, a loving warm bright light blinds me completely as if covering me, embracing, welcoming me. Peacefully.

At this moment, I see my whole life with clarity. All of my life's memorable moments display's around me, swirling cinematically. I see Beatrice's green eyes in the wheat field, peacefully gazing at me, her long brown hair floating in the wind. And now it's all clear to me. In my life's final moment, love was always within me. At last, I truly did give love a chance.

Epilogue

Beatrice

2 YEARS LATER …

TWO YEARS HAVE PASSED since Liam's tragic accident. A couple of weeks after Liam's funeral, I discovered I was pregnant. I was delighted to be expecting. I cradled the thought of having a piece of Liam growing inside me. I welcomed a baby boy and named him Tristan D'Fiori. He is the spitting image of his father.

Tristan got me through the mourning of my beloved Liam, and if it was not for Tristan, I don't know if I would've been able to hold on for as long as I did. My parents love Tristan just as much as I do. Tristan breathed new life into our family home, which is now filled with laughter, hope, and happiness.

Tristan and I are in the front garden, playing, when my mother walks up to us, phone in hand. She seems nervous. I give her a puzzled look.

"Is everything okay?"

"I think that you are going to want to take this," my mother says before handing me the phone and leaving.

"Hello?" I say into the phone.

There is silence, and then an unfamiliar female voice says, "Hello. Is this Bia?"

"Yes, it is. Who is this?" I ask.

"You probably won't know me, but I know you. My name is Michelle, and I was a friend of Liam's." The lady gets all choked up and then clears her throat before continuing, "I hope it is okay that I called you. Liam loved you very much, and he dedicated his very first manuscript to you. I found it after he left and decided to speak to one of my friends in publishing. They loved it, and the book was published. I have sent you the first copy of his book with the sales profits. Bia, the book is a huge success. Liam has made headlines once again with his first bestseller. You should be extremely proud."

I am dumbstruck.

"I hope that his legacy will live on through you and this book," Michelle continues. "Anyway, I must go now. My condolences to you."

"Thanks, Michelle," I whisper, and the line goes dead. I hug my knees, still in shock from the conversation that just happened. I take Tristan inside and find Di in the kitchen.

"Di, can you please get me a fresh bunch of white roses?" I ask.

"Of course," Di says and walks out to the garden. I pull on my riding boots and take the flowers from Di. Tristan and I ride Snowy up Lovers Mountains to our secret spot. Standing at the edge of the cliff, holding Tristan's little hand, I watch as the sun sets on the busy little town below.

All of them are going on with their lives, unaware of the tragic loss that this world has suffered. But not me; I will never forget. Bending down, I place the bouquet at the cliff's edge and whisper to the wind, "I will always love you, my Liam." Standing there with tears streaming down my face, I think about all the fun times and special moments we shared. Just then, a gust of wind blows, breaking off a petal. The wind carries the white petal, and it drifts away, swirling high into the clear sky. Into the lights of the stars.

"Daddy," Tristan says suddenly. I pick him up and hug him fiercely.

"It is him. I know it is."

This is his way of showing me that even though he isn't with me physically, I will never be alone. Smiling, Tristan and I sit on a fallen-down log and enjoy the amber hues of the sun as it sets behind the mountain.

Now Listen, you who say, "Today or tomorrow we will go to this or that city, spend a year there, carry on business and make money." Why, you do not even know what will happen tomorrow. What is your life? You are a Mist that appears for a little while and then vanishes.

—James 4:13-14